大学英语拓展阅读教程

（进阶篇）

总主编　董连忠　董丽娜

主　编　宋红辉

编　者　张　鑫　宋红辉　王　猛

　　　　邵　帅　董连忠

上海交通大学 出版社

内 容 提 要

本教程旨在通过教师课上指导、学生课下自主学习的方式拓宽学生视野、培养他们的终生学习能力。全教程由基础篇、进阶篇、提高篇、高阶篇和精阶篇五册组成,每册十个单元。每单元设计一个主题的形式,单元中各模块的设计符合学生的阅读规律,如阅读知识面拓展、技巧训练、能力培养、实战演练和兴趣开发。练习题型的设计主要是帮助学生阅读过程中猜测生词词义、预测文章内容,运用"相互关联"(Interactive)阅读模式,将"用法"(Usage)与"运用"(Use)有机地结合。同时,为适应 CET 4/6 考试要求,增加了快速阅读和细读(In-depth reading)真题训练,达到"学"以致"用"的目的。

本教程适用于本、专科学生,也可作为英语学习爱好者的案头读物。

图书在版编目(CIP)数据

大学英语拓展阅读教程. 进阶篇/ 宋红辉主编. —上海:
上海交通大学出版社,2010
ISBN 978-7-313-06735-7

Ⅰ. 大… Ⅱ. 宋… Ⅲ. 英语—阅读教学—高等学
校—教材 Ⅳ. H319.4

中国版本图书馆 CIP 数据核字(2010)第 154785 号

大学英语拓展阅读教程
(进阶篇)

宋红辉 主编
上海交通大学出版社出版发行
(上海市番禺路 951 号 邮政编码 200030)
电话:64071208 出版人:韩建民
常熟市梅李印刷有限公司 印刷 全国新华书店经销
开本:787mm×1092mm 1/16 印张:12 字数:293 千字
2010 年 9 月第 1 版 2010 年 9 月第 1 次印刷
印数:1~3 030
ISBN 978-7-313-06735-7/H 定价:28.00 元

序

　　中国劳动关系学院的董连忠老师送来他和董丽娜主任合作编写的《大学英语拓展阅读教程》书稿，请我写几句话。我很高兴有机会浏览这套新编的英语泛读教材。我学习和教授英语快有 40 年了。我做学生的时候，特别喜欢阅读课外书，1979 年，系主任分配我教泛读课。当时最大的问题就是没有教材。我记得，我从图书馆筛选内容有趣、语言难度与学生英语水平相当的英语图书作为课外读物提供给学生，让大家课后阅读，读完后，分小组交流，或写读书报告。另外，我还挑选一些英语短文，编制一些问答题或选择题，作为课堂快速阅读的材料，每次上课前，发给大家，根据文章长度，限定阅读时间，等学生读完后，核对阅读练习题。虽然很忙碌，但是当时泛读教学的这种经历给我留下很多美好的回忆，我也对英语阅读产生了浓厚的兴趣。后来，我参加了英语泛读教材和英语快速阅读教材的编写工作，我认为大量阅读是中国学生在国内学好英语的重要途径之一。我赞成以大量阅读为基础，综合提高学生听说读写技能的主张。我也愿就此机会，谈谈我对英语阅读的体会：

　　1. 阅读是一种综合技能

　　怎样才能提高自己的阅读能力，仅仅靠阅读或多读是不够的。我的体会是：① 要扩大自己的词汇量，阅读能力的高低和词汇量的大小是分不开的，不少学生阅读困难是因为他们的英语词汇量偏少。要采用构词记忆、联想记忆、大量阅读记忆，以及通过上下文记忆等方法，不断扩大自己的词汇量；② 要善于整合和利用自己的语法知识，理清阅读材料中令人费解的长句、难句，以及与我们母语思维差异较大的英语句式；③ 要读得快，读得懂，还要有丰富的文化背景知识和生活知识，要不断丰富和拓宽自己的知识面；④ 要善于把握和判断所读材料的语篇类型、语篇结构和文体风格。

　　2. 培养阅读能力要注重发展阅读策略

　　多年的阅读经历使我体会到，要能读得好，须要读得巧。我的体会是：① 阅读是一种技能，要多实践、勤体验。每天阅读 30 分钟优于平时不经常读而周末读上几小时的做法；② 要熟悉快读、精读、寻读和略读的技能，培养自己根据需要，采取适当阅读策略的能力；③ 要发展自己的推测生词词义的能力(Inference skill, to know words you don't know based on words you know)。在实际阅读过程中，我们会遇到生词，即使学过的单词，有时也要根据不同的语境，确定单词的意思。所以要培养自己能根据上下文或文中其他词汇的信息推测生词意思的能力，要善于根据上下文线索和构词法等知识进行推测。④ 培养阅读能力不是一朝一夕就能完成的任务，需要时间和耐心，要持之以恒。

　　3. 阅读能力要与其他语言学习技能协调发展

　　整体语言教学理论强调语言是一个整体。语言教学要从整体着手。整体语言教学不是一种简单的语言教学方法，而是涉及语言、语言学习、语言教学、教学内容及学习环境的理念。我个人的体会是：读完一篇文章或材料，如果能够有所思考，写写体会或感想，或提出问题，或做一点练习，或与人交流讨论，都能有效提高阅读的能力和效率。

4. 通过阅读学习语言,很重要的一个因素是选择合适的阅读材料

合适的阅读材料一是要难易适度。材料过难,读不懂大意,容易失去阅读信心,从而影响对英语阅读的兴趣;材料过于简单,没有阅读激情,觉得学不到东西,容易失去阅读兴趣,从而影响英语阅读能力的提高。二是要内容有趣,要尽量为学生提供与他们兴趣、生活、年龄和心理联系密切的阅读材料。

我简要归纳了我自己在英语阅读教学方面的体会,以及英语泛读在英语学习中的重要性。从这个角度来看这套《大学英语拓展阅读教程》,我们就会发现,它有几个鲜明的特色:

(1)《大学英语拓展阅读教程》注重拓宽学生的文化视野和知识范围,整套教材题材广泛、内容丰富,涉及科技、文化、经济、体育、跨文化交际,以及与青年大学生兴趣和生活关系密切、大学生喜闻乐见的话题,这既有助于提高阅读兴趣,又能丰富和拓宽学生的知识面,进而提高阅读能力。特别值得一提的是,本套教程还专门设计和收入了有关中国文化的素材,为学生在跨文化交流中用英语介绍和表达自己的文化提供了语言支持,有助于提高其跨文化交际的能力。

(2)《大学英语拓展阅读教程》注重培养学生的阅读策略。每个单元设置了专门的"阅读策略实践"。为学生提供了经常性的、与单元内容有关的、真实的英语阅读策略实践和指导。

(3)《大学英语拓展阅读教程》体例设计新颖、活泼。每章开始,都有章节起始页,醒目的标题、活泼的图片、简洁的说明和本章篇目标题,给人为之一新的感觉。阅读材料后面的注释、练习和部分译文,为阅读提供了方便的帮助。每篇文章后面,都提供了问答题、选择题、填空题等形式的练习,是一套便教利学、目标明确、不可多得的大学英语泛读教程。

我们衷心期望这套英语泛读教程能为国内学生在国内学习英语提供阅读素材,以及发展阅读能力的指导,让我们的学生在英语学习过程中,体验阅读的快乐和成功,并以此为基础,综合提高英语学习的效率和综合运用英语的能力。

田贵森

北京师范大学外文学院教授

2010 年 6 月 30 日

Preface

I take it as an honor to be asked to write a preface for this set of *Extensive Reading* textbooks. My first reaction when I went through the five volumes was: Finally, someone is focusing on extensive reading and lifelong learning abilities! For years, I have been frustrated by Chinese teachers' focus on the intensive studying of English as a foreign language in China. Despite all its merits, "intensive reading" textbooks and courses do not push learners beyond the boundaries of a foreign language learner. It is when students are encouraged to use the language being learned, e. g. , for extensive reading or other useful purposes, that we begin to see hope for the students' use of English as a tool after they go out of the classroom and after their formal schooling.

With a wide array of topics that are of interest to Chinese university students, which I believe will help entice learners to the world of reading in English, a key characteristic of this set of textbooks is the express focus on reading strategies, learner autonomy, and lifelong reading skills. I encourage teachers to go further. In addition to the skimming and scanning strategies most prominently featured throughout these volumes, other important reading strategies such as summarizing, inferencing and predicting may well prove to be useful tools as well in the development of students' reading abilities.

I see at least three levels of reading: 1) read and understand, 2) read and remember, and 3) read and integrate. At the first level, a reader is able to decode the text being read and understand what the literal textual meaning is. Beginners of a foreign language will struggle for a long time in order to decode every word and every sentence before arriving at a general level of comprehension. Real reading never stops here. Many times we read for various functional purposes, for example, to read between the lines for the author's real intentions behind the text, to learn more about the content, and to share with each other the joys and sorrows of life. We remember the content as a natural result of reading. This is the second level. The overwhelming majority of readers will reach this level. The best readers, however, will read at level three where they enter into a dialogue with the writer. In other words, ideal readers not only read with understanding and memory, they also integrate what they read into their own knowledge structure, critically analyze the text and see if they agree with the author or how they would write their own message if they were the author. Nobody is born with these reading skills, and all three levels of reading will need to be trained. I hope that teachers who go through the trouble of reading this preface will explore different ways in cultivating their students' reading abilities at all these levels.

Extensive or intensive reading, let's not forget that the ultimate purpose of learning English as a foreign language for non-English majors at the tertiary level in China is to be able to function independently in their respective future careers not only in Chinese, but also in a language that has become a de facto world language. In other words, we are all engaged in a great enterprise of educating the next generation of Chinese workforce that is globally competitive and future-ready. As such, their English language ability will not and should not stop at Band 4 or Band 6 of CET. Reading extensively, being able to read and learn competently after they graduate from universities, and being able to use English as a tool for international communication and professional development is the target we should all aim for.

GU Yongqi
School of Linguistics and Foreign Language Studies
Victoria University of Wellington
New Zealand
July, 2010

前　言

　　《大学英语拓展阅读教程》是在充分研究了国内外英语教材编写的原则和特点的基础上，应用最新英语教学理论，吸纳最新英语教学方法、以培养学生阅读策略和自主学习能力为目标而编写的一套理念创新、体系科学、内容实用的阅读教材。其选材既注重科学性、人文性、可读性，又侧重培养学生的阅读技能和综合应用能力，符合我国大学英语教学改革的最新要求及发展趋势。其主要特色如下：

　　一、选材广泛，内容新颖

　　本教程立足教学实际、博采众长，突出了语言输入与输出功能的结合。选材以英语国家社会、政治、经济、文化等方面内容为主，同时辅以相应的中国文化元素，让学生在浩瀚的知识海洋中，多方汲取营养。所选文章语言规范，题材多样，贴近生活，可读性强，适合不同专业学生的学习需求。

　　二、个性鲜明，针对性强

　　本教程广泛汲取了国内外同类教材的精华，针对非英语专业学生英语水平和教学实际，充分体现了国家教育部有关大学英语教学改革的精神，彰显了英语教学个性化风格。

　　三、理念先进，题型多样

　　本教程旨在通过教师课上指导、学生课下自主学习的方式拓宽学生视野、培养他们的终生学习能力。单元中各模块的设计符合学生的阅读规律，如阅读知识面拓展、技巧训练、能力培养、实战演练和兴趣开发。练习题型的设计主要是帮助学生阅读过程中猜测生词词义、预测文章内容，运用"相互关联"(Interactive)阅读模式，将"用法"(Usage)与"运用"(Use)有机地结合。同时，为适应 CET 4/6 考试要求，增加了快速阅读和细读(In-depth reading)真题训练，达到"学"以致"用"的目的。

　　四、独特设计、实用创新

　　本教程由五册组成，每册十个单元。采用每单元设计一个主题的形式，在选材及练习设计上秉承循序渐进的原则，将其分为基础篇、进阶篇、提高篇、高阶篇和精阶篇。一切从有利于学生打好语言基础和提高语言应用能力出发，前后按照由浅入深、循序渐进的原则系统而连贯地设计完成。各册互相渗透，形成科学有机的整体。

　　五、中西相融、学练相长

　　本教程的创新之处在于中、西文化元素相融，"学"、"练"相长。学生在吸纳西方文化精华的同时，补以母语(中国)文化的"乳汁"，使学生所学知识得以融会贯通、相得益彰，从而提高其文化鉴赏能力和批判阅读能力。

　　本教程的基础篇、进阶篇、提高篇和高阶篇分别用于两年(四个学期)的大学英语基础教学；精阶篇用于三、四年级备考英语六级和研究生入学英语考试的选修课程。使用过程中，可根据本校学生实际情况灵活掌握。

　　本教程总主编为董连忠、董丽娜副教授。编写组成员分别为张鑫、宋红辉、王猛、邵帅和董连忠。他们每位担任一册教材的主编，同时负责每册教材两个单元的编写工作。教程的编写还得到了同事和朋友的支持。北京师范大学博士生导师田贵森教授和新西兰维多利亚大学顾永琪博士为本教程的编写给予了指导并撰写了序言;廊坊师范学院和北华航天学院的部分教师在试用过程中提出了宝贵的反馈意见;董丽娜主任对整体设计给予了精心指导;外语教学部的巫正洪、周风燕、陈劲、邓小莉、乔晓芳、安静、康春杰、李群、范恭华、刘磊、宋炳、訾华东老师作了校读并提出了宝贵意见,吕京红老师在编写和试用过程中做了大量基础工作。另外,作为中国劳动关系学院教改立项的部分成果,本教程得到了学院的资助,使其得以问世,在此我们一起表示衷心的感谢。

　　本教程适用于本、专科学生,也可作为英语学习爱好者的案头读物。作为我国大学英语教学改革实践的创新成果,虽经我们精心编写,但由于编者的水平和经验有限,错误和缺点在所难免,恳请各位专家和读者提出宝贵意见,以便在修订中日臻完善。

编者

2010 年 8 月

Contents

Unit One	**Cultural Differences** / 1
	Part One Beauty: The Korean Way / 2
	Part Two American Culture: Myths & Realities / 7
	Part Three Myths and Realities of Thanksgiving / 11
	Part Four The Frugal Gourmet Cooks American / 15
	Part Five American Table Manners / 17

Unit Two	**The Olympic Games** / 20
	Part One China Ties Olympic Gold to Quest for Worldwide Esteem / 21
	Part Two Michael Phelps — Biography / 26
	Part Three The Olympic Games / 29
	Part Four A Research on Referees' Errors / 33
	Part Five Summer Olympic Mascots / 35

Unit Three	**Interracial and Intercultural Marriage** / 38
	Part One The Love Letter / 39
	Part Two Love Story / 43
	Part Three After 40 Years, Interracial Marriage Flourishing / 46
	Part Four Mobility and Family Disorganization / 50
	Part Five Zhaojun Departs the Frontier / 52

Unit Four	**True Love** / 55
	Part One True Love / 56
	Part Two The Mystery of Love / 60
	Part Three Writing a Love Letter / 62
	Part Four What Will Happen if the World Was Suddenly No Emotion / 66
	Part Five Chinese Men in the Western Eyes / 68

Unit Five	**Parenting** / 71
Part One	Do You Expect Too Much of Your Kids / 72
Part Two	Letting Kids Be Kids / 77
Part Three	Parenting and Children's Development / 81
Part Four	Bringing up Children / 83
Part Five	Children's Day / 85

Unit Six	**Stereotype** / 87
Part One	Prejudice Against the Obese and Some of Its Situational Sources / 88
Part Two	Name Discrimination! How It Affects Job and Career Choices, Life Status, Overall Success / 91
Part Three	Beauty Contestant Fights for Right of Self-improvement / 95
Part Four	Moral Decline / 98
Part Five	Sayings about Proper Names and Nicknames / 99

Unit Seven	**"Work Smart, Not Hard"** / 102
Part One	Mayhew / 103
Part Two	U. S. Workers Feel Burn of Long Hours, Less Leisure / 108
Part Three	Six Secrets of High-Energy People / 111
Part Four	Stress / 114
Part Five	Are You a Workaholic / 115

Unit Eight	**More to Life than Work** / 118
Part One	What Do Young Jobseekers Want? / 119
Part Two	How to Become a World Citizen, before Going to College / 123
Part Three	Writing High Impact Resumes / 127
Part Four	What Youngsters Expect in Life / 130
Part Five	Life Description of a Chinese College Student / 132

Unit Nine   **Success Doesn't Come Easy** / 135

Part One   The Secret of My Success / 136

Part Two   Be Strong: How to Deal with Pain and Hardships in Your Life / 141

Part Three   Bosses Say 'Yes' to Home Work / 145

Part Four   The Business of America Is Business / 149

Part Five   Two Chinese Idioms / 151

Unit Ten   **Peace, Not War** / 154

Part One   Why Did President Truman Drop the Atomic Bomb? / 155

Part Two   There Will Never Be a "Victor" in Iraqi War / 161

Part Three   Beginning Anew / 164

Part Four   A New Era Began at Alamogordo / 167

Part Five   Meng Jiangnv Weep over the Great Wall / 168

Key   / 172

Unit One

Cultural Differences

Cultural differences between people do exist and will continue. They can cause argument and criticism sometimes. But if we don't have them, the whole world will be a boring place. "Variety is the spice of life".

In this unit, you will read:

- Beauty: The Korean Way
- American Culture: Myths & Realities
- Myths and Realities of Thanksgiving
- The Frugal Gourmet Cooks American
- American Table Manners

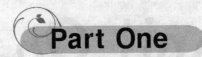

Part One

> **Pre-reading Questions**
> 1. Why do you think many people would like to undergo plastic surgery?
> 2. What do you know about plastic surgery?
> 3. What do you think is the standard for beauty?

Beauty: The Korean Way

Julia Yoo

1   "Thank goodness! You have ssang-ku-pool! Your parents saved a lot of money." said a close family friend when I was five years old. Ssang-ku-pool is the line above the **eyelid**, which almost every **Caucasian** has but is rare among Northeast Asians. According to Sandy Cobrin, only 25% of Koreans are born with the double eyelid **crease**, and she describes eyelid **surgery** as "**stitching** a permanent crease into the eyelid." After observing the Korean trends and Korean pop culture idols for many years from a Korean-American perspective, I think I have figured out the meaning of Korean beauty. It is a very complicated and profound one. Beauty means having big eyes, a pale **complexion**, a sharp and pointed nose, a taller height, and a small chin and mouth. **Essentially**, South Korean beauty means looking as "white" or Caucasian as possible.

2   I never quite understood how having lines above my eyelids saved my parents money until the summer of 1998 when I visited Korea and saw my aunt in Korea whom I hadn't seen for years. She just had eyelid surgery a year before, and I noticed how the lines above her eyes opened them up so that they appeared a bit rounder. She was **beaming** as she was telling me how she got a discount on the surgery, paying only $700 because she knew the surgeon. I felt fortunate; I had saved seven hundred dollars. But instead of yelling this aloud, I remained silent. For the first time in my life, I felt a bit ashamed of my race.

3   **Plastic surgery** has some kind of magical appeal to many Koreans — the promise of beauty. In this **mystical** and arduous **quest** for good looks, women are often **convinced** that suffering and **sacrificing** is necessary and worthy in order to bear the fruits of beauty. And this suffering is not for nothing. With good looks, the Korean society believes that beauty leads to attracting a better-looking partner, which leads to a better lifestyle and better-looking children. Oh, and of course, better looks equals better chances for competitive jobs, especially in the business field. Essentially, they believe that physical beauty equals happiness.

4   And in Korea, we impossibly apply the same standards for beauty as the Western world does. A woman should be tall, thin, with a milky complexion; **chiseled** facial features, long legs, nice big eyes, and the perfectly-angled nose. Ann Shin's film, "**Western Eyes**" thoroughly and accurately captures the essence of the struggle for Asian-American women striving for Western beauty. The **protagonists resort** to **cosmetic** surgery in search of beauty and acceptance, believing that their appearance, especially their eyes, will alter the way others perceive them. The immigrant women believe cosmetic surgery is the key to their assimilation in a **predominantly** white town. However, the Asian immigrants in the movie are different from the women in Korea, such as my aunt, who do not live around white people, yet experience similar internal **dilemmas** with their appearance. So if environment is not the primary cause of this drive to look "whiter," then what is it?

5   The next closest thing to living around white people is seeing them all over TV, **billboards**, and magazines. With globalization alive and well in South Korea, Western pop culture has mushroomed into every corner of the country. Lacoste, Estee Lauder, Ralph Lauren, Louis Vuitton, and Chanel are only a few of the heavily sought-out Western brands. The Koreans exchange their advanced electronic devices through companies such as LG, Samsung, Hyundai, and Kia in return for Western clothing, cosmetics, and pop idols such as Britney Spears and Justin Timberlake. However, Koreans do not just admire these Western idols. They do not only want to purchase their albums and clothes, but they also want to look like them. Maybe this explains why the majority of Korean celebrities have gone under the knife at least once.

6   This rush for Western beauty has not only plagued South Korea, but is **seeping** into other parts of Asia, such as Japan and China. Korean pop culture is **dominating** Asia today with its soap opera series, movies, cosmetics, and technology. In 2004, after the hit TV show "Dae-jang-geum," many Japanese and Taiwanese women flocked to South Korean cosmetic clinics asking to look like the hit's main character, Young-Hae Lee, who is known for her big round eyes, small chin, and high nose. *Newsweek* describes the westernization of beauty standards: "Eastern and Western tastes have been **cross-pollinating** with a **vengeance**... The **zaftig** Indian goddesses and the heart-shaped face of the Chinese beauty are yielding to round eyes, **oblong** faces and lean figures." But perhaps this **surge** for Western beauty is just an **ephemeral** trend, like skinny-legged jeans.

7   Much evidence indicates that this beauty ideal is not a trend, but a very real standard that is growing deeper into Korean society. Appearance is starting to play a bigger role in the workplace, to the extent that men are starting to resort to cosmetic surgery also. The most popular surgeries among these men are almost identical to those for women—eyelid and nose jobs. In other words, this shows that the standards for beauty not only apply to women, but also to men. According to a Men's Health Research, "86 percent of South Korean men between age 25 and 37 believe their competitiveness for jobs would be increased by having a good appearance and healthy body," and over half the South Korean male population are dissatisfied with their appearance. Therefore, the continuing high rates of cosmetic surgeries, and the

growing number of Korean celebrities who look almost "white" as a result of these procedures, indicate the extent to which Western beauty standards have been ingrained into South Korea.

8 Perhaps the quest for western beauty is political as well as cultural. Going back to the **Imperialist** era in the 1800s, the notion of white **supremacy** is still alive in our minds since Western nations, such as the United States, are still the most powerful and wealthiest. Perhaps even the notions of "walking, talking, and looking" like the white race still exist to the **subtlest** extents. For instance, many countries around the world, including South Korea, are required to speak English, the language of the world power—the United States—as their second language. As a result, most South Korean students are reasonably fluent in English by the time they reach high school.

9 Perhaps the **obsession** with beauty is due to the fact that human nature always strives for what is thought to be better. So Koreans associate beauty with people of countries that are wealthier than they are, and as a result strive to be more like them. In essence, this quest for beauty is no different than the quest for any other **greed** in life, such as money and fame. There is always someone more beautiful, richer, taller, and smarter. We always want what we can't have. We cannot help but wonder about people and places that we will never be or see. Our **elusive** journey toward the complete perfection that we can never achieve begins.

10 The solution to this plague is starting with the transformation of one individual at a time in South Korea. The fact that nearly half the population is somehow displeased with their appearance and willing to undergo cosmetic surgery shows that something is culturally wrong here. But before these individuals can change, the change needs to begin with the role models in Korea, the celebrities and other media figures. Essentially, the face of Korean media needs to change. They need to stop sending the message that beauty means Nicole Kidman and Britney Spears, and instead show that true Asian characteristics are beautiful too. They need to realize that smaller eyes, rounder faces, and flatter noses can be beautiful. By continuing to have eyelid surgeries and nose jobs, the Koreans are rejecting their natural Asian beauties and perpetuating the notion that western features are more beautiful.

Words and Expressions

eyelid *n.* each of the upper and lower folds of skin which cover the eye when closed 眼皮,眼睑

crease *n.* a line or ridge produced on paper, cloth or skin (纸,布或皮肤的)折痕,褶皱

surgery *n.* the branch of medicine concerned with treatment of injuries or disorders of the body by incision or manipulation, esp. with instruments 外科学,外科手术

stitch *v.* make, mend, or join (sth.) with stitches 缝,缝补,缝合

complexion *n.* the natural color, texture, and appearance of a person's skin, esp. of the face 天然肤色(尤指面色)

essentially *ad.* used to emphasize the basic, fundamental, or intrinsic nature of a person, thing, or situation 基本上,本质上

beam *v.* smile radiantly 面露喜色,满脸堆笑

plastic surgery the process of reconstructing or repairing parts of the body by the transfer of tissue, either in the treatment of injury or for cosmetic reasons 整形手术

mystical *a.* inspiring a sense of spiritual mystery, awe, and fascination 使人敬畏的，使人迷恋的，使人感到玄秘的

quest *v.* a search for sth. 寻求，探求

convince *v.* cause (someone) to believe firmly in the truth of sth. 使确信，使信服

sacrifice *v.* give up (sth. important or valued) for the sake of other considerations 牺牲，献出

chisel *v.* cut or shape (sth.) with a chisel 凿，镌，雕

protagonist *n.* the leading character or one of the major characters in a drama, film, novel, or other fictional text 主人公

resort *v.* turn to and adopt 采取，诉诸

cosmetic *a.* designed or serving to improve the appearance of the body, esp. the face 化妆用的；美容的

predominantly *ad.* mainly, for the most part 主要地，大部分地

dilemma *n.* a situation in which a difficult choice has to be made between two or more alternatives, esp. ones that are equally undesirable (进退两难的)困境，窘境

billboard *n.* a large outdoor board for displaying advertisements (户外)广告牌，广告招贴板

seep *v.* flow or leak slowly through porous material or small holes(液体)渗出，渗漏

dominate *v.* have a commanding influence on; exercise control over 支配，控制

cross-pollinate *v.* pollinate (a flower or plant) with pollen from another flower or plant 异花受粉

vengeance *n.* punishment inflicted or retribution exacted for an injury or wrong 报仇，复仇，报复

zaftig *a.* having a full, rounded figure; plump 体态丰盈的，丰满的

oblong *a.* having an elongated and typically rectangular shape 长方形的

surge *v.* a powerful rush of an emotion or feeling(感情)汹涌，翻腾

ephemeral *a.* lasting for a very short time 短暂的，昙花一现的

imperialist *a.* 帝国主义的

supremacy *n.* the state or condition of being superior to all others in authority, power, or status 至高无上，最高地位

subtle *a.* (esp. of a change or distinction) so delicate or precise as to be difficult to analyze or describe 微妙的，细微的，难以描述的，难以分析的

obsession *n.* the state of being obsessed with sb. or sth. 着迷

greed *n.* intense and selfish desire for sth., esp. wealth, power, or food 贪婪，贪心，贪欲

elusive *a.* difficult to find, catch, or achieve 难以分辨(或捉摸、得到)的

Background Information

1. Caucasian: In common use in American English, the term "Caucasian" (rarely supplemented with the word "race") is sometimes restricted to Europeans and other lighter-skinned populations within these areas, and may be considered equivalent to the varying definitions of white people. The term continues to be widely used in many scientific and general contexts, usually with its more restricted sense of "white", specifically White American in a US context.

2. Western Eyes: This documentary presents two Canadian women of Asian descent who are contemplating eyelid surgery. Maria and Sharon, of Philippine and Korean heritage respectively, believe their looks—specifically their eyes—get in the way of how people see them. Layering their stories with pop culture references to beauty icons and supermodels, filmmaker Ann Shin looks at the pain that lies deep behind the desire for plastic surgery.

Learn about Words

Often you can tell the meaning of a word from its context — the words around it. Please find the word in the paragraph that means:

1. lasting or intended to last or remain unchanged indefinitely (1)
2. demanding deep study or thought (1)
3. involving or requiring strenuous effort; difficult and tiring (3)
4. becoming absorbed and integrated (4)
5. increase, spread, or develop rapidly (5)
6. a famous person (5)
7. cause continual trouble or distress to (6)
8. go together in a crowd (6)
9. firmly fix or establish (a habit, belief, or attitude) (7)
10. make (sth., typically an undesirable situation or an unfounded belief) continue indefinitely (10)

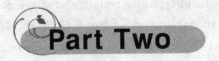

Part Two

Reading Skill — Reading for the Main Idea in a Paragraph

The particular reading skill introduced in this unit is reading for the main idea of a paragraph. This skill is one of the most useful reading skills students can develop. Finding the main idea is necessary for the understanding of a piece of writing.

The main idea of a paragraph is usually stated by one of the sentences in the paragraph. The main idea sentence is commonly known as "a topic sentence" or "a topic statement". Most frequently the first sentence of a paragraph states the main idea. However, the main idea sentence may also appear in other places: in the middle or at the end of a paragraph. Sometimes, there is no sentence in a paragraph that directly states the main idea. The main idea is simply left unstated or implied.

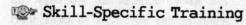 Skill-Specific Training

Read the passage and try to sum up the main idea of the specific paragraph.

American Culture: Myths & Realities

1   From your reading, from American films and TV and from talking with Americans in your country, you have probably formed some idea of life in the United States. Some of what you have seen and heard is true; some of it is probably distorted or just plain fiction. To help you distinguish fantasy from fact, we include several common "mythical" statements about life in the United States, followed by our view of the reality behind the myths. Remember though, that each person's experience is different, and part of the value of your experience abroad will be your own discovery of America and Americans.

Main idea of Para. 1: _____

MYTH: Life is easy in the United States.

2   **REALITY:** While it is true that the material standard of living in the United States is high, this has not resulted in a leisurely pace of life. Visitors to the United States are often surprised at how hard most Americans work, at their long work hours and short vacations, and at the fast pace of American life in general. Even leisure time is often devoted to activities such as sports, exercise, or other hobbies that involve intense activity and effort. Many Americans are uncomfortable with true leisure and feel guilty about doing nothing or spending long periods of time relaxing or talking with friends.

Main idea of Para. 2: _____

MYTH: America is "the land of the free" so I can do whatever I want there.

3   **REALITY:** Individual freedom is an important American value, but newcomers may find themselves overwhelmed by the legal and **bureaucratic** restrictions on their activities and confused by the complexities of social interaction.

4   Throughout their 300-year history, Americans have been trying to balance the freedom of the individual with the well being of society, sometimes with odd results. Often the right of a majority to freedom from something wins out, as in anti-smoking laws, where the right of non-smokers to be free **overrides** the right of smokers to smoke. International students are often

shocked by the number of rules governing their behavior as foreigners, as students, as motorists, as bicyclists—any of the roles they may assume during their stay in the United States.

5　The rules of social behavior in the United States can be equally confusing. There is a strong **dose** of **Puritanism** mixed in with generally **laissez-faire** American attitude, which makes it difficult to predict how people will behave or react to others, which means that values may differ widely from one social group to another and from one individual to another. Sometimes it may seem that no rules apply and that "anything goes", but a newcomer should be wary of making assumptions about what is acceptable, especially in the area of sexual relations.

Main idea of Para. 5: _____

MYTH: Americans are racist/ Americans are tolerant.

6　**REALITY**: The contradictory stereotypes exist side by side, and both have elements of truth. In general you need not fear that you will encounter **overt** racism in the United States, particularly within the university or college community.

7　In regions where there are many immigrants you may find yourself blending in suffering more from indifference than intolerance. In other more isolated and **homogeneous** areas, you may be an object of curiosity, noticed and welcomed, but perhaps not always understood. Because of America's relative geographical isolation, many Americans are quite ignorant about the rest of the world and may be rather **chauvinistic** (have a sense of national superiority). This can be irritating but you will find that hostility towards foreigners is rare.

8　Racial and ethnic prejudice is unfortunately a reality in the United States and occasionally a foreign student experiences hostility, even violence, of this nature. It would be wise to be aware of the tensions that may exist in the communities you visit in the United States, but do not fear that this will be a common or frequent problem. Pay attention to the news, listen to the advice of friends, and perhaps take a class on race relations in the United States. This is a complex issue that reflects many of the **paradoxes** of American history.

Main idea of Para. 8: _____

9　Be aware also that you may have been influenced by racial stereotyping in American films. Visitors to the United States are sometimes surprised to find that the African-Americans they meet in the United States have nothing in common with the violent stereotype so often projected in the movies.

MYTH: The United States has a classless society.

10   **REALITY:** Although the United States does not have a history or tradition of rigidly defined social classes, distinctions among economic classes in the United States result in **de facto** social **stratification**. Although the majority of Americans can be considered to belong to the middle class, there is a small, wealthy upper class and a growing underclass. Still, the American ideal of equal educational opportunity and the belief that hard work and ability should be rewarded make for a society in which upward mobility is still common.

Main idea of Para. 10: _____

MYTH: Americans are rude and loud.

11   **REALITY:** This is the image of the "ugly American" who, when abroad, demands in loud English to be understood. Although you may find examples of this stereotype on your campus, they will probably be few. It is true that Americans are often less **inhibited** socially than people from some other cultures. It is equally true that directness, or saying what one thinks, is acceptable behaviour. Americans value honesty and frankness. They are generally not embarrassed or angered by being told they are wrong, as long as the criticism is stated in a friendly and respectful way. They would generally prefer an honest argument or refusal to polite but insincere agreement.

12   The definition of "rudeness" varies widely from one culture to another. Do not jump to hasty conclusions about the intention behind someone's words or behaviour that may seem very rude to you. Someone who tells you that you have done something wrong, including your professor, is probably trying to help you, not embarrass or hurt you.

MYTH: All Americans are rich and drive fast cars.

13   **REALITY:** In the United States, as in any country, there is a wide **spectrum** of economic status. You may be surprised to find American students at your university who come from very modest **means** and who struggle daily with money issues. Many American students go deeply into debt to obtain a university degree.

14   Some of the students you meet will, in fact, be rich, but you may find it hard at first to tell the rich from the poor. Even "poor" American students own a lot of things, from cars and computers to stereo and **skis**. Material goods are easy to acquire in a consumer-orientated, credit-driven society, but they do not necessarily indicate great wealth. A car may be a practical necessity for a student who works long hours after classes or who lives with his or her

family in another town.

MYTH: American students are less prepared academically than students from my country, and I will not have to work very hard in class.

15 **REALITY:** Some American students are less prepared academically than others. While it may be tempting to think that you will not have much competition in the classroom, **rest assured** that there are many, many academically prepared and highly competitive American students. Do not underestimate the effect a change in language or a change in classroom style can have on your performance. In general, American students have a lot of experience in test taking and at expressing their opinions in class. You may come from an academic system that does not emphasize those skills.

Main idea of Para. 15: _____

MYTH: American professors are casual, sometimes even asking students to address them by their first names.

16 **REALITY:** It is true that your American professors may ask you to address them by their first names, but this does not mean they do not expect your respect. The ways in which **courtesy** and respect are shown to an American professor may well differ from how they are expressed in your country. Respect in a U. S. classroom includes a willingness to participate in class debate and to ask questions when you do not understand something that has been said. Spend time watching how your American classmates interact with the professors. You will catch on quickly to the unique mix of **formality** and structure.

MYTH: American students use illegal drugs.

17 **REALITY:** Some do, most do not.

📖 Words and Expressions

bureaucratic *a.* 官僚的，官僚主义的，官僚作风的

override *v.* be more important than 优先于，重要性超过

dose *n.* a quantity of a medicine or drug taken or recommended to be taken at a particular time 一剂，一服，一点，一份

Puritanism *n.* 清教主义

laissez-faire *a.* 〈法〉自由放任的，放任主义的

overt *a.* done or shown openly; plainly or readily apparent, not secret or hidden 公开的，明显的

homogeneous *a.* consisting of parts all of the same kind 由同种组成的

chauvinistic *a.* 沙文主义的

paradox *n.* a situation, person, or thing that combines contradictory features or qualities 有矛盾特点的情景(或人),怪事,怪人

de facto *a.* 〈拉〉实际上存在的

stratification *n.* 层化,成层,阶层的形成

inhibit *v.* hinder, restrain, or prevent 阻碍,制止,防止,禁止

spectrum *n.* a range 范围,幅度

means *n.* money, financial resources 金钱,收入

ski *n.* 滑雪板

rest assured 确信无疑,放心

courtesy *n.* politeness in one's attitude and behaviour towards others 礼貌,谦恭

formality *n.* the rigid observance of rules of convention or etiquette 拘泥形式,遵守礼节

Comprehension of the Text

1. Why are many Americans uncomfortable with true leisure?

_____.

2. Why can't newcomers do whatever they want in America?

_____.

3. What is the social stratification like in America?

_____.

4. Will Americans feel angry if they are told they are wrong?

_____.

5. Can you tell the rich students from the poor ones easily at first?

_____.

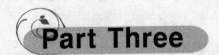

Part Three

> **Reading Comprehension (Skimming and Scanning)**
>
> **Directions:** *In this part, you will have 15 minutes to go over the passage quickly and answer the questions. For questions 1~7, choose the best answer from the four choices marked A), B), C) and D). For statements 8~10, complete the sentences with the information given in the passage.*

Myths and Realities of Thanksgiving

Martin Kelly

In America today, Thanksgiving is generally seen as a time to get together with loved ones, eat a ridiculously large amount of food, watch some football, and of course give thanks for all the blessings in our lives. Many homes will be decorated with horns of plenty, dried corn, pumpkins and other symbols of Thanksgiving. Schoolchildren across America will reenact Thanksgiving by dressing as either pilgrims or Wampanoag Indians and sharing a meal of some sort. All of this is wonderful for helping create a sense of family, national identity, and of course remembering to say thanks at least once a year. However, as with many other holidays and events in American History, many of these commonly believed traditions about the origins and celebration of this holiday are based more on myth than fact. Let's look at the truth behind our celebration of Thanksgiving.

Origins of Thanksgiving

The first interesting thing to point out is that the feast shared with the Wampanoag Indians and the first mention of Thanksgiving are really not the same event. During the first winter in 1621, 46 of the 102 pilgrims died. Thankfully, the following year resulted in a plentiful harvest. The pilgrims decided to celebrate with a feast that would include 90 natives who helped the pilgrims survive during that first winter. One of the most celebrated of those natives was a Wampanoag who the settlers called Squanto. He taught the pilgrims where to fish and hunt and where to plant New World crops like corn and squash. He also helped negotiate a treaty between the pilgrims and chief Massasoit.

This first feast included many fowl, though it is not certain that it included turkey, along with venison, corn, and pumpkin. This was all prepared by the four women settlers and two teenage girls. This idea of holding a harvest feast was not something new to the pilgrims. Many cultures throughout history had held feasts and banquets honoring their individual deities or simply being thankful for the bounty. Many in England celebrated the British Harvest Home tradition.

The First Thanksgiving

The first actual mention of the word thanksgiving in early colonial history was not associated with the first feast described above. The first time this term was associated with a feast or celebration was in 1623. That year the pilgrims were living through a terrible drought that continued from May through July. The pilgrims decided to spend an entire day in July fasting and praying for rain. The next day, a light rain occurred. Further, additional settlers and supplies arrived from the Netherlands. At that point, Governor Bradford proclaimed a day of Thanksgiving to offer prayers and thanks to God. However, this was by no means a yearly occurrence.

The next recorded day of Thanksgiving occurred in 1631 when a ship full of supplies that was feared to be lost at sea actually pulled into Boston Harbor. Governor Bradford again ordered a day of Thanksgiving and prayers.

Was the Pilgrim Thanksgiving the First

While most Americans think of the Pilgrims as celebrating the first Thanksgiving in America, there are some claims that others in the New World should be recognized as first. For example, in Texas there is a marker that says, "Feast of the First Thanksgiving—1541." Further, other states and territories had their own traditions about their first thanksgiving. The truth is that many times when a group was delivered from drought or hardship, a day of prayers and thanksgiving might be proclaimed.

Beginning of the Yearly Tradition

During the mid-1600s, Thanksgiving as we know it today began to take shape. In Connecticut valley towns, incomplete records show proclamations of Thanksgiving for September 18, 1639, as well as 1644, and after 1649. Instead of just celebrating special harvests or events, these were set aside as an annual holiday. One of the first recorded celebrations commemorating the 1621 feast in Plymouth colony occurred in Connecticut in 1665.

Growing Thanksgiving Traditions

Over the next hundred years, each colony had different traditions and dates for celebrations. Some were not annual though Massachusetts and Connecticut both celebrated Thanksgiving annually on November 20 and Vermont and New Hampshire observed it on December 4. On December 18, 1775, the Continental Congress declared December 18 to be a national day of Thanksgiving for the win at Saratoga. Over the next nine years, they declared six more Thanksgivings with one Thursday set aside each fall as a day of prayers.

George Washington issued the first Thanksgiving Proclamation by a President of the United States on November 26, 1789. Interestingly, some of the future presidents such as Thomas Jefferson and Andrew Jackson would not agree to resolutions for a national day of Thanksgiving because they felt it was not within their constitutional power. Over these years, Thanksgiving was still being celebrated in many states, but often on different dates. Most states, however, celebrated it sometime in November.

Sarah Josepha Hale and Thanksgiving

Sarah Josepha Hale is an important figure in gaining a national holiday for Thanksgiving. Hale wrote the novel Northwood, or Life North and South in 1827 which argued for the virtue of the North against the evil slave owners of the South. One of the chapters in her book discussed the importance of Thanksgiving as a national holiday. She became the editor of the *Ladies' Magazine* in Boston. This would eventually become the *Lady's Book and Magazine*, also known as *Godey's Lady's Book*, the most widely distributed magazine in the country during the 1840s and 50s. Beginning in 1846, Hale began her campaign to make the last Thursday in November a Thanksgiving national holiday. She wrote an editorial for the magazine about this each year and wrote letters to governors in every state and territory. On September 28, 1863 during the Civil War, Hale wrote a letter to President Abraham Lincoln "as Editress of the 'Lady's Book'" to have the day of annual Thanksgiving made a National and fixed Union Festival. Then on October 3, 1863, Lincoln, in a proclamation written by Secretary of State William Seward, proclaimed a nationwide Thanksgiving Day as the last Thursday of November.

The New Deal Thanksgiving

After 1869, each year the president proclaimed the last Thursday in November as Thanksgiving Day. However, there was some contention over the actual date. Each year individuals tried to change the date of the holiday for various reasons. Some wanted to combine it with Armistice Day, November 11 commemorating the day when the armistice was signed between the allies and Germany to end World War I. However, the real argument for a date change came about in 1933 during the depths of the Great Depression. The National Dry Retail Goods Association asked President Franklin Roosevelt to move the date of Thanksgiving that year since it would fall on November 30. Since the traditional shopping season for Christmas then as now started with Thanksgiving, this would leave a short shopping season reducing possible sales for the retailers. Roosevelt refused. However, when Thanksgiving would again fall on November 30, 1939, Roosevelt then agreed. Even though Roosevelt's proclamation only set the actual date of Thanksgiving as the 23rd for the District of Columbia, this change caused a furor. Many people felt that the president was messing with tradition for the sake of the economy. Each state decided for itself with 23 states choosing to celebrate on the New Deal date of November 23 and 23 staying with the traditional date. Texas and Colorado decided to celebrate Thanksgiving twice!

The confusion of the date for Thanksgiving continued through 1940 and 1941. Due to the confusion, Roosevelt announced that the traditional date of the last Thursday in November would return in 1942. However, many individuals wanted to insure that the date would not be changed again. Therefore, a bill was introduced that Roosevelt signed into law on November 26, 1941 establishing the fourth Thursday in November as Thanksgiving Day. This has been followed by every state in the union since 1956.

1. Which of the following may NOT be the symbols of Thanksgiving?
   A. Horns.   B. Cotton.   C. Corn.   D. Pumpkins.
2. During the first winter in 1621, how many pilgrims died?
   A. 102.   B. 90.   C. 82.   D. 46.
3. What might the native Squanto NOT do?
   A. He taught the pilgrims where to fish and hunt.
   B. He taught the pilgrims where to plant crops.
   C. He taught the pilgrims how to cook.

    D. He helped the pilgrims negotiate a treaty.

4. When was the term Thanksgiving first associated with a feast?
    A. In 1621.   B. In 1623.
    C. In 1631.   D. In 1639.

5. Where did Thanksgiving begin to be set aside as an annual holiday?
    A. In Massachusetts.   B. In Vermont.
    C. In Connecticut.   D. In New Hampshire.

6. Who issued the first Thanksgiving Proclamation by a President of the United States?
    A. George Washington.   B. Thomas Jefferson.
    C. Andrew Jackson.   D. Abraham Lincoln.

7. When is Thanksgiving Day celebrated now?
    A. On November 11.   B. On November 23.
    C. On November 30.   D. On the fourth Thursday in November.

8. Thomas Jefferson and Andrew Jackson would not agree to resolutions for a national day of Thanksgiving because _____.

9. Sarah Josepha Hale, an important figure in gaining a national holiday for Thanksgiving, wrote the novel *Northwood*, *or Life North and South* in 1827 which argued for _____.

10. _____ asked President Franklin Roosevelt to move the date of Thanksgiving that year since it would fall on November 30.

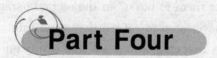

Part Four

> **Directions**: *There is a passage in this section. This passage is followed by some questions. For each of them there are four choices marked A), B), C) and D). You should decide on the best choice.*

The Frugal Gourmet Cooks American

    Our real American foods have come from our soil and have been used by many groups — those who already lived here and those who have come here to live. The Native Americans already had developed an interesting cuisine using the abundant foods that were so prevalent.

    The influence that the English had upon our national eating habits is easy to see. They were a tough lot, those English, and they ate in a tough manner. They wiped their mouths on the tablecloth, if there happened to be one, and they ate until you would expect them to burst.

European travelers to this country in those days were most often shocked by American eating habits, which included too much fat and too much salt and too much liquor. Not much has changed! And, the Revolutionists refused to use the fork since it marked them as Europeans. The fork was not absolutely common on the American dinner table until about the time of the Civil War, the 1860s. Those English were a tough lot.

Other immigrant groups added their own touches to the preparation of our New World food products. The groups that came still have a special sense of self-identity through their ancestral heritage, but they see themselves as Americans. This special self-identity through your ancestors who came from other lands was supposed to disappear in this country. The term melting pot was first used in reference to America in the late 1700s, so this belief that we would all become the same has been with us for a long time. Thank goodness! It has never worked. The various immigrant groups continue to add flavor to the pot, all right, but you can pick out the individual flavors easily.

The largest ancestry group in America is the English. There are more people in America who claim to have come from English blood than there are in England. But is their food English? Thanks to God, it is not! It is American. The second largest group is the Germans, then the Irish, the Afro-Americans, the French, the Italians, the Scottish, and the Polish. The Mexican and American Indian groups are all smaller than any of the above, though they were the original cooks in this country.

1. Which of the following statements is nearly identical in meaning with the sentence "they ate until you would expect them to burst" in the second paragraph?

   A. You bet they would never stop to eat till they were full.

   B. What you can expect is that they would not stop eating unless there was no more food.

   C. The only thing you would expect is that they wouldn't stop eating till they had had enough of the food.

   D. The only thing you would expect is that they wouldn't stop eating till they felt sick.

2. Which of the following statements is NOT true?

   A. English people had bad table manners.

   B. American food was exclusively unique in its flavors and varieties.

   C. American diet contained a lot of fat, salt and liquor.

   D. Europeans were not at all accustomed to the American way of eating.

3. The author's attitude towards the American food is that _____.

   A. American food is better than foods from other countries

   B. American food is superior to European food

   C. European food has helped enrich the flavors and varieties of American food

   D. people from other countries can still identify from the American foods the food that is unique to their countries

4. Immigrant groups, when they got settled down in the United States, still have had their

own sense of self-identity because _____.

A. their foods are easily identified among all the foods Americans eat

B. their foods stand out in sharp contrast to foods of other countries

C. they know pretty well what elements of the American food are of their own countries' origin

D. they know pretty well how their foods contribute to American cuisine

5. Which of the following statements is true?

A. People from other cultures or nations start to lose their self-identity once they get settled down in America.

B. The "melting pot" is supposed to melt all the foods but in reality it doesn't.

C. The special sense of self-identity of people from other countries can't be maintained once they become Americans.

D. The "melting pot" finds it capable of melting all the food traditions into the American tradition.

Part Five

Reading for Pleasure

American Table Manners

Manners in every country are different. What is polite in China may not be polite in the United States. These basic rules will help you enjoy western food with your American friends.

Always put the napkin on your lap first. Before you leave the table, fold your napkin and put it beside your plate.

As the meal is served, use the silverware farthest from the plate first. When eating something in a bowl, do not leave the spoon in the bowl. Put it on the plate beneath the bowl. Soup, as well as all American food is eaten quietly. Do not slurp the soup. The soup spoon is used by moving the spoon away from you. Do not over fill the spoon. The bowl may be tipped slightly away from you to allow the last bit of soup to be collected on the spoon. Do not pick the bowl up to hold it closer to your mouth. When you have finished your meal, place your knife and fork side by side on the plate. This signals that you have finished eating.

Wait until everyone has been served to begin eating. Everyone begins to eat at the same time. The host or hostess may invite you to start eating before everyone is served. Some foods may be cold if you are required to wait until everyone is served. If invited to begin before others are served, wait until three or four people have been served before starting to eat. While eating, remember not to talk with your mouth full of food.

During the meal, the host or hostess will offer you a second helping of food. Sometimes they will ask you to help yourself. When they offer you food, give a direct answer. If you refuse the first time, they might not ask you again.

At the table, ask others to pass you dishes that are out of your reach. Good phrases to know are: "Please pass the _____" or "Could you hand me the _____, please?" If asked to pass the salt to someone, you should pass both the salt and pepper which are placed on the table together. Hand the salt and pepper to the person seated next to you. Do not reach over the person next to you to pass anything to others.

Sit up straight at the table. Bring the food up to your mouth. Do not lean down to your plate.

Cut large pieces of meat, potatoes and vegetables into bite size pieces. Eat the pieces one at a time.

When eating spaghetti, wind the noodles up on your fork. You may use your spoon to assist in winding the noodle on your fork. The spaghetti on your fork should be eaten in one bite. It is very impolite to eat half your noodles and allow the other half to fall back on your plate.

Some foods may be eaten with your fingers. If you are not sure if it is proper to eat something by picking it up with your fingers watch what others do before doing so yourself. Examples of foods which can be eaten with your fingers include: bacon which has been cooked until it is very crisp; bread should be broken rather than cut with a knife; cookies; sandwiches; and small fruits and berries on the stem. Most fast foods are intended to be eaten with your fingers.

Do not lean on your arm or elbow while eating. You may rest your hand and wrist on the edge of the table.

In America, people do not use toothpicks at the table.

Some of the rules mentioned here may be somewhat relaxed in informal settings. The best way to learn good manners is to watch others. Observe the way your western friends eat. This is the best way to avoid making mistakes when you are unsure of what to do.

Humor Prepared for You

In European Heaven:
Cooks are French;
Mechanics are German;
Cops are British;
Bosses are Swiss;
Lovers are Italian.

In European Hell:
Cooks are British;
Mechanics are French;
Cops are German;
Lovers are Swiss;
Bosses are Italians.

Famous Sayings

When in Rome, do as the Romans do.
入乡随俗

The value of culture is its effect on character. It avails nothing unless it ennobles and strengthens that. Its use is for life. Its aim is not beauty but goodness.

——*Somerset Maugham, British novelist and dramatist*

文化的价值在于它对人类品性的影响。除非文化能使品性变得高尚、有力,否则将一无是处。文化的作用在于裨益人生。它的目标不是美,而是善。

—— 英国小说家、戏剧家 毛姆

Unit Two

The Olympic Games

The Olympic Games are a major international event featuring summer and winter sports, in which thousands of athletes participate in a variety of competitions. The Games are currently held every two years, with Summer and Winter Olympic Games alternating. Originally, the ancient Olympic Games were held in Olympia, Greece, from the 8th century BC to the 5th century AD. In the late 19th century, Baron Pierre de Coubertin was inspired by Olympic festivals to revive the Games. For this purpose, he founded the International Olympic Committee (IOC) in 1894, and two years later, the modern Olympic Games were established in Athens.

In this unit, you will read:
- China Ties Olympic Gold to Quest for Worldwide Esteem
- Michael Phelps — Biography
- The Olympic Games
- A Research on Referee's Errors
- Summer Olympic Mascots

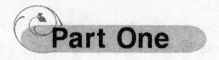

Part One

Pre-reading Questions

1. What are the benefits of holding Olympic Games?
2. What are the drawbacks of holding Olympic Games?
3. Some people think that if you are second in Olympic Games, then you are a loser. What's your opinion?

China Ties Olympic Gold to Quest for Worldwide Esteem

Calum MacLeod

1   Photos of Olympic champions line the walls of a table tennis hall at Beijing Shichahai Sports School, where children battle across 30 tables and hundreds of balls litter the floor. A red **banner** with Chinese characters reads: "Future champions go from here to the world."

2   Sun Kun, 10, practices table tennis for more than five hours a day as a resident of Shichahai, which trains athletes in a variety of sports, including **gymnastics**, weightlifting and volleyball. "My parents give me a lot of pressure. They want me to be a world champion," says Sun, who has trained in China's sports schools since he was 6.

3   Sun's family pays $ 6,450 a year for his training here. Their hope is Shichahai officials will think enough of his talent to elevate him from trainee to student status, so the state will begin picking up most of the costs of taking part in a rigorous training system modeled after the old Soviet sports machine.

4   Shichahai is one of thousands of sports schools in China, which together train more than 6 million young athletes. It's part of an increasingly aggressive sports program the Chinese hope to **showcase** in the 2008 Summer Olympics, which begin here next August. For a Communist nation of 1.3 billion people that for generations largely avoided involvement with the West, the Olympics represent a chance to announce itself as a modern athletic and economic power — and boost national pride.

5   So there is an unmistakable urgency at Shichahai and many other sports schools that identify and train athletic Chinese children as potential **Olympians**. Such schools employ a strict, no-nonsense approach to training that has been criticized as abusive.

6   But many Chinese families — those that can afford it and particularly low-income ones attracted by the potential for better health care and education for their children — enthusiastically join the pursuit of glory through sports.

7   "I hope he'll be a champion; this place can develop him," says Sun's mother, Zhao Shixia.

"Everyone said it was the best at table tennis and other sports. He needs to be conscientious. I hope we'll get some payback."

8   A visit to Shichahai provides a rare glimpse into China's training of its athletes, which is mostly secret. He Yi, an official for the Beijing Sports Bureau, a branch of the National Sports Ministry, says government sports officials "are like the U.S. colleges supporting sport."

9   "We study Western methods, but we still have the inertia of the planned economy," says He, a former swimming national champion and sports school graduate. "We can learn experience and skills from Western countries, but the actual sports system is tied to our country's political system."

10   Ren Hai, director of the Chinese sports ministry's Olympic Studies Center, estimates that at least 70% of China's full-time athletes graduated from specialized state schools. "The schools still provide the basis of sport in China," Ren says.

11   The Chinese training methods have drawn scrutiny. After a visit to Shichahai in 2005, Matthew Pinsent, an Olympic **rowing** champion for Britain and former International Olympic Committee member, reported that gymnasts were being physically abused.

12   Some young Chinese athletes say they are accustomed to some abuse but defend the practice as part of training to be the best.

13   School director Liu Hongbin says abuse isn't condoned: "However, the concept of beating and abuse are different in different cultures and countries."

14   China's recent rise in medals comes despite the fact it "is not a sports country," says Josef Capousek, a former German coach who leads China's Olympic canoe and **kayak** team. "Unlike in the USA or Germany, you don't see people jogging or rowing for fun. Everything is performance sport — or nothing."

15   Each year, authorities identify children who show athletic promise to train in sports schools, often in sports unknown to most Chinese.

16   Kayaker Zhang Jinmei says she fell out of a kayak as a teenager when a coach took her out for a trial run in Qinhuangdao.

17   "I had never rowed a boat before; I didn't know what a kayak looked like," Zhang says. "And I couldn't even swim."

18   The former discus thrower says she was picked for kayaking because she is "tall and stout, with good upper-body strength." Now 25, Zhang won a 2004 World Cup race and hopes to win an Olympic medal next summer.

Funding the elite

19   China's system for developing elite athletes contrasts with that of the USA, where top Olympic prospects receive no government funding. Athletes receive money from the U.S. Olympic Committee (USOC) and several other sources, including corporate sponsorships, appearance fees and winnings.

20   China does not make public what it spends on sports programs, but Steve Roush, the

USOC's chief of sport performance, estimates China is spending ＄400 million to ＄500 million to train elite athletes in the four years leading up to the 2008 Games. That doesn't include younger athletes training in sports schools. The USOC and the sports' national governing bodies will spend ＄200 million to ＄225 million during that period, Roush says.

21　Much of China's funding for the Beijing Olympics is going to 100 to 150 athletes, while the USA is funding 2,500 to 3,000 potential 2008 Olympians, Roush says. "I think now they are targeting their very best with the most resources."

22　"There is big political pressure in China to do well," Capousek says. "China wants to show how strong it is."

23　Shichahai cost ＄4 million to operate in 2006, with most of the money coming from the government. Student fees and sponsorships also feed the school's budget, Liu says.

24　"We are a developing country. Our economic basis and national conditions are different from the USA, so we need preferential policies" that attract promising young athletes to sports schools, Liu says. "There are very poor conditions in the countryside, and some students cannot afford to pay."

'I want to be a world champion'

25　The Shichahai school was established in 1958, during a decade in which newly communist China copied much from the Soviet Union, including its sports system, which feeds, clothes and houses its chosen athletes.

26　Besides athletic training, elementary students attend classes in literature, math, English, natural science, **ideology** and morality. On Saturdays they can go home to their families for the night.

27　Lang Ping, head coach of the U.S. women's volleyball team and a former Chinese national team member and coach, was 13 when she first went to a sports school in Beijing to train in volleyball.

28　She remembers getting up at 6 a.m. three days a week to train before classes. After school she would train for three more hours every day except Sunday.

29　Sacrifice is part of the path to greatness, Shichahai director Liu says. "Our students want to be champions for our school, for Beijing and for the country. We teach them to be **patriotic**. If you win glory for the nation, the nation will reward you."

📖 Words and Expressions

esteem *n.* respect and admiration, typically for a person 尊敬,敬重

banner *n.* a long strip of cloth bearing a slogan or design, carried in a demonstration or procession or hung in a public place 旗,旗帜;横幅

gymnastics *n.* 体操;体操训练

showcase *v.* exhibit; display 展示;表现

Olympian *n.* 奥运会选手

rowing *n.* 赛艇运动；划船

kayak *n.* 皮艇

ideology *n.* a system of ideas and ideals, esp. one which forms the basis of economic or political theory and policy(尤指构成经济、政治理论、政策基础的)思想，思想体系

patriotic *a.* having or expressing devotion to and vigorous support for one's country 爱国的；显示爱国精神的；有爱国心的

📖 Background Information

China sent its first Olympian to the 1932 Summer Games, but the Chinese do not have a long history of Olympic achievement.

At the 1984 Games in Los Angeles, China claimed its first gold medal when shooter Xu Haifeng won the 50-meter rifle event. That summer the Chinese won 15 gold medals and 32 overall, fourth in the gold medal count behind the USA, Romania and West Germany in a year in which the Soviet Union boycotted the Olympics.

Four years later, in the Seoul Olympics, China's gold medal total dipped to five.

A two-decade surge in sports investment — along with the breakup of the Soviet Union's Olympic powerhouse — has since vaulted China in the medal standings. In the 2004 Athens Games, China was second to the USA in the gold medal count with 32 golds and had 63 medals overall. The USA won 36 golds and 102 medals overall.

2008 Summer Olympic Games

	Medal Standings	Gold	Silver	Bronze	Total
1	China	51	21	28	100
2	USA	36	38	36	110
3	Russia	23	21	28	72
4	GBR	19	13	15	47
5	Germany	16	10	15	41

📖 Learn about Words

Often you can tell the meaning of a word from its context — the words around it. Please choose the choice with the same meaning to the word used in the article.

1. make (a place) untidy with rubbish or a large number of objects left lying about (1)

2. raise to a more important or impressive level (3)

3. (of a rule, system, etc.) strictly applied or adhered to (3)

4. help or encourage (sth.) to increase or improve (4)

5. (of a person) wishing to do what is right, esp. to do one's work or duty well and thoroughly (7)

6. a tendency to do nothing or to remain unchanged (9)

7. critical observation or examination (11)

8. approve or sanction (sth.), esp. with reluctance (13)

9. rather fat or of heavy build (18)

10. a group of people considered to be the best in a particular society or category, esp. because of their power, talent, or wealth (19)

Part Two

Reading Skill — Finding out Word Meanings

Before you can start thinking critically about what you read, you have to understand the meanings of the words you are reading. You will often come across words whose meanings you do not know. What is the best way to figure out the meaning of a new word? Do you always need to get out a dictionary and spend time looking the word up?

Fortunately, there is another way that often works. You may be able to figure out the meaning of a word from its context. That is, by looking carefully at the rest of the sentence or at the sentences around it, and seeing how the word fits in.

Suppose, for example, you are told that someone has used legumes to prepare a vegetable soup. By looking at the context of the word "legumes," you can easily guess that legumes are some kind of vegetable. This meaning for "legumes" fits in best with the context of the rest of the sentence.

Skill-Specific Training

Now, figure out the meanings of the following words from their context.

1. stroke

    A. a sudden serious illness when a blood is blocked

    B. a single successful action or event

    C. a style of swimming

2. ADHD

    A. a name of an illness

    B. a name of an organization

    C. a name of swimming style

3. floor

    A. to surprise or confuse somebody

    B. to make sb. fall down by hitting them

    C. to provide a building or room with a floor

Michael Phelps — Biography

Ever hear the saying about swimmers with big hands and feet? They're **sunk** unless they've got the ability and heart to match. Not a problem for Michael Phelps, the greatest **all-around** competitor in the history of his sport. Every time he **splashes** into the water he's determined to produce a once-in-a-lifetime performance — according him rock-star status among swim fans and drawing a tidal wave of attention from the **non-chlorinated** world, as well. Iron Mike's goal heading into the 2008 Olympics was to become the gold standard for aspiring champions for generations to come. He left Beijing as something substantially more than that. This is his story...

GROWING UP

Michael Phelps was born on June 30, 1985 to Fred and Debbie Phelps. His parents already had two daughters, Hilary and Whitney. The family lived in Maryland, just outside of Baltimore. Fred was a state **trooper**, and Debbie was a middle-school teacher who was twice named Maryland's "Teacher of the Year."

Fred was a good athlete, and passed his ability on to his kids. All three got into swimming at an early age. Hilary showed real promise, particularly in the butterfly, but eventually gave up the sport. Whitney stuck with it much longer. One of the better swimmers in her area, she tried out for the U. S. Olympic team in 1996 at the age of 15. Michael was among those in attendance to cheer her on. When Whitney didn't qualify, he was left **devastated** like the rest of the family. Ultimately, her career was cut short by a series of **herniated disks**.

Michael learned a lot from his sisters, particularly the value of hard work. Hilary started swimming the year he was born, and Michael spent many afternoons in a stroller watching her practice. He eventually followed both sisters into the pool, though initially with great hesitancy. As a seven-year-old, he refused to put his face in the water. Sensing Michael's fear, his instructors allowed him to float around on his back. Not surprisingly, the first stroke he mastered was the backstroke.

Focus was never a problem for Michael in the pool. He spent hour after hour in the water. In school, however, Michael struggled at times. He was diagnosed with **ADHD** after his ninth birthday. Michael worked with Debbie to overcome the condition.

One of the turning points for Michael came when he saw swimmers Tom Malchow and Tom Dolan compete at the 1996 Summer Games in Atlanta. The 11-year-old began to dream of becoming a champion himself.

By then, Michael's home life had changed **drastically**. After years of fighting, his parents divorced. The kids went to live with Debbie. Michael grew very close to his mother, while Fred did what he could to keep a foothold in his children's lives. Today Michael has very little contact with his father.

A new male presence entered Michael's life in 1996. He had started his swimming career at Towson's Loyola High School pool. But when it became clear he needed better facilities and more professional coaching, he moved on to the North Baltimore Aquatic Club. There he met Bob Bowman. The coach recognized Michael's potential immediately.

Bowman told Debbie that her son was a rare talent. Long-limbed with big hands and feet, he took to instruction very well, loved to work hard and never seemed nervous in competition. He hated to lose, and reacted angrily on the odd occasions when he did. Once Michael flung his **goggles** away in disgust after finishing behind a swimmer of the same age. Bowman pulled him aside, and warned him never to act that way again.

Because Towson didn't have a swim team, Michael continued competing for the **NBAC**. He performed well in his sophomore year, which convinced him that he could be something truly special in the water. He picked up his training **regimen** considerably as a junior, working out 10 times a week.

ON THE RISE

In 1999, Michael earned a spot on the U.S. National B Team. At the Junior Nationals, he broke a record in the 200-meter butterfly for the 20-year-old age group. At 15, Michael became the youngest swimmer to compete for the U.S. in the Olympics in 68 years. He **acquitted** himself well, touching the wall in fifth place in the 200-meter butterfly. Michael ended the year ranked 7th in the world in the 200-meter butterfly and 44th in the 400-meter individual **medley**.

Michael entered 2001 **poised** to take another huge step in his career, and staged his coming out party at the Phillips 66 National Championships that August. First he set a world record in 200-meter butterfly at 1:54.92. Then he captured the gold in the 100-meter butterfly. Running fifth at the midway point, Michael turned on the jets down the stretch for the victory.

After graduating from high school in 2003, Michael shifted his focus to the U.S. Spring National Championships. There he floored **onlookers** by becoming the first man to win in three different strokes at one national event. His victories came in the 200-meter freestyle, 200-meter backstroke and 100-meter butterfly.

...

MAKING HIS MARK

Michael enrolled at the University of Michigan in 2005, after Coach Bowman accepted the **varsity** coaching job in Ann Arbor. He served as Bowman's assistant, and started working toward a degree in sports marketing and management.

Coming out of the Olympics, Michael had his sights set on more than Olympic glory and a big payday. He wanted to transform his sport the way other great athletes like Michael Jordan and Tiger Woods had. Now he had to wait until he re-entered the spotlight.

That opportunity came in March of 2007, at the World Championships in Melbourne, Australia. Competing in the backyard of Thorpe — the man who owned the record for six gold medals in this competition — Michael won seven events and **obliterated** world records in five by **jaw-dropping** margins. He also set personal bests in all seven events.

Michael won 100 and 200 butterfly, the 200 freestyle, the 200 and 400 individual medley, and both freestyle relays he entered. In the 400 individual medley, Michael shattered the record he set in the 2004 Summer Games by more than two seconds.

The 2008 season, of course, was all about the Olympics. Michael was primed to become the leading gold medalist in the history of the Olympics, and had a chance of winning eight golds in Beijing. That meant qualifying in eight events: 400 individual medley, 4 × 100 freestyle relay, 200 freestyle, 200 butterfly, 4 × 200 freestyle relay, 200 individual medley, 100 butterfly and 4 × 100 medley relay. Michael put forth a **glitch**-free performance in Omaha and made all eight events.

His physique **notwithstanding**, endurance may be Michael's single greatest asset. He's able to hold his stroke under pressure and when fatigue begins to creep in. From a mind over matter standpoint, Michael is also off the charts. His ability to relax, focus and block out the pain all at once is unique in his sport. He never seems nervous before a race, yet his intensity on the starting block is unmatched.

Comprehension of the Text

1. How many members are there in Michael Phelps's family?

   _____

2. What was Michael's first stroke?

   _____

3. Who is the coach of Michael Phelps?

   _____

4. In 2003, Michael won in three different strokes at one national event, and what were they?

   _____

5. What is Michael's greatest valuable quality?

   _____

Words and Expressions

sink *v.* go down below the surface of sth. , esp. of a liquid; become submerged 下沉；沉没
all-around *a.* many-sided 全面的，综合性的
splash *v.* to scatter (liquid) about in blobs 使(液体)溅起
non-chlorinated *a.* 无氯的
trooper *n.* a state policeman 警官
devastate *v.* to destroy or overwhelm, as with grief or shock 在感情上(精神上、财务上等)压垮
herniated disks 椎间盘突出
ADHD *n.* 小儿多动症
drastically *ad.* in a drastic manner 大大地；彻底地
goggles *n.* close-fitting glasses with side shields, for protecting the eyes from glare, dust,

water，etc.（用以挡光、防尘、防水等的）护目镜

NBAC *n.* 醋酸正丁酯

regimen *n.* a systematic way of life or course of therapy, often including exercise and a recommended diet（为病人规定的）生活规则，养生法

acquit *v.* to perform(one's part) 使(自己)作出某种表现

medley *n.* 混合泳接力

poise *v.* to be or cause to be balanced or suspended 体态，姿态；使平衡，使平稳

onlooker *n.* a person who observes without taking part 观看者

varsity *n.* a team representing a college or university（学校的）代表队

obliterate *v.* destroy utterly; wipe out 摧毁；抹除

jaw-dropping *a.* （informal）amazing（非正式）令人吃惊的，令人惊奇的

glitch *n.* an unexpected setback in a plan（计划）受到的意外挫折

notwithstanding *prep.* in spite of 尽管，虽然

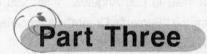

Part Three

Reading Comprehension（Skimming and Scanning）

Directions： *In this part, you will have 15 minutes to go over the passage quickly and answer the questions. For questions 1~7, mark Y (for YES) if the statement agrees with the information given in the passage; N (for NO) if the statement contradicts the information given in the passage. For questions 8~10, complete the sentences with the information given in the passage.*

The Olympic Games

Origins

The ancient Greeks first had the idea of getting men together every four years to hold and witness sporting events（in those days women did not participate, though they had their own, independent, events）. The idea was to have the best athletes from all over Greece gather in one field and compete every four years. All wars and fighting had to stop while the athletes and their supporters came together in the town of Olympia for a few days to compete in a few events, mostly related to warfare（throwing the javelin, running, wrestling, boxing and chariot racing）.

The first written reference to the Games is 776 BC. They lasted until 389 AD. The idea of having the modern Games was suggested in the mid 19th century but there weren't a world event until 1896. Besides being postponed because of wars, they have been held since then every four years in different cities around the world.

Symbols

The Olympic Games have many important symbols that most people recognize. The five rings that appear on the Olympic flag （colored yellow, green, blue, black and red） were introduced in 1914. They represent the five continents of Africa, the Americas, Australia, Asia and Europe. The flag is raised in the host city and then flown to the next one where it is kept until the next Games. The Olympic torch, a major part of the ancient Games, was brought back in 1928 and is carried with great fanfare and publicity to the host city where it lights the burning flame of the Games. It is kept burning until the close of the Games. The torch symbolizes purity, the drive for perfection and the struggle for victory.

Music

The rousing Olympic anthem is the simply named "Olympic Music" by John Williams, who wrote it for the 1984 Olympics, held in Los Angeles. What you hear first are the forty or so notes played on horns which form the "Bugler's Dream" （also called "Olympic Fanfare"） by Leo Arnaud, first played in the 1968 Games.

The torch, fanfare and flag are clearly evident in the Opening Ceremony, when everyone formally welcomes the participants and the Games can begin. Here we find the dramatic and colorful March of Nations, in which all the athletes from each country go into the venue to the sound of their country's anthem and march behind their flags, thus becoming representatives of their countries.

Athlete's Oath

One part of the Opening Ceremony that tries to keep the spirit of the Games and sportsmanship alive is when one athlete, representing all those participating, takes the Athlete's Oath:

"In the name of all the competitors, I promise that we shall take part in these Olympic Games, respecting and abiding by the rules which govern them, in the true spirit of sportsmanship, for the glory of sport, and the honor of our teams."

Medals

In the ancient Games, only the winner was celebrated. Each winner was given a simple crown of olive leaves to wear on his head. This was the only reward for his victory. Those who came in second or third got nothing. Interestingly, when the Games started again in 1896, silver medals were given to the first place winners. Later in 1904 in the St. Louis Games, gold was the top prize. Now, of course we have gold for first place, silver for second and bronze for third.

Motto

The Olympics' official motto is "Citius, Altius, Fortius". This is Latin for "Swifter, Higher, and

Stronger". This is said to represent the Olympic spirit, supposed to be present throughout the Games and generally held to be a celebration of brotherhood, competition, sportsmanship, goodwill and peace. The Games help us see how similar we are, and help us celebrate our humanity.

People

As in ancient times, those who participate in the Games are famous for the rest of their lives. Today, it's estimated that some 100,000 people have competed in the Games. These athletes, all supposed to be amateurs (people who play and get no money for their play), have to qualify or win regional and national events. They often play on their countries' national teams. If they are ill or can't make it for an event, they have substitutes. When they start playing, they become competitors or opponents on the playing field.

Officials, referees, scorekeepers and umpires monitor their play, and judges score their performances. Spectators watch the events, and fans cheer the athletes on.

Helping the athletes in their chosen sports are their trainers and coaches. Helping the athletes in their business affairs are their agents and managers. Sometimes athletes have sponsors and after the Games are over the athletes become spokesmen for companies.

The Olympic Games also require people to take on the jobs of announcers, commentators and broadcasters. These people comment on, report and describe the events that are happening and tell us about the standings of the countries and the athletes who play the Games.

Unfortunate events in world history (the 1972 Munich Olympics and 9/11) mean that security is a major concern for the Games. Thus the Olympics also employs those who are responsible for the safe-being of the athletes and spectators, including police (city, provincial and federal) and even national troops or soldiers. They are pitted against "common" criminals (thieves, pickpockets, vandals...) and terrorists.

In addition, the support staffs get the fields, grounds and arenas ready and help to maintain the equipment and facilities.

The nationalities you hear of in the Olympics fall mostly into certain suffix groups, for example:

ish (mostly European)	ese (mostly Asian)	i (mostly Middle Eastern)	an/ian	ch	other
British	Burmese	Bahraini	American	Czech	Filipino
Finnish	Chinese	Iraqi	Australian	Dutch	Greek
Irish	Japanese	Israeli	Canadian	French	Icelandic
Polish	Portuguese	Kuwaiti	German	—	Swiss
Spanish	Vietnamese	Pakistani	Indonesian	—	Thai
Turkish	—	Saudi	Korean	—	Malagasy

Events

The ancient Games had only a few events. Foot racing was in every game and each race had a variety of lengths — the longest being the marathon named after the Greek city and famous battle. The pentathlon, supposedly developed by Jason of Golden Fleece fame, had five events (running, jumping, wrestling, discus throwing and javelin throwing) which were all scored together. Three pentathlon events were important and popular enough to have their own events. Wrestling, discus throwing and the javelin were all recorded in the Homeric poems and were seen as vital for all men to be skilled in. The javelin throw was separated into two categories: length and accuracy (aimed at a specific target). Boxing was one of the oldest events and was written about by Homer. Finally there was the pancration, a combination of boxing and wrestling and various events with horse racing.

Today, of course, there are many more events. The chart below lists the most popular modern events in the Summer and Winter Olympics.

Summer		Winter	
kayaking	boxing	down hill skiing	snowboarding
swimming	diving	hockey	speed skating
equestrian	hurdles	curling	bobsledding
gymnastics	track & field	figure skating	luge
volleyball	basketball	biathlon	ski jumping
tennis	wrestling	skeleton	cross country skiing

NB. The following summer sports have been recently recognized and are now legitimate events: air sports; automobile; bandy; billiards; boules; bowling; bridge; chess; dancesport; golf; karate; korfball; life saving; motorcycle racing; mountaineering and climbing; netball; orienteering; pelote basque; polo; racquetball; roller sports; rugby; squash; surfing; tug of war; underwater sports; water skiing; wushu.

Competition

Athletes compete or play against each other in hopes of winning. That might mean crossing the finish line first or putting on a perfect performance. Throughout the Games, the contestants are supposed to play with a spirit of sportsmanship, which can be defined as the character and conduct worthy of a sportsman. This means that they are to play with honour, seeking only to do their very best in their sport, and not specifically to defeat the other players.

When the playing begins, the events have preliminaries, or official trials or contests, in which athletes have to meet specified minimum requirements. This is for the setting of standards and for athletes to gain the right to compete in the final contest.

Sometimes it seems that the spirit and the joy of the Games have been lost to commercialism and the overpowering desire to focus only on victory. When controversy and partisanship take over, it's good to remember what a churchman once said during the 1908 London Games, which is still true today:

"*The important thing is not so much winning as taking part.*"

Unfortunately, some athletes and coaches have taken to cheating or doping, in an attempt to gain an unfair advantage. Steroids, drugs that encourage muscle strength and stamina, are one of the banned substances that give athletes an extra, and illegal, advantage.

In spite of the problems of cheating and doping, and nationalism which can be divisive, the Games carry on and remain popular. This is possibly because the Games show us what we as humans are capable of and that humanity is capable of engaging in friendly competition. We should keep in mind what the father of the modern Games, Baron Pierre de Courbertin, once said: "*Olympism is not a system, it is a state of mind.*"

1. Most of the sporting events in ancient Greeks are related to the war.
2. The Olympic torch is kept burning until the close of the Games.
3. Every athlete should take the Athlete's oath in order to keep the spirit of the Games and sportsmanship alive.
4. In the ancient Games, only the winner was given the reward, so those who came in second or third got nothing.
5. The 1972 attack led to increased security for the Games.
6. Sometimes, the spirit and the joy of the Games have been lost to commercialism and the overpowering desire to focus only on victory.
7. The Games has lost its popularity because of the problems of cheating and doping.
8. The Olympics' official motto is "_____, higher, and stronger".
9. Some athletes and coaches have taken to cheating or _____ in order to gain an unfair advantage.
10. Steroids, one of the banned substances, can encourage muscle strength and _____.

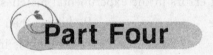

Part Four

> **Directions:** *There is a passage in this section. This passage is followed by some questions. For each of them there are four choices marked A), B), C) and D). You should decide on the best choice.*

A Research on Referee's Errors

Long after the 1998 World Cup was won, disappointed fans were still cursing the disputed *refereeing* (裁判) decisions that denied victory to their team. A researcher was appointed to study the performance of some top referees.

The researcher organized an experimental *tournament* (锦标赛) involving four youth teams. Each match lasted an hour, divided into three periods of 20 minutes during which different referees were in charge.

Observers noted down the referees' errors, of which there were 61 over the tournament.

Converted to a standard match of 90 minutes, each referee made almost 23 mistakes, a remarkably high number.

The researcher then studied the videotapes to analyse the matches in detail. Surprisingly, he found that errors were more likely when the referees were close to the incident. When the officials got it right, they were, on average, 17 meters away from the action. The average distance in the case of errors was 12 meters. The research shows the *optimum*（最佳的） distance is about 20 meters.

There also seemed to be an optimum speed. Correct decisions came when the referees were moving at a speed of about 2 meters per second. The average speed for errors was 4 meters per second.

If FIFA, football's international ruling body, wants to improve the standard of refereeing at the next World Cup, it should encourage referees to keep their eyes on the action from a distance, rather than rushing to keep up with the ball, the researcher argues.

He also says that FIFA's insistence that referees should retire at age 45 may be misguided. If keeping up with the action is not so important, their physical condition is less critical.

1. The experiment conducted by the researcher was meant to _____.
   A. review the decisions of referees at the 1998 World Cup
   B. analyse the causes of errors made by football referees
   C. set a standard for football refereeing
   D. reexamine the rules for football refereeing

2. The number of refereeing errors in the experimental matches was _____.
   A. slightly above average   B. higher than in the 1998 World Cup
   C. quite unexpected   D. as high as in a standard match

3. The findings of the experiment show that _____.
   A. errors are more likely when a referee keeps close to the ball
   B. the farther the referee is from the incident, the fewer the errors
   C. the more slowly the referee runs, the more likely will errors occur
   D. errors are less likely when a referee stays in one spot

4. The word "officials" (Line 3, Para. 4) most probably refers to _____.
   A. the researchers involved in the experiment
   B. the inspectors of the football tournament
   C. the referees of the football tournament
   D. the observers at the site of the experiment

5. What is one of the possible conclusions of the experiment?
   A. The ideal retirement age for an experienced football referee is 45.
   B. Age should not be the chief consideration in choosing a football referee.
   C. A football referee should be as young and energetic as possible.
   D. An experienced football referee can do well even when in poor physical condition.

Part Five

Reading for Pleasure

Summer Olympic Mascots

Matching the mascot to the corresponding Olympic Games.

Waldi — mascot of 1972 Olympic
Summer Games in Munich, Germany

Amik — mascot of the 1976 Olympic
Summer Games in Montreal, Canada

Misha — mascot of the 1980 Olympic
Summer Games in Moscow

Sam the Eagle — mascot of the 1984 Olympic
Summer Games in Los Angeles, USA

Hodori — mascot of the 1988 Olympic
Summer Games in Seoul, Korea

Cobi — mascot of the 1992 Olympic
Summer Games in Barcelona, Spain

Izzy — mascot of the 1996 Olympic
Summer Games in Atlanta, USA

Syd, Olly and Millie — mascots of the 2000
Olympic Summer Games in Sydney, Australia

Athena and Phevos — mascots of the 2004 Olympic Summer Games in Athens, Greece

Fuwa — mascots of the 2008 Olympic Summer Games in Beijing, China.

Humor Prepared for You

The teacher told the class the story of a man who swam a river three times before breakfast.

Johnny laughed.

"Do you doubt that a good swimmer could do that?" asked the teacher.

"No, sir," answered Johnny, "but I wonder why he did not swim it four times and get back to the side where his clothes were."

Famous Sayings

Share the Spirit of Olympic Games 共享奥运精神

You are my adversary, but you are not my enemy. For your resistance gives me strength, your will gives me courage, your spirit ennobles me. And though I am to defeat you, should I succeed I will not humiliate you, instead, I will honor you. For without you, I am a lesser man.

你是我的对手,但不是敌人。因为,你的竞争给予我力量,你的意志带给我勇气,你的精神使我崇高。我要尽力击败你,但即使我胜利了,我也不会羞辱你。相反,我将以你为荣。因为如果没有你,我就无法达成今天的成就。

Unit Three

Interracial and Intercultural Marriage

Interracial marriage is the term used to describe marriages that take place between people who are from different racial or ethnic groups. Intercultural marriages are defined as marriages between people who come from two different cultural backgrounds. A marriage between a woman from China, whose culture emphasizes the needs of the family over the needs of the individual, and a man from the United States, whose culture emphasizes individual autonomy, would be an example of an intercultural marriage. Whereas relationships between people from different ethnic and cultural groups are becoming increasingly common, there are substantial increases in the number of individuals engaging in interracial or intercultural marriages.

In this unit, you will read:
- The Love Letter
- Love Story
- After 40 Years, Interracial Marriage Flourishing
- Mobility and Family Disorganization
- Zhaojun Departs the Frontier

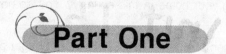

Part One

Pre-reading Questions
1. What will be written in a love letter?
2. What problems will a mixed couple encounter?
3. Are you in favor of the mixed marriage? Why or Why not?

The Love Letter

1　I was always a little in awe of Great-aunt Stephina Roos. Indeed, as children we were all frankly terrified of her. The fact that she did not live with the family, preferring her tiny cottage and solitude to the comfortable but rather noisy household where we were brought up added to the respectful fear in which she was held.

2　We used to take it in turn to carry small **delicacies** which my mother had made down from the big house to the little cottage where Aunt Stephina and an old colored maid spent their days. Old Tnate Sanna would open the door to the rather frightened little messenger and would usher him — or her — into the dark **voor-kamer**, where the shutters were always closed to keep out the heat and the flies. There we would wait, in trembling but not altogether unpleasant.

3　She was a tiny little woman to inspire so much **veneration**. She was always dressed in black, and her dark clothes melted into the shadows of the voor-kamer and made her look smaller than ever. But you felt the moment she entered that something vital and strong and somehow indestructible had come in with her, although she moved slowly, and her voice was sweet and soft.

4　Tante Sanna would bring in dishes of sweet sticky candy, or a great bowl of grapes or peaches, and Great-aunt Stephina would converse gravely about happenings on the farm, and, more rarely, of the outer world.

5　When we had finished our **sweetmeats** or fruit she would accompany us to the **stoep**, bidding us thank our mother for her gift and sending **quaint**, old-fashioned messages to her and the Father. Then she would turn and enter the house, closing the door behind, so that it became once more a place of mystery.

6　As I grew older I found, rather to my surprise, that I had become genuinely fond of my **aloof** old great-aunt. But to this day I do not know what strange impulse made me take George to see her and to tell her, before I had confided in another living soul, of our engagement. To my astonishment, she was delighted.

7   "An Englishman," she exclaimed. "But that is splendid, splendid." "And you, "she turned to George," you are making your home in this country? You do not intend to return to England just yet?"

8   She seemed relieved when she heard that George had bought a farm near our own farm and intended to settle in South Africa. She became quite animated and chattered away to him.

9   After that I would often slip away to the little cottage. Once she was somewhat disappointed on hearing that we had decided to wait for two years before getting married, but when she learned that my father and mother were both pleased with the match she seemed reassured.

10   Still, she often appeared anxious about my love affair, but I was quite unprepared for her outburst when I mentioned that George thought of paying a lightning visit to England before we were married. "He must not do it," she cried. "Ina, you must not let him go. Promise me you will prevent him." She was trembling all over. I did what I could to console her, but she looked lonely and pathetic, and for the first time I wondered why no man had ever taken her and looked after her and loved her.

11   She paused, as though she did not quite know how to begin. Then she seemed to give herself, mentally, a little shake. "You must have wondered", she said, "why I was so upset at the thought of young George's going to England without you. I am an old woman, and perhaps I have the silly fancies of the old, but I should like to tell you my own love story, and then you can decide whether it is wise for your man to leave you before you are married."

12   "I was quite a young girl when I first met Richard Weston. He was an Englishman who boarded with the Van Rensburgs on the next farm, four or five miles from us. Richard was not strong. He had a weak chest, and the doctors had sent him to South Africa so that the dry air could cure him. We loved one another from the first moment we met, though we did not speak of our love until the evening of my eighteenth birthday. That was the happiest birthday of my life, for while we were resting between dances Richard took me outside into the cool, moonlit night, and there, under the stars, he told me he loved me and asked me to marry him. Of course I promised I would, for I was too happy to think of what my parents would say. My father hated the **Uitlanders**, and he never liked Richard, though he was always polite to him. One day, when I reached the homestead after paying a visit to Driefontein, we heard that Richard had gone back to England. His father had died, and now he was the heir and must go back to look after his estates."

13   "I do not remember very much more about that day, except that the sun seemed to have stopped shining. Late that afternoon, Jantje, the little **Hottentot** herd boy, came up to me and handed me a letter, which he said the English **baas** had left for me. It turned all my bitterness and grief into a peacefulness which was the nearest I could get, then, to happiness. I knew Richard still loved me, and somehow, as long as I had his letter, I felt that we could never be really parted, even if he were in England and I had to remain on the farm. I have it yet, and though I am an old, tired woman, it still gives me hope and courage."

14　"It must have been a wonderful letter, Aunt Stephina," I said.

15　The old lady came back from her dreams of that far-off romance. "Perhaps," she said, hesitating a little, "perhaps, my dear, you would care to read it?"

16　"I should love to, Aunt Stephina," I said gently.

17　The letter, faded and yellow with age, the edges of the envelope worn and frayed as though it had been much handled. But when I came to open it I found that the seal was unbroken.

18　"Open it, open it," said Great-aunt Stephina, and her voice was shaking.

19　I broke the seal and read.

20　It was not a love letter in the true sense of the word, but pages of directions of how "my sweetest Phina" was to elude her father's vigilance and follow her lover to Cape Town and from there to England, "where, my love, we can be married at once. But if, my dearest, you are not sure that you can face lift with me in a land strange to you, then do not take this important step, for I love you too much to wish you the smallest unhappiness. If you do not come, and if I do not hear from you, then I shall know that you could never be happy so far from the people and the country which you love. If, however, you feel you can keep your promise to me, but are too timid and modest of a journey to England unaccompanied, then write to me, and I will, by some means, return to fetch my bride."

21　I read no further.

22　"But Aunt Phina!" I gasped. "Why... why...?" The old lady was watching me with trembling eagerness, her face flushed and her eyes bright with expectation. "Read it aloud, my dear," she said. "I want to hear every word of it. There was never anyone I could trust... Uitlanders were hated in my young days... I could not ask anyone."

23　"But, Auntie, don't you even know what he wrote?"

24　The old lady looked down, troubled and shy like a child who has **unwittingly** done wrong.

25　"No, dear," she said, speaking very low. "You see, I never learned to read."

🐾 Words and Expressions

delicacy *n.* a choice or expensive food 精美的食物,美味,佳肴

voor-kamer *n.* （荷兰语）客厅

veneration *n.* respect 尊敬,崇敬,崇拜

sweetmeats *n.* candies 糖果

stoep *n.* (S. African)a terraced veranda in front of a house （南非）屋前游廊

quaint *a.* attractively unusual or old-fashioned 古色古香的;奇特而有趣的

aloof *a.* not friendly or forthcoming; cool and distant 不友好的,不友善的;冷淡的,疏远的

Uitlander *n.* a British immigrant living in the Transvaal who was denied citizenship by the Boers for cultural and economic reasons [南非]外国人,外侨(尤指英国侨民)

Hottentot *a.* 霍屯督人(的)(用于指科伊科伊人)

baas *n.* (S. African, offensive)a boss or master, esp. a white man in charge of coloreds or blacks (南非,冒犯)(尤指管理有色人和黑人的白人)老板;主人

unwittingly *a.* not done on purpose; unintentional 非故意的,无心的

🔊 Background Information

1. Uitlanders (Afrikaans, "outsiders"), the non-Boer immigrants into the Transvaal, who came after the discovery of gold (1886). They were denied citizenship, were heavily taxed, and excluded from government.

2. The Boer Wars (known in Afrikaans as Vryheidsoorloe? [lit. "freedom wars"]) were two wars fought between Britain and the two independent Boer republics, the Orange Free State and the South African Republic (Transvaal Republic).

🔊 Learn about Words

Often you can tell the meaning of a word or phrase from its context — the words around it. Please find the word in the paragraph that means.

1. the state or situation of being alone (1)
2. show or guide (sb.) somewhere (2)
3. create (a feeling, esp. a positive one) in a person (3)
4. not able to be destroyed (3)
5. tell sb. about a secret or private matter while trusting them not to repeat it to others (6)
6. full of life or excitement; lively (8)
7. comfort (sb.) at a time of grief or disappointment (10)
8. a person legally entitled to the property or rank of another on that person's death (12)
9. (of a fabric, rope, or cord) unravel or become worn at the edge, typically through constant rubbing (17)
10. evade or escape from (a danger, enemy, or pursuer), typically in a skilful or cunning way (20)

Part Two

> **Reading Skill — Distinguishing Between Facts and Opinions**
>
> Most reading passages contain ideas based on facts and opinions. The ability to recognize differences between facts and opinions can help us to achieve a deeper level of understanding in our reading. Fact is statement that tells what really happened or what really is the case. Opinion is statement of belief, judgment or feeling. It shows what someone thinks or feels about a subject.

🐢 Skill-Specific Training

Before you read Part Two, decide whether the following statement is fact or opinion.

1. I had forgotten that Italians like Jenny feel strongly about their parents.
2. It's impossible to hurt Oliver Barrett the Third.
3. Your name and your number are part of what you are.
4. This means that we were surrounded by his people. His old college friends. His admirers.
5. Old Stonyface was clearly delighted that I had remained in my seat.

Love Story

Erich Segal

"Jenny, he isn't exactly going to be President of the United States, after all!"

We were at last — thank God — driving back to Cambridge.

"Even so, Oliver, you weren't very nice to him about it."

"I said Well Done."

"That was very big of you, I'm sure!"

"Dammit, what did you expect me to say?"

"Oh God," she replied, "the whole thing makes me physically sick."

"That makes two of us," I added. We drove along for a long time without saying a word. But something was wrong.

"What whole thing makes you sick?" I asked her at last.

"The horrible way you behave towards your father!"

"What about the horrible way he behaves towards me?"

I had forgotten that Italians like Jenny feel strongly about their parents. Jenny gave me a long lecture.

"You're horrible to him," she said. "You hurt him, and hurt him and hurt him, all the time."

"He does the same to me, Jen. Or didn't you notice that?"

"I think you'd do *anything*, just to hurt your old man."

"It's impossible to hurt Oliver Barrett the Third."

There was a strange little silence before she replied, "Unless maybe you marry Jennifer Cavilleri..."

I stayed cool long enough to drive into the car park of a roadside seafood restaurant. I then turned to Jenny. I was angrier than I had ever been before.

"Is that what you think?" I demanded.

"I think it's part of it," she said very quietly.

"Jenny, don't you believe I love you?" I shouted.

"Yes," she replied, still quietly. "But in a stupid, wrong-headed way you also love the fact that socially I'm just zero."

I couldn't think of anything to say except "No." I said it several times, in several ways. I mean, I was so terribly hurt and angry that I even considered that there just might be some truth in her suggestion.

But Jenny wasn't exactly feeling wonderful, either.

"I can't judge you, Ollie. I just think that is part of it. I mean, I know that I love you, *and* your name, *and* your number." She looked away, and I thought that perhaps she was going to cry. But she didn't. She finished what she had to say: "After all, your name and your number are part of what you are."

I sat there for a while, watching the electric sign outside the restaurant that said "Frank's Fresh Fish".

The thing that I loved so much about Jenny was her ability to see right inside me. She understood things that I never needed to put into words. She was still doing it now. But was I brave enough to face the fact that I wasn't perfect? My God, she had already faced that fact, *and* the fact that she wasn't perfect either. My God, how small I felt!

I didn't know what to say.

"Would you like some fresh fish, Jen?"

"Would you like me to knock your teeth out, **Preppie**?"

"Yes," I said. She closed her hand up tight, like a boxer. Then she placed it gently against my cheek. I kissed her hand. As I reached over to put my arms around her, she hit me hard on the nose, and shouted, like someone in an old film: "Just drive, Preppie. Get back to the wheel and drive! Fast!"

I did. I did.

My father's argument against our marriage was that I was doing things too fast. I forget his exact words. But I know that the subject of his lecture during our lunch at the **Harvard Club** was *Doing Things in a Hurry*. He started by suggesting that I ate too fast. I politely suggested that I was an adult, and that he no longer had any right to speak about — my behavior. He argued that even world leaders needed helpful suggestions now and again.

We were, as I said, eating lunch in the Harvard Club, Boston. (I was eating mine too fast if we accept my father's opinion.) This means that we were surrounded by his people. His old college friends. His admirers. Of course, Oliver Barrett the Third had planned it that way.

We were having another of our non-conversations. But I knew what was really worrying him, because he did not mention it until I did.

"Father, you haven't said a word about Jennifer."

"What is there to say? You seem to have decided everything for yourself."

"But what do *you* think, Father?"

"I think Jennifer is admirable. For a girl from her position in society to get all the way to **Radcliffe**..."

"Get to the point, Father!"

"The point has nothing to do with the young lady," he said, "and everything to do with you. "

"What?" I said.

"You are rebelling, son. "

"Father, I fail to see how, by marrying a beautiful, very clever girl from Radcliffe, I am rebelling. "I raised my voice a little.

"Father, what worries you most about her? That she's **Catholic**? Or that she's poor?"

He replied in a whisper, leaning a little towards me.

"What do you *like* most about her?"

I wanted to get up and I told him so.

"Stay here and talk like a man," he said. I stayed. Old Stonyface was clearly delighted that I had remained in my seat. I mean, I could tell that he saw it as another of his many victories over me.

"All I ask, son, is that you wait a while," said Oliver Barrett III.

"What do you mean by 'a while', please?"

"Finish law school. If this is real, it will pass the test of time. "

"It is real, but why do I have to test it?"

I was rebelling now, and he knew it. I was rebelling against his desire to control me, to control my life.

"Oliver," he started again. "You're still under twenty-one. In the eyes of the law you are not yet an adult. "

"Stop talking like a lawyer, dammit!"

Perhaps some people at the neighboring tables heard me say this, Oliver III realized this, and he aimed his next words at me in a biting whisper:

"Marry her now, and you will get nothing from me. "

I said, "Father, you've got nothing I want. "

Love Story is a 1970 romantic drama film written by Erich Segal and directed by Arthur Hiller. The film, well-known as a tragedy, is considered one of the most romantic of all time by the American Film Institute (♯ 9 on the list), and was followed by a sequel, Oliver's Story during 1978.

The novel also includes the double meaning of a love story between Oliver and his father.

🕮 Words and Expressions

Preppie *n*. 大学预科生

catholic *a*. of or relating to the historic doctrine and practice of the Western Church(有关)西派教会历史性教义(或实践)的

🕮 Background Information

1. **The Harvard Club of New York**, incorporated in 1887, is housed in adjoining lots at 27

West 44th Street and 35 West 44th Street. Anyone who has attended Harvard University may apply to become a member. The Club publishes a Bulletin and a Newsletter. The HCNY Foundation has a scholarship fund that helps support twenty undergraduates at Harvard College and several students in graduate programs, as well as international student exchange programs. It offers rooms for visiting alumni. 哈佛私人会所

2. Radcliffe College was a women's liberal arts college in Cambridge, Massachusetts, and was the coordinate college for Harvard University. It was also one of the Seven Sisters colleges.

Comprehension of the Text

1. Who are the main characters in this story? And what are they?

   _____.

2. How do the father and the son get along with each other?

   _____.

3. Why does the father disagree with his son's idea of getting married?

   _____.

4. At the beginning of the story, Jennifer said "That was very big of you, I'm sure!" What does that mean?

   _____.

5. When the father and the son sit together in a club, the son writes "We were having another of our non-conversations." What does that mean?

   _____.

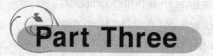

Part Three

> **Reading Comprehension (Skimming and Scanning)**
>
> **Directions:** *In this part, you will have 15 minutes to go over the passage quickly and answer the questions. For questions 1~7, mark Y (for YES) or N (for NO). For question 8~10, complete the sentences with the information given in the passage.*

After 40 Years, Interracial Marriage Flourishing

Since landmark 1967 ruling, unions have moved from radical to everyday

The charisma king of the 2008 presidential field. The world's best golfer. The captain of the New York Yankees. Besides superstardom, Barack Obama, Tiger Woods and Derek Jeter have another common bond: Each is the child of an interracial marriage.

It was only 40 years ago — on June 12, 1967 — that the U.S. Supreme Court knocked down a Virginia statute barring whites from marrying nonwhites. The decision also overturned similar bans in 15 other states.

Since that landmark Loving v. Virginia ruling, the number of interracial marriages has soared; for example, black-white marriages increased from 65,000 in 1970 to 422,000 in 2005, according to Census Bureau figures.

Stanford: 7 percent of couples interracial

Factoring in all racial combinations, Stanford University sociologist Michael Rosenfeld calculates that more than 7 percent of America's 59 million married couples in 2005 were interracial, compared to less than 2 percent in 1970.

Coupled with a steady flow of immigrants from all parts of the world, the surge of interracial marriages and multiracial children is producing a 21st century America more diverse than ever, with the potential to become less stratified by race.

From exotic to commonplace

The boundaries were still distinct in 1967, a year when the Sidney Poitier film "Guess Who's Coming to Dinner" —

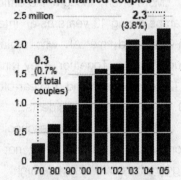

Growing diversity

The number of interracial married couples in the U.S. has soared more than 667 percent since 1970.

Interracial married couples

By race and origin of spouses, in millions of couples

COUPLE	'70	'05	%CHG
Black/other	0.01	0.1	900%
White/other	0.2	1.7	750%
White/black	0.1	0.4	300%
Hispanic/other	0.6	2.2	267%

SOURCE: U.S. Census Bureau   AP

a comedy built around parents' acceptance of an interracial couple — was considered groundbreaking. The Supreme Court ruled that Virginia could not criminalize the marriage that Richard Loving, a white, and his black wife, Mildred, entered into nine years earlier in Washington, D.C.

But what once seemed so radical to many Americans is now commonplace.

Many prominent blacks — including Supreme Court Justice Clarence Thomas, civil rights leader Julian Bond and former U.S. Sen. Carol Moseley Braun — have married whites. Well-known whites who have married blacks include former Defense Secretary William Cohen and actor Robert DeNiro.

Last year, the Salvation Army installed Israel Gaither as the first black leader of its U.S. operations. He and his wife, Eva, who is white, wed in 1967 — the first interracial marriage between Salvation Army officers in the United States.

Opinion polls show overwhelming popular support, especially among younger people, for interracial marriage.

That's not to say acceptance has been universal. Interviews with interracial couples from around the country reveal varied challenges, and opposition has lingered in some quarters.

Bob Jones University in South Carolina only dropped its ban on interracial dating in 2000; a year later 40 percent of the voters objected when Alabama became the last state to remove a no-longer-enforceable ban on interracial marriages from its constitution.

Taunts and threats, including cross burnings, still occur sporadically. In Cleveland, two white men were sentenced to prison earlier this year for harassment of an interracial couple that included spreading liquid mercury around their house.

Tough times for some multiracial families

More often, though, the difficulties are more nuanced, such as those faced by Kim and Al Stamps during 13 years as an interracial couple in Jackson, Miss. Kim, a white woman raised on Cape Cod, met Al, who is black, in 1993 after she came to Jackson's Tougaloo College to study history. Together, they run Cool Al's — a popular hamburger restaurant — while raising a 12-year-old son and 10-year-old daughter in the state with the nation's lowest percentage (0.7) of multiracial residents.

The children are homeschooled, Kim said, because Jackson's schools are largely divided along racial lines and might not be comfortable for biracial children. She said their family triggered a wave of "white flight" when they moved into a mostly white neighborhood four years ago — "People were saying to my kids, 'What are you doing here?'"

"Making friends here has been really, really tough," Kim said. "I'll go five years at a time with no white friends at all."

Her own parents in Massachusetts have been supportive, Kim said, but she credited her mother with foresight.

"She told me, 'Your life is going to be harder because of this road you've chosen — it's going to be harder for your kids,'" Kim said. "She was absolutely right."

'In-your-face racism is pretty rare'

It's been easier, if not always smooth, for other couples.

Major Cox, a black Alabamian, and his white wife, Cincinnati-born Margaret Meier, have lived on the Cox family homestead in Smut Eye, Ala., for more than 20 years, building a large circle of black and white friends while encountering relatively few hassles.

"I don't feel it, I don't see it," said Cox, 66, when asked about racist hostility. "I live a wonderful life as a nonracial person."

Meier says she occasionally detects some expressions of disapproval of their marriage, "but flagrant, in-your-face racism is pretty rare now."

Sometimes, a blend of nationalities

In many cases, interracial families embody a mix of nationalities as well as races. Michelle Cadeau, born in Sweden, and her husband, James, born in Haiti, are raising their two sons as Americans in racially diverse West Orange, N.J., while teaching them about all three cultures.

"I think the children of families like ours will be able to make a difference in the world, and do things we weren't able to do," Michelle Cadeau said. "It's really important to put all their cultures together, to be aware of their roots, so they grow up not just as Swedish or Haitian or American, but as global citizens."

Love can take its toll

The stresses on interracial couples can take a toll. The National Center for Health Statistics says their chances of a breakup within 10 years are 41 percent, compared to 31 percent for a couple of the same race.

In some categories of interracial marriage, there are distinct gender-related trends. More than twice as many black men marry white women as vice versa, and about three-fourths of white-Asian marriages involve white men and Asian women.

C.N. Le, a Vietnamese-American who teaches sociology at the University of Massachusetts, says the pattern has created some friction in Asian-American communities.

"Some of the men view the women marrying whites as sellouts, and a lot of Asian women say, 'Well, we would want to date you more, but a lot of you are sexist or patriarchal,'" said Le, who attributes the friction in part to gender stereotypes of Asians that have been perpetuated by American films and TV shows.

'Encouraging development'

Kelley Kenney, a professor at Kutztown University in Pennsylvania, is among those who have bucked the black-white gender trend. A black woman, she has been married since 1988 to a fellow academic of Irish-Italian descent, and they have jointly offered programs for the American Counseling Association about interracial couples.

Kenney recalled some tense moments in 1993 when, soon after they moved to Kutztown, a harasser shattered their car window and placed chocolate milk cartons on their lawn. "It was very powerful to see how the community rallied around us," she said.

Kenney is well aware that some blacks view interracial marriage as a potential threat to black identity, and she knows her two daughters, now 15 and 11, will face questions on how they identify themselves.

"For older folks in the black community," she said, "it's a feeling of not wanting people to forget where they came from."

Yet some black intellectuals embrace the surge in interracial marriages and multiracial families; among them is Harvard law professor Randall Kennedy, who addressed the topic in his latest book, "Interracial Intimacies: Sex, Marriage, Identity, and Adoption."

"Malignant racial biases can and do reside in interracial liaisons," Kennedy wrote. "But against the tragic backdrop of American history, the flowering of multiracial intimacy is a profoundly moving and encouraging development."

1. Barack Obama and Tiger Woods have one thing in common: either is the child of an

interracial marriage.

2. According to Census Bureau figures, more than 7 percent of America's 59 million married couples in 2005 were black-white marriage.

3. Opinion polls show overwhelming popular support, especially among black people, for interracial marriage.

4. In 2001, 40 percent of the voters objected when Alabama removed a ban on interracial marriages from its constitution.

5. Life is harder for Kim's children because they are biracial.

6. Some people harbor reservations on Cox and Meier's marriage.

7. Michelle Cadeau wants her sons to be brought up as Americans.

8. C. N. Le attributes the friction in part to _____ of Asians that have been perpetuated by films and TV shows.

9. Kelley Kenny believed that some blacks view interracial marriage as a possible threat to _____.

10. Randall Kennedy thought the flowering of _____ is a profoundly moving development.

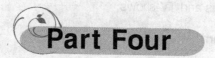

Part Four

> **Directions:** *There is a passage in this section. This passage is followed by some questions. For each of them there are four choices marked A), B), C) and D). You should decide on the best choice.*

Mobility and Family Disorganization

Mobility of individual members and family groups tends to split up family relationships.

Occasionally the movement of a family away from a situation which has been the source of friction results in greater family organization, but on the whole mobility is disorganizing.

Individuals and families are involved in three types of mobility: movement in space, movement up or down in social status, and the movement of ideas. These are termed respectively spatial, vertical, and ideational mobility.

A great increase in spatial mobility has gone along with improvements in rail and water transportation, the invention and use of the automobile, and the availability of airplane passenger service. Spatial mobility results in a decline in the importance of the traditional home with its emphasis on family continuity and stability. It also means that when individual family members or the family as a whole move away from a community, the person or the family is removed from the pressures of relatives, friends, and community institutions for conventionality and stability. Even more important is the fact that spatial mobility permits some members of a family to come in contact with and possibly adopt attitudes, values, and ways of thinking different from those held by other family members. The presence of different attitudes, values, and ways of thinking within a family may, and often does, result in conflict and family disorganization. Potential disorganization is present in those families in which the husband, wife, and children are spatially separated over a long period, or are living together but see each other only briefly because of different work schedules.

One index of the increase in vertical mobility is the great increase in the proportion of sons, and to some extent daughters, who engage in occupations other than those of the parents.

Another index of vertical mobility is the degree of intermarriage between racial classes. This occurs almost exclusively between classes which are adjacent to each other. Engaging in a different occupation, or intermarriage, like spatial mobility, allows one to come in contact with ways of behavior different from those of the parental home, and tends to separate parents and their children.

The increase in ideational mobility is measured by the increase in publications, such as newspapers, periodicals, and books, the increase in the percentage of the population owning radios, and the increase in television sets. All these tend to introduce new ideas into the home.

When individual family members are exposed to and adopt the new ideas, the tendency is for conflict to arise and for those in conflict to become psychologically separated from each other.

1. What the passage tells us can be summarized by the statement:
   A. social development results in a decline in the importance of traditional families.
   B. potential disorganization is present in the American family.
   C. family disorganization is more or less the result of mobility.
   D. the movement of a family is one of the factors in raising its social status.
2. According to the passage, those who live in a traditional family _____.
   A. are less likely to quarrel with others because of conventionality and stability
   B. have to depend on their relatives and friends if they do not move away from it
   C. can get more help from their family members if they are in trouble
   D. will have more freedom of action and thought if they move away from it
3. Potential disorganization exists in those families in which _____.
   A. the husband, wife, and children work too hard
   B. the husband, wife, and children seldom get together
   C. both parents have to work full time
   D. the family members are subject to social pressures
4. Intermarriage and different occupations play an important role in family disorganization because _____.
   A. they enable the children to travel around without their parents' permission

B. they allow one to find a good job and improve one's social status

C. they enable the children to better understand the ways of behavior of their parents

D. they permit one to come into contact with different ways of behavior and thinking

5. This passage suggests that a well-organized family is a family whose members _____.

A. are not psychologically withdrawn from one another

B. never quarrel with each other even when they disagree

C. often help each other with true love and affection

D. are exposed to the same new ideas introduced by books, radios, and TV sets

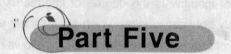

Part Five

Reading for Pleasure

Zhaojun Departs the Frontier

Wang Qiang (王墙 also 王檣；王嬙), more commonly known by her style name Wang Zhaojun (王昭君) was the consort of the Xiongnu shanyu Huhanye (呼韩邪). She is famed as one of the Four Beauties of ancient China.

Wang Zhaojun in History

Wang Zhaojun was born to a prominent family of Zigui country, Nan county (now Xingshan county, Hubei) in the south of the Western Han Dynasty. She entered the harem of Emperor Yuan probably after 40 BC. During her time in the Lateral Courts, Wang Qiang was never visited by the emperor and remained as a palace lady-in-waiting. When choosing a new wife, the Emperor was first presented with portraits of all the possible women. Wang Zhaojun's portrait was either never viewed by the Emperor, or was not in its true form, and therefore the Emperor overlooked her.

In 33 BC, Huhanye visited Chang'an on a homage trip, as part of the tributary system between the Han and Xiongnu. He took the opportunity to ask to be allowed to become an imperial son-in-law. Instead of honouring the shanyu with a princess, Huhanye was presented with five women from the imperial harem, one of whom was Wang Zhaojun.

A story from the *Hou Han Shu* relates that Wang Zhaojun volunteered to join the shanyu. When summoned to court, her beauty astonished the emperor's courtiers and made the emperor reconsider his decision to send her to the Xiongnu.

Wang Zhaojun became a favourite of the Huhanye shanyu, giving birth to two sons. Only one of them seemed to have survived, Yituzhiyashi（伊屠智牙师）. They also had at least one daughter, Yun（云）, who was created Princess Yimuo and who would later become a powerful figure in Xiongnu politics. When Huhanye died in 31 BC, Wang Zhaojun requested to return to China. Emperor Cheng, however, ordered that she follow Xiongnu levirate custom and become the wife of the next shanyu, the oldest brother (or her stepson, born by her husband's first wife) of her husband. In her new marriage she had two daughters.

Wang was honoured as Ninghu Yanzhi（宁胡阏氏 "Hu-Pacifying Chief-Consort"）.

Wang Zhaojun in Legend

According to other legends, she commits suicide after her husband's death as her only resort in order to avoid marrying his son.

Her life became the story of "Zhaojun Departs the Frontier"（昭君出塞）. Peace was maintained for over 60 years between China and the Xiongnu. However, China eventually lost touch with her and her descendants.

Since the 3rd century the story of Zhaojun had been elaborated upon and she had been touted as a tragic heroine. The Communist government of the People's Republic of China uses her as a symbol of the integration of Han Chinese and ethnic minorities of China. Zhaojun Tomb still exists today in Inner Mongolia.

Humor Prepared for You

Right and Wrong

A man and wife had argued. Finally the wife said she would say she was wrong if the man would say she was right. He agreed but said she should go first.

So she said, "I was wrong."

The man then said, "You're right."

The Husband Has an Affair with Somebody

Lady A: If your husband has an affair with somebody, what will you do?

Lady B: I will open one eye and close the other.

Lady A: Wow, you are so generous!

Lady B: No, I'm aiming my gun at him.

Famous Sayings

Keep your eyes open before marriage, and half-shut afterwards.

—*Benjamin Franklin*

婚前睁大眼，婚后半闭眼。

——富兰克林

Love is an ideal thing, marriage is a real thing; a confusion of the real with the ideal never goes unpunished.

—*Goethe*

爱情是理想化的，婚姻是现实的。把二者混为一谈就要遭殃。

—— 歌德

Man's love is of man's life a part; it is a woman's whole existence.

—*Lord Byron*

男人的爱是男人生活的一部分，它却是女人生活的全部。

——拜伦

Unit Four

True Love

Some people believe it's true love if you are willing to look beyond the person's looks or financial background, and others believe true love is the unconditional love that sustains and nurtures life, joy, peace, and freedom. When a little girl is asked to define love, she says love is when you see people sad you try to make them smile and that when you see them cry you reach out and make them stop crying. Without necessarily being right or wrong, everyone has a different definition. Then the only question remains: what is yours?

In this unit, you will read:

- True Love
- The Mystery of Love
- Writing a Love Letter
- What Will Happen if the World Was Suddenly No Emotion
- Chinese Men in the Western Eyes

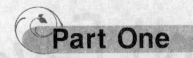

Part One

Pre-reading Questions

1. How would you define true love?
2. Do you believe that one can find true love online?
3. How would you comfort those whose hearts were broken in their difficult road of finding true love?

True Love

1   What is attracting you to a person, is it the money, or the looks. If neither of these **features** as number one on your list, then you should know that you love the person truly. It's true love if you are willing to look beyond the person's looks or financial background. If the person you love also does not look at the looks and money matters then you should be sure that what the person feels for you is true love.

True love symbols

2   There are so many love symbols in the world, but when they are sent by someone who really loves you it is a true love symbol. So if someone sent you a **cupid** it means that he or she loves you. A cupid is sometimes **depicted** as a picture of a baby naked and **blindfolded** with wings. It is referred to as **Putto**. It is said to be the son of the Goddess of love. It has a bow and arrow aimed at a heart. When someone sends you this symbol, they simply mean that they love you and somehow, you have made a mark in their heart. Legend has it that when someone is hit by the cupid's arrow they fall in love without them even wanting to. So if you are lucky enough to get hit by a cupid arrow you are on your way to falling in love with someone.

3   A heart is another true love symbol that is used to depict that someone loves you. A heart is a very important organ of a human being. Most people say 'I love you with all my heart'. You would never hear someone saying 'I love you with all my **kidneys** or liver'. A heart is a symbol of love and if someone sent you a heart symbol you should know for sure that the person intended to say that they love you.

4   The butterflies are also a true love symbol that people send to their husbands and wives. However, there are people who still send them to their partners. This is because a butterfly is said to represent a soul and in the Asian culture it means a happy marriage. There cannot be a happy marriage if two people do not love each other. People who love each other and intend to get married always send each other butterflies to **signify** that they love each other and they

have given their soul.

True love lasts

5   True love lasts in more ways than you can imagine. When you love someone, no matter how far they go from you and no matter where they are the love you feel for them will always remain. This love you feel for them might even get stronger with distance. You will feel that you miss the person when he is not around and you will be able to keep the communication longer. As for the saying "distance makes the heart fonder", I think it is meant for people who really love each other and not just for people who have a liking for you and when you get out of the door they'll forget you.

6   True love lasts forever because that is the way it was meant to be. When some people get married, they realize that they cannot stand each other. The men will stop coming home early and the women will stop respecting their husbands almost immediately after getting married. It is as if they discover something that is not **appealing** at all in the other person and they wish they could get out of the marriage. Most of the time when you observe these couples you will notice that they entered into **matrimony** for reasons other than love. Some of them got married because the society expects them to get married at a particular age while some of them get married because of the material possession that their partners have. If they loved each other, they would not be thinking of leaving each other, they would stick around for better or worse because true love is forever.

True love online

7   A lot of people are busy. They are busy trying to **make their ends meet**. There are bills to get paid and they cannot afford to sit at home or go to places and have fun unless it is during the holiday. Finding someone perfect in this busy schedule can almost be impossible but thanks to technology it is no longer hard to find someone special. Many people have been known to find true love online because there are thousands of people registered here. With this great number, you cannot go wrong in looking for love. Your true love could be among these people. If you look in the right places, that is, in the right dating site, you will not miss him or her. True love can be found the traditional way or the online way. Whichever method works for you is what you should use to find true love.

8   When you finally decide it is time to meet this person you get to know online, make sure that you take the necessary **precautions**. Meet in a public place. If not, carry a friend with you to this meeting. There are very many Internet **predators** that are waiting to take advantage of people who are looking for true love online. They might hurt you physically or financially if they do not succeed in hurting you emotionally. Before you meet up with them, it is important that you get some little details about them. Check to see for any **inconsistencies** in the answers that they give you and determine for yourself if the person can be trusted or not. Remember to always trust your **instincts**, they are rarely wrong. And anyway, you would rather be safe and

wrong than be unsafe.

Never let go

9   True Love can never be found easily. Many people gave up on love after discovering that it hurts more than anything else in the world. Most of them **resorted** never to give their hearts to anyone just in case they get really hurt again. Many are all familiar with the feeling of being hurt. It is a pain that no one can put a finger on yet it is a pain that is so painful that there are people who are not willing to go through it again. When love turns sour, a lot of people get hurt. Some have even taken **desperate** measures of committing suicide so as to escape from the hurt they felt. However that is not the solution. Just because someone hurt you it doesn't mean that you need to **terminate** your life. Life is too precious, once you finish, it is done, and it cannot be **reversed**.

10   After going through many heart breaks, a lot of people who have resorted never to give their hearts out to anyone again. To them, giving someone their heart to break it into small pieces does not appeal much. You surely cannot blame them. That is why true love today is very rare. However, whenever you get hold of a true love, you need to stick to it and never let go. When you finally fall in love, do not be afraid of loving with all your heart. You might get hurt, it is actually inevitable but when you love truly you end up enjoying life even more. Broken hearts get healed and I am sure you know that. They might take long but they surely get healed.

📖 Words and Expressions

feature *v.* have as a trait 以……为特色

depict *v.* to represent by or as if by drawing 描写，描绘

blindfold *v.* to prevent (a person or animal) from seeing by covering (the eyes) 蒙住……的眼睛

Putto *n.* a representation of a small boy, esp. in painting or sculpture 天使像

kidney *n.* either of two bean-shaped organs at the back of the abdominal cavity in man 肾脏

signify *v.* to indicate, show, or suggest 表示，象征，意味

appealing *a.* attractive or pleasing 引人注意的，讨人喜欢的

matrimony *n.* the state or condition of being married 婚姻生活

make ends meet *v.* 使收支平衡

precaution *n.* an action taken to avoid a dangerous or undesirable event 预防措施

predator *n.* someone who attacks in search of booty 捕食者；掠夺者

inconsistency *n.* lack of consistency or agreement 矛盾

instinct *n.* inborn pattern of behavior often responsive to specific stimuli 本能，直觉

resort *v.* to have recourse (to) for help, use 求助；依赖

desperate *a.* showing extreme urgency because of great need or desire 不顾一切的

terminate *v.* put an end (to) 使结束，使终止

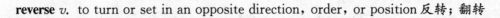

reverse *v.* to turn or set in an opposite direction, order, or position 反转；翻转

 Background Information

Cupid the Roman god of love, represented as a winged boy with a bow and arrow, with which he shot at humans to inflict wounds that inspired love or passion.

Learn about Words

Often you can tell the meaning of a word from its context — the words around it. Please find the word in the paragraph that means:

1. having the body completely unclothed; undressed (2)
2. a popular story handed down from earlier times (2)
3. to stand as an equivalent of; correspond to (4)
4. the feeling of a person who likes; fondness (5)
5. concerned with worldly rather than spiritual interests (6)
6. the act of having and controlling property (6)
7. a plan of procedure for a project (7)
8. the act of rising upward into the air (9)
9. the act or an instance of killing oneself intentionally (9)
10. incapable of being avoided or prevented (10)

Part Two

> **Reading Skill — Recognizing Word Meanings**
>
> Students will develop the ability to interpret word meanings through various methods.
> 1. Using context clues — the context clues that might be helpful include: definition, example, synonyms and antonyms.
> 2. Using word part clues — try to get the clue of the meaning of a new word from its prefix, stem and suffix like the word *mis-understand-ing*.
>
> Most often, you can not guess the precise meaning of a new word you come across, but as long as you have an idea that the new word has a positive or negative sense in the context, you should have no trouble understanding the overall meaning of the text.

Skill-Specific Training

*Explain the meaning of the words in **bold** in both English and Chinese, using the underlined words as reference. The first word is explained as an example.*

The Mystery of Love

It is a mystery why we fall in love, how it happens, and when it comes. It is a mystery why some love grows and it is a mystery why some love fails.

You can analyze this mystery and look for reasons and causes, but you will never do anymore than take the life out of the experience. Just as life itself is more than the sum of the bones and muscles and electrical **impulses** in the body, love is more than the sum of the interests and attractions and **commonalities** that two people share. And just as life itself is a gift that comes and goes in its own time, so too, the coming of love must be taken as an **unfathomable** gift that cannot be questioned in its ways.

1. unfathomable: impossible to be understood 深奥的

Sometimes, hopefully at least once in your life — the gift of love will come to you in full flower. Take hold of it and celebrate it in all **inexpressible** beauty. This is the dream we all share. More often, it will come and take hold of you, celebrate you for a brief moment, then move on.

2. inexpressible: _____

When this happens to young people, they too often try to grasp the love and hold it to them, refusing to see that it is a gift that just as freely, moves away. When they fall out of love, or the person they love feels the spirit of love leaving, they try **desperately** to *reclaim the love that is lost* rather than accepting the gift for what it was, then moving on.

3. reclaim: _____

They want answers where there are no answers. They want to know what is wrong in them that makes the other person no longer love them, or try to get their love to change, thinking that if some small things were different, love would **bloom** again. They blame their **circumstances** and say that if they go far away and start a new life, their love will grow.

They try anything to give meaning to what has happened. But there is no meaning beyond the love itself, and until they accept its own mysterious ways, they live in a sea of misery and *distress*.

4. distress: _____

You need to know this about love, and accept it. You need to treat what it brings you with kindness. If you find yourself in love with someone who does not love you, be gentle with yourself. There is nothing wrong with you. <u>Love just didn't choose to rest or **berth** in the other person's heart</u>.

5. berth: _____

   If you find someone else in love with you but you don't love him back, feel honored that love came and called at your door, but gently **decline** <u>the gift you cannot return</u>. Do not take advantage; do not cause pain. How you deal with love is how you deal with yourself. All our hearts feel the same pains and joys, even if our lives and ways are different.

6. decline: _____

   If you fall in love with another, and he falls in love with you, and then love chooses to leave. You should not try to reclaim it or to **assess** blame. Let it go. There is a reason and there is a meaning. You will know in time.

   Remember that you don't choose love. Love chooses you. All you can really do is accept it for all its mystery when it comes into your life. Feel the way it <u>fills</u> you to **overflowing**, then reach out and give it away. Give it back to the person who brought it alive in you. Give it to others who find it poor in spirit. Give it to the world around you in any way you can.

7. overflowing: _____

   There is where many lovers go wrong. Having been so long without love, they understand love only as a need. They see their hearts as empty places that will be filled by love, and they begin to look at love as something that flows to them rather than from them.

   The first **blush** of new love is filled to overflowing, but as their love cools, they **revert** to seeing their love as a need. They cease to be someone who **generates** love and instead become someone who seeks love. They forget that the secret of love is that it is a gift, and that it can be made to grow only by giving it away.

   Remember this and keep it to your heart. <u>Love has its time, its own season, its own reason for coming and going</u>. You cannot bribe it or **coerce** it, or reason it into staying. You can only embrace it when it arrives and give it away when it comes to you. But if it chooses to leave from your heart or from the heart of your lover, there is nothing you can do and there is nothing you should do. Love always has been and always will be a mystery. Be glad that it came to live for a moment in your life.

8. coerce: _____

   If you keep your heart open, it will come again. . . .

🔊 Words and Expressions

impulse *n.* a sudden desire 冲动

commonality *n.* sharing of common attributes 共性

desperately *ad.* with great urgency 不顾一切的

bloom *v.* produce or yield flowers 开花；繁盛

circumstance *n.* a condition of time, place, etc. 情况，形势；环境

assess *v.* to judge the worth, importance, etc. 评估

blush *n.* sudden reddening of the face 脸红，红晕

revert *v.* to go back to a former practice, condition, belief 回复；恢复

generate *v.* to produce or bring into being；create 产生

Comprehension of the Text

1. What seem to be the author's explanation of "the mystery of love" according to Para. 2?

   _____

2. What should young people do when they fall out of love according to the author?

   _____

3. What if you find someone in love with you but you don't love him back?

   _____

4. What does the author mean by saying "love is a gift"?

   _____.

5. What should you do if love chooses to leave from your heart? Why?

   _____

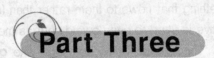

Part Three

> **Reading Comprehension（Skimming and Scanning）**
>
> **Directions：** *In this part, you will have 15 minutes to go over the passage quickly and answer the questions on Answer Sheet 1. For questions 1～7, choose the best answer from the four choices marked A), B), C) and D). For questions 8～10, complete the sentences with the information given in the passage.*

Writing a Love Letter

A love letter is a romantic way to express feelings of love in written form. Delivered by hand, by mail or romantically left in a secret location, the letter may be anything from a short and simple message of love to a lengthy explanation of feelings.

Why to write a love letter?

Sometimes letters are preferable to face-to-face contact because they can be written as the thoughts come to the author's mind. This may allow feelings to be more easily expressed than if the writer were in the beloved's presence. Further, expressing strong emotional feelings to paper or some other permanent form can be an expression within itself of desire and the importance of the beloved and the lover's emotions. The expression of feelings may be made to an existing love or in the hope of establishing a new relationship. The increasing rarity and consequent emotional charm of personal mail may also serve to emphasize the emotional importance of the message.

Other times, especially in the past before the wide use of telecommunications, letters were one of the few ways for a couple to remain in contact. When one of them was posted or stationed some distance from the other, the "being apart" often intensified emotions and many times a desired normal communication could lead to a letter expressing love, longing and desires. This was especially the case with large numbers of young men and women were separated during times of war. During these times, "love letters" were the only means of communication, and soldiers even swapped addresses of desirable young ladies so that an initial communication and possible start of a relationship could be initiated.

After the end of a relationship, returning love letters to the sender or burning them can symbolize the hurt felt. In the past, love letters also needed to be returned as a matter of honor: a love letter, particularly from a lady, could be compromising or embarrassing later in life.

How to write a love letter?

With the increasing popularity of email, short messaging, blogging, and other forms of communication, the act of letter writing has started to become a lost art. There are times, however, when a person needs to know how to write a love letter in order to express a much deeper emotion. Writing a love letter, especially in this day and age, often involves using an intimate and heightened writing style closer to poetry than prose. The sender should want to write a love letter which leaves a lasting impression on the recipient, or inspires the recipient to return the sentiments. One historically popular love letter structure is the form of a sonnet. William Shakespeare's sonnets are often cited as good examples of how to write emotional themes. Structure and suggestions of love letters have formed the subject of many published books, such as the anthology *Love Letters of Great Men*. In German speaking countries, love letters were painted by hand on delicately cut high quality paper and writing such letters was considered a folk art.

It would be difficult to write a love letter without using some heightened or romantic language, but the sentiment behind the language should still ring true and not sound artificial. "I love the way your hair shimmers in the moonlight, and the way your eyes sparkle whenever you laugh." would be perfectly acceptable in a modern love letter, but using archaic or flowery language would not be. "Your eyes are bluer than the deepest azure waves of a distant ocean, and your lips are glazed with the dew of a thousand morning glories." might work in a collection of 18th century love poems, but not necessarily in a modern love letter. It is more important to express feelings of deep emotion or high praise for the letter's recipient in the writer's own language than to recreate an Elizabeth Barrett-Browning love poem.

When really get started, some people like to choose paper and envelopes specifically for love letters produced by stationery companies. Some of these are scented, though some people spray them with their own perfume to strengthen the impact of the letter. At the very least, you should use some heavy-stock, elegant-looking paper, and if you must use an ordinary pen, choose one with a classy color of ink.

What to keep in mind while writing a love letter?

When writing a love letter, it helps to be in love. This means the writer should be in an emotional state where deeper feelings and even some sense of vulnerability can be experienced first-hand. The focus should be on the recipient and only the recipient. What qualities does this person possess which the writer finds to be inspirational or intriguing? Those romantic qualities and attributes should form the framework of the love letter, going from the general to the specific. A husband may admire his wife's compassion for others, for example, then provide more personal details: "I love the way you show your compassion for others, like the time you took in that stray kitten and nursed it back to health, or when I was discouraged about life and you just held my hand and listened."

There may also be times when it is better to write a love letter rather than leave romantic matters unresolved. A person saying goodbye to a loved one may want to share all of the things he or she will miss about her or him while away. This type of love letter should be very honest and straightforward, since it may be the last communication for a long time. Such a letter should include a few specific things the writer will remember while he or she is away, along with some positive affirmation that the relationship will survive during the time the couple must be apart. A love letter should also end on a positive note about the future, including long-term romantic hopes and aspirations.

A love letter isn't like a high-school essay, with an introduction, expository text, and recapitulation. What you're aiming for here is an inexhaustible, stream-of-consciousness recitation of the virtues of your beloved, contrasted with your own inimitable shortcomings. As a general rule: the higher the virtue-to-shortcoming ratio, the classier the letter.

However, sometimes a quality love letter doesn't necessarily need to read as a flowery or romantic correspondence to be effective. As long as the writer expresses his or her most honest emotions in a way the recipient should instinctively recognize and appreciate, he or she has written the perfect love letter.

1. What makes letters preferable than face-to-face contact sometimes?
   A. People could not express their feelings through face-to-face contact.
   B. Emotional feelings become stronger in written words.
   C. Letters allow feelings to be more easily expressed than face-to-face contact.
   D. A letter is more of a formal way to express feelings.

2. What made letter more important in the past?
   A. There was no wide use of telecommunications.
   B. Letters were the only way for a couple to remain in contact.
   C. There were more wars in the past.
   D. Letters could help young men and women start a relationship.

3. What might NOT be the reason why letter writing has started to become a lost art?
   A. The increasing popularity of email.
   B. The increasing popularity of short messaging.
   C. The increasing popularity of blogging.
   D. The increasing popularity of the Internet.

4. What is true about love letters in German speaking countries in the past?
   A. All love letters were written in the structure of Shakespeare's sonnets.
   B. Love letters were into the anthology Love letters of Great Men.
   C. Love letters were painted by hand on high quality paper.
   D. People had to ask artists to write love letters for them.

5. What language would be appropriate in modern love letter?
   A. "I love the way your eyes sparkle whenever you laugh. "
   B. "Your eyes are bluer than the deepest azure waves of a distant ocean. "
   C. Archaic and flowery language.
   D. Language from a collection of 18th century love poems.

6. Which one of the following statements is true according to the author?
   A. When writing a love letter, one must be in love.
   B. When writing a love letter, one should be in an emotional state.
   C. When writing a love letter, the focus should be on the sender.
   D. When writing a love letter, the focus should be on the sender and the recipient.

7. What should NOT be included in a letter from a person who has to be away from his or her lover for a period of time?
   A. Very honest and straightforward words.
   B. A few specific things the writer will remember.
   C. Some positive affirmation that the relationship will survive.
   D. Some affirmation that their relationship might not survive.

8. At the end of a love letter, one should write a positive note about the future, including long-term romantic _____.

9. One doesn't have to write all the parts of introduction, expository text, and recapitulation in a love letter like a _____.

10. A quality love letter doesn't have necessarily to be romantic, and it would be perfect as long as the writer expresses his or her _____.

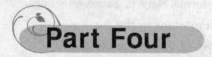

Part Four

> **Directions**: *There is a passage in this section. This passage is followed by some questions. For each of them there are four choices marked A), B), C) and D). You should decide on the best choice.*

What Will Happen if the World Was Suddenly No Emotion

Imagine a world in which there was suddenly no emotion — a world in which human beings could feel no love or happiness, no terror or hate. Try to imagine the consequences of such a transformation. People might not be able to stay alive: knowing neither joy nor pleasure, anxiety nor fear, they would be as likely to repeat acts that hurt them as acts that were beneficial. They could not learn: they could not benefit from experience because this emotionless world would lack rewards and punishments. Society would soon disappear: people would be as likely to harm one another as to provide help and support. Human relationships would not exist: in a world without friends or enemies, there could be no marriage, affection among companions, or bonds among members of groups. Society's economic *underpinnings* (支柱) would be destroyed: since earning $ 10 million would be no more pleasant than earning $ 10, there would be no incentive to work. In fact, there would be no incentives of any kind. For as we will see, incentives imply a capacity to enjoy them.

In such a world, the chances that the human species would survive are next to zero, because emotions are the basic instrument of our survival and adaptation. Emotions structure the world for us in important ways. As individuals, we categorize objects on the basis of our emotions. True we consider the length, shape, size, or texture, but an object's physical aspects are less important than what it has done or can do to us—hurt us, surprise us, anger us or make us joyful. We also use categorizations colored by emotions in our families, communities, and overall society. Out of our emotional experiences with objects and events comes a social feeling of agreement that certain things and actions are good and others are bad, and we apply these categories to every aspect of our social life — from what foods we eat and what clothes we wear to how we keep promises and which people our group will accept. In fact, society exploits our emotional reactions and attitudes, such as loyalty

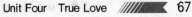

morality, pride shame, guilt, fear and greed, in order to maintain itself. It gives high rewards to individuals who perform important tasks such as surgery, makes heroes out of individuals for unusual or dangerous achievements such as flying fighter planes in a war, and uses the legal *penal* (刑法的) system to make people afraid to engage in antisocial acts.

1. The reason why people might not be able to stay alive in a world without emotion is that
   _____.
   A. they would not be able to tell the texture of objects
   B. they would not know what was beneficial and what was harmful to them
   C. they would not be happy with a life without love
   D. they would do things that hurt each other's feelings
2. According to the passage, people's learning activities are possible because they _____.
   A. believe that emotions are fundamental for them to stay alive
   B. benefit from providing help and support to one another
   C. enjoy being rewarded for doing the right thing
   D. know what is vital to the progress of society
3. It can be inferred from the passage that the economic foundation of society is dependent on
   _____.
   A. the ability to make money
   B. the will to work for pleasure
   C. the capacity to enjoy incentives
   D. the categorizations of our emotional experiences
4. Emotions are significant for man's survival and adaptation because _____.
   A. they provide the means by which people view the size or shape of objects
   B. they are the basis for the social feeling of agreement by which society is maintained
   C. they encourage people to perform dangerous achievements
   D. they generate more love than hate among people
5. The emotional aspects of an object are more important than its physical aspects in that
   they _____.
   A. help society exploit its members for profit
   B. encourage us to perform important tasks
   C. help to perfect the legal and penal system
   D. help us adapt our behavior to the world surrounding us

Part Five

Reading for Pleasure

Chinese Men in the Western Eyes

Not many western women know much about the Chinese men, except Bruce Lee and Jackie Chen. But normally in their eyes, Chinese men are divided into two groups. One group are of the virtues of (有……优点) thrift (节俭) and hard work. They put all their money in the bank, and buy nothing but important things. The other group is the new youth, they are living in the fast developing areas, and they feel the poor conditions and good conditions. So in order to attempt new life, new things, new place and new strangers, they like the exciting and the latest, and don't care about their profit and cost.

While getting to know them, western women may find a Chinese man very honest, and he might be shy when he meets a new girl. In western eyes, Chinese men are very clever, since they know themselves and the world culture and most of them want to get romantic love. Chinese men are also known as being of vivid character: they will like, love, hate, cry and forgive.

In the western eyes, a Chinese man would rather afford the duty as a father. They will support whole family, including their parents, kids and wives. It is high expression for Chinese men that they are glad to afford everything, even if losing life. Mostly Chinese men work hard: they wake up early in the morning, and stay up late in the evening, and they are especially laborious (勤劳的) when they become a real father.

Humor Prepared for You

The Love Test

One day, two colleagues Henry and Peter were having their lunch. Just then Henry started having hiccups (打嗝). When Peter asked him the reason, he replied that it was due to his wife's love. When his wife missed him a lot, he had loud hiccups.

Peter thought how lucky Henry was to have such a loving wife. He hurried back to his house and started scolding his wife for not missing him. Then he narrated (叙述) to her the whole matter. His wife understood where the problem was.

Next day, she mixed a lot of chilli powder (辣椒粉) in the lunch. When Peter sat down to eat, he had hiccups. He thought, Oh dear! Don't miss me so much. Henry laughed seeing Peter's condition.

Only for Love

Two donkeys (驴) who were friends, met at a crossroad. One donkey was healthy and the other malnourished (营养不良的). The healthy donkey asked the weak one: "What has happened to you? Why do you seem so weak?"

The weak donkey replied: "My master makes me work the whole day and doesn't give me enough food to eat and also beats me."

"Oh", exclaimed the healthy donkey, "then why don't you run away from your master's house?"

He replied: "I think my job has better prospects (前景；前途). My master beats his only daughter, too. And whenever he does so, he says to her, 'I'll marry you off to this donkey.' For this reason I'm not running away."

Three Words

Girl: Do you really love me?

Boy: Of course I do.

Girl: I wanna (= want to) hear you say it.

Boy: I don't have to.

Girl: Why not?

Boy: Because...

Girl: I just want to hear you say it in words.

Boy: I can't...

Girl: Then you don't love me... (*The girl started to cry softly.*)

(*The two continued to walk in silence. They reached the girl's home.*)

Girl: Why?

Boy: Do you really want to know?

Girl: (*Hesitantly*) Yes.

(*He hugged her gently, kissed the tip of her nose and whispered in her ear.*)

Boy: Because three words are not enough...

Famous Sayings

Spread love everywhere you go: first of all in your own house. Give love to your children, to your wife or husband, to a next door neighbor... Let no one ever come to you without leaving better and happier.

—*Mother Theresa*

随处散播你的爱心，就从对你的家人开始，多一分关爱给你的孩子，你的另一半，然后你的邻居……让每个接近你的人都有如沐春风的感觉。

——特蕾莎

If you judge people, you have no time to love them.

—*Mother Theresa*

总是审视别人的话，你就没有时间爱他们。

——特蕾莎

A loving heart is the truest wisdom.

—*Charles Dickens*

拥有爱心才是真正的智慧。

——查尔斯·狄更斯

If you would be loved, love and be lovable.

—*Benjamin Franklin*

想被人爱，就要去爱别人，并让自己可爱。

——本杰明·富兰克林

The course of true love never did run smooth.

—*William Shakespeare*

真爱的路途充满坎坷。

——威廉·莎士比亚

Love test

Believe it or not, here is a test that measures whether you are in love with someone.

1. Do you call them more than once a day just to hear their voice?　　no　　yes
2. Is it impossible to imagine life without them?　　no　　yes
3. Could you never lie to them?　　no　　yes
4. Do you have trouble remembering your life before them?　　no　　yes
5. Would you give your last chocolate to them?　　no　　yes
6. Do you feel happy, sad, hot and cold all at the same time?　　no　　yes
7. Do you put them first in your life, even before you?　　no　　yes
8. Do presents from them seem more enjoyable than any other gift, even before you know what they are?　　no　　yes
9. Have you ever posted pictures of them all over your walls, leaving little qr no wall visible?　　no　　yes
10. Have you ever called them to hear their voice, only to hang up before speaking?　　no　　yes

—If you have got 6 or more than 6 yeses, you are in love.

Unit Five

Parenting

Building a positive relationship between parents and child is one that requires work and effort to make it strong and successful. Parenting is a tough job, and maintaining close relationships and open communications help to ensure parents and their children stay connected through all ages of their upbringing.

In this unit, you will read:

- Do You Expect Too Much of Your Kids
- Letting Kids Be Kids
- Parenting and Children's Development
- Bringing up Children
- Children's Day

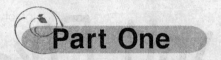

Part One

Pre-reading Questions

1. What are your parents' expectations to you?
2. What do you think you will expect of your future children?
3. What skills do you know for educating children?

Do You Expect Too Much of Your Kids

1　When asked which is his favorite school subject, Jason Abrams, 11, doesn't **hesitate** "Lunch!" The mischief in his voice gives away that he knows his answer will get a laugh. But his parents, Jane and Stuart, are concerned that Jason isn't taking school more seriously. They wonder if their son's marks — good but not outstanding — might keep him from getting accepted into an advanced programme. "You want the best for your kids" says Jane. "We know Jason could do better if he applied himself."

2　But could he? "Most parents make well-meant efforts to set high goals to **motivate** and stimulate their children's learning and good behavior," observes Sam Goldstein, a psychologist **specializing** in child development at **the University of Utah**. "But many don't understand their own child's limitations or strengths."

3　In fact, many potentialities and limitations — in intelligence, **temperament** and mental health — are laid down prior to birth, says David Cohen, a recently retired psychology professor at **the University of Texas**. We may want our son or daughter to do better than we did at the same age, but if it's not **in the cards**, or **coaxing** will move them much beyond their natural gift. In fact, the pressure may have the opposite effect.

4　Goldstein talks of Sally, a shy eight-year-old whose mother was also quite as a child but hoped to help her daughter become more **outgoing** "Telling a child of this makeup to make friends is **equivalent** to asking a child unable to float to swim in two-metre-deep water!" Her mum's exhortations only added to Sally's anxiety.

5　Trouble arises when we ignore the signs that a child isn't ready or able to live up to our expectations. "Let's face it, too many parents are living **vicariously** through their children," says Christine Ziegler, professor of psychology at **Kennesaw State University**. "But if a child is not really good at what his parents are pushing him to do. That can do **irreparable** damage. This is the antithesis of developing self-esteem."

6　Repeated failures may cause some children to set the bar too low for themselves, withdrawing from new experiences and missing out on opportunities to guarantee they won't fail again, warns Goldstein.

7　"When a child doesn't meet expectations, the parent may feel **resentment**, which shows up as anger or frustration," says Ronald P. Rohner, director of the Centre for the Study of Parental Acceptance and Rejection at **the University of Connecticut**. Children may see their parents' disappointment as rejection, and these feelings can lead to hostility, emotional withdrawal, a sense of incompetence and conduct problem or **delinquency**.

8　Thirteen-year-old George was referred to Goldstein because he'd set a fire at his school. It became apparent that the incident was **triggered** by George's anger towards his parents for their resentment about his poor marks and his not being like his sister, a popular, gifted student. Through counseling, the parents eventually learned to let go of their image of the ideal son and to encourage George in the one area where he showed interest and talent gardening.

9　The bottom line is that we must accept our children for who they are and allow them to become what they will be. However, Ziegler warns, "don't misinterpret acceptance as permissiveness." Letting children do what they want when they want does no one any good; homework must be done, family rules respected and consideration shown. It comes down to a **delicate** balance of control and acceptance, says Rohner.

10　Jayson Abrams may **balk** at his parents' **strictures** (not too much candy, TV or **teasing** his sister), but he knows they understand the other things he enjoys as well, biking with his dad, sharing a **roller-coaster** ride with his mum and even being allowed to dye the tips of his hair. And Mum and Dad nurture Jayson's **eclectic** interest in music, which led to his playing the **clarinet** in school.

11　Other kids will give us the clues we need to help them set and achieve realistic goals. The benefits of your child may surprise you. When parents are accepting, loving and supportive, says Goldstein, "children are often motivated to exceed your expectation." Jason proved as much to his parents. His test scores qualified him for a special advanced programme.

12　No one ever said raising a child was an exact science. But according to the experts, here's what to do to sharpen your skills.

Know your child

13　"We parents fall short when we try to make our children more intelligent, **assertive**, graceful or accomplished than they are naturally **disposed** to be," Cohen points out. "We fail them just as much when we ignore or deny their real talents and temperament."

Know yourself

14　Examine your motives in wanting more from your child. "Parents may have their own shame or unmet needs that they **project** onto their children," says Rohner.

15　Do you want your children to take dance lessons because your parents forced them on you? Were you a mediocre athlete but hope for a **trophy** winner in the next generation?

Educate yourself

16   Talk to other parents and your **paediatrician**, and read child-development books to learn what you can reasonably expect from your child at each stage of his life.

Empathize

17   Take time to see yourself through your child's eyes. Do you act embarrassed by him? Do you point out only his mistakes? Would you want to be treated that way?

Make adjustments

18   "No one responds well to someone who is **accusatory** or judgmental," says Goldstein. If you find yourself **harping on** what your child can't do, refocus on her strengths. Once you change your attitude, you may find that she changes too.

Collaborate

19   Create a partnership with you in which he can participate in setting appropriate goals and solving problems, says Frances Stott, psychologist and dean of **the Erikson Institute in Chicago**.

20   Read how your child feels. Your child's behaviour — anger, **fidgeting procrastination** — says a lot about whether she is being asked to do more than she can manage.

Explore possibilities

21   A good way to encourage is to expose your children to a variety of environments, including sports, the arts, nature and science. Let your child find out what she enjoys.

Keep your eye on the end goal

22   "A parent's main objective should be to raise a child who loves well, works well and takes pleasure in life," advises Stott. "You don't want to **stifle** curiosity, **initiative** and confidence."

Avoid comparisons

23   A style of parenting that works for one child may **backfire** for his **sibling**. "Every child has his own personality," says Ziegler.

🔊 Words and Expressions

hesitate *v.* pause before saying or doing sth. , esp. through uncertainty 犹豫,踌躇

motivate *v.* stimulate (someone's) interest in or enthusiasm for doing sth. 激发(某人的)积极性

specialize *v.* concentrate on and become expert in a particular subject or skill 专攻,专门从事

temperament *n.* a person's or animal's nature, esp. as it permanently affects their behaviour 性格,性情,气质

in the cards 可能的

coax *v.* persuade (sb.) gradually or by flattery to do sth. 劝诱,哄

outgoing *a.* friendly and socially confident 对人友好的,开朗的

equivalent *a.* equal in value, amount, function, meaning, etc. 相等的,相当的

vicariously *ad.* for another 代理地,担任代理者地

irreparable *a.* (of an injury or loss) impossible to rectify or repair 不能修复的,不可弥补的

resentment *a.* bitter indignation at having been treated unfairly 愤恨,不满,怨恨

delinquency *a.* minor crime, esp. that committed by young people 不良行为,少年犯罪

trigger *v.* cause (an event or situation) to happen or exist 引发,引起,导致

delicate *a.* requiring sensitive or careful handling 难以处理的,微妙的

balk *v.* hesitate or be unwilling to accept an idea or undertaking 畏缩不前,犹豫

stricture *n.* a sternly critical or censorious remark or instruction 苛评,指责

tease *v.* make fun of or attempt to provoke (a person or animal) in a playful way 取笑,戏弄,逗弄

roller-coaster *n.* 过山车

eclectic *a.* deriving ideas, style, or taste from a broad and diverse range of sources 兼收并蓄的,不拘一格的

clarinet *n.* 单簧管,竖笛

assertive *a.* having or showing a confident and forceful personality 果敢的,有冲劲的

dispose *v.* arrange in a particular position 安置,安排

project *v.* throw or cause to move forward or outward 投掷,发射,喷射

trophy *n.* a cup or other decorative object awarded as a prize for a victory or success 奖杯,奖品,胜利纪念品,战利品

paediatrician *n.* 儿科医师

empathize *v.* understand and share the feelings of another 有同感,产生共鸣,表示同情

accusatory *a.* indicating or suggesting that one believes a person has done sth. wrong 指责的

harp on 喋喋不休

fidget *v.* be impatient or uneasy 烦躁,坐立不安

procrastination *n.* delay or putting off doing sth. 拖延,耽搁

stifle *v.* prevent or constrain (an activity or idea) 阻止,抑制

initiative *n.* the ability to assess and initiate things independently 首创精神,创造力

backfire *v.* have the opposite effect to what was intended 事与愿违,产生反作用,发生回火

sibling *n.* a brother or sister 兄弟,姐妹

📖 Background Information

1. The University of Utah: The University of Utah, also known as the U or the U of U, is a public, coeducational research university in Salt Lake City, Utah, United States. The university was established in 1850 as the University of Deseret by the General Assembly of the provisional State of Deseret, making it Utah's oldest institution of higher education. It received its current name in 1892, four years before Utah attained statehood, and moved to its current location in 1900. It is one of the ten institutions that make up the Utah System of Higher Education.

2. The University of Texas: The University of Texas is a public research university located in Austin, Texas, United States, and is the flagship institution of the University of Texas System. Founded in 1883, the university has over 50,000 undergraduate and graduate students and 16,500 faculty and staff. It currently holds the largest enrollment of all colleges in the state of Texas.

3. Kennesaw State University: Kennesaw State University is a public, coeducational, comprehensive university that is part of the University System of Georgia. The university is well known for academic programs in business, education and nursing.

4. The University of Connecticut: The University of Connecticut is a public research university in the U.S. state of Connecticut. Founded in 1881 as a land-grant university, it serves more than 28,000 students on its six campuses, including nearly 8,000 graduate students in multiple programs.

5. The Erikson Institute in Chicago: The institute was founded in 1966. It is a graduate school in child development located in downtown Chicago, Illinois. It is named for the noted psychoanalyst and developmental psychologist, Erik Erikson.

Learn about Words

Often you can tell the meaning of a word from its context — the words around it. Please find the word in the paragraph that means:

1. playfulness that is intended to tease, mock, or create trouble (1)
2. encourage interest or activity in (a person or animal) (2)
3. latent qualities or abilities that may be developed and lead to future success or usefulness (3)
4. an address or communication emphatically urging sb. to do sth. (4)
5. a person or thing that is the direct opposite of sb. or sth. else (5)
6. the provision of assistance and guidance in resolving personal, social, or psychological problems and difficulties, esp. by a professional (8)
7. allowing great or excessive freedom of behaviour (9)
8. care for and encourage the growth or development of (10)
9. be better than, surpass (11)
10. of only moderate quality; not very good (15)

Part Two

> **Reading Skill — Reading for the Main Idea in a Paragraph**
>
> Figurative language or speech contains images and it is not intended to be interpreted in a literal sense. The writer or speaker describes something through the use of unusual comparisons, for effect, interest, and to make things clearer. The result of using this technique is the creation of interesting images.

🐾 Skill-Specific Training

Each of the following sentences from the passage contains one or more figurative expressions (the underlined parts). Explain in your own words what each expression means.

1. The poor player is <u>a nervous wreck</u> by the end of each game. (Para. 2)

   Explanation: _____

2. The drive home from each game is <u>a play-by-play rundown</u> of what the kid should have done during the game. (Para. 2)

   Explanation: _____

3. A track team member's parents are certain their daughter can become <u>the next big thing</u>. (Para. 4)

   Explanation: _____

4. They are <u>frustrated "weekend warriors"</u> living out their own dreams of glory through their children. (Para. 6)

   Explanation: _____

5. They need to be praised for trying their best and for <u>putting themselves "out there."</u> (Para. 8)

   Explanation: _____

6. As parents and coaches, we have been entrusted with <u>the incredible gift</u> and awesome responsibility of being part of the "making" of the men and women whom our children will become. (Para. 9)

   Explanation: _____

Letting Kids Be Kids

Nancie Menapace

1. We all know them, don't we? "Those" parents — the ones no one wants to sit with in the **bleachers** because they're so irritating. Recognize any of these folks?

2　A young basketball coach has to call his own father for advice after he struggles with a "bleacher dad" who persists in coaching his son from the sidelines. The poor player is a nervous **wreck** by the end of each game, between trying to follow his coach's directions and hearing his dad's constant from-the-side input, which is sometimes contrary to what the coach has told him to do. Finally, the coach pulls the dad aside and tells him that he needs to stop, that he's damaging his son's nerves and **undermining** the coach's authority. After being **chastised** by the coach, the dad makes a large show during games of folding his arms, pressing his lips and not saying a word, but the drive home from each game is a **play-by-play rundown** of what the kid should have done during the game.

3　A baseball coach is enthusiastically supportive and encouraging to all of the players, except his own son, who is a strong, but **erratic pitcher**. When other players come up to bat, the coach is there to **high-five** them as they leave the field, whether they hit well or strike out. When his own son is up to bat or pitching, however, Coach Dad is a **study** in disgust and frustration, rolling his eyes at any error, sighing deeply, shouting, "Oh, come on," when his son fails to strike out a pitcher or make at least a **base hit**. Coach Dad has placed such impossibly high expectations on his son that his son inevitably becomes **rattled** and makes even more mistakes than ever.

4　A track team member's parents are certain their daughter can become the next big thing; she just needs to work harder, receive better coaching, get leaner. They hire personal coaches to work with her, **enroll** her in summer camps to train and tell her if she would just push herself harder, she'd be a star. She isn't allowed to attend a friend's midnight **bowling** party because she has to be up early to train the next day. Track Girl does everything she's told to do. She also throws up before every meet and secretly writes long poems about frustration, weakness and worthlessness.

5　They're just kids.

6　I wish I could say these **scenarios** are fiction, but they are simply **fictionalized** versions of all-too-common examples of parents who place far too much emphasis on their children's athletic achievements. What is the cause of this overemphasis? First, it can **stem from** the parents' own attitudes, either they were successful and driven athletes who want to see the same from their own children or they are frustrated "weekend warriors" **living out** their own dreams of glory through their children.

7　Competitiveness is introduced far too young in many sports. **Aspiring** players are either cut or **relegated** to the bench while their bodies and their abilities are still developing. Even the children who will never grow into athletic success need to be given the opportunities and encouragement to find personal **bests**, to experience small successes, to feel part of a team. One of the most rewarding sights for parents is to see the **interplay** among teammates when it's done right — kids who may not actually **socialize** with each usually, who may not even like each other, can really warm your heart when you see them supporting each other on the field, the track or the court. Being a fair, supportive, equal part of a team can be **superb** preparation for all kinds of things life will bring as children grow into **adulthood** and take their places in society. Taught properly, by coaches and parents, every member of the team can be made to feel that he or she has the responsibility to look after the good of the team, to make his or her best contribution and to be **unfailingly** respectful of his or her teammates.

8　In the meantime, kids still need to be kids. They need to play. They need to be praised for trying their best and for putting themselves "out there." In no other part of their childhood do we expect them to have adult **motivations** and success, but too often, in the sports **arena**, we expect just that.

9　As parents and coaches, we have been **entrusted** with the **incredible** gift and **awesome** responsibility of being part of the "making" of the men and women whom our children will become. They have the rest of their lives to learn to absorb the hits of losing and the **thrills** of winning; how about a little consideration while they are young?

Words and Expressions

bleacher *n.* a cheap bench seat at a sports ground, typically in an outdoor uncovered stand （尤指露天运动场的廉价）长条凳座位

wreck *n.* a person whose physical or mental health or strength has failed 受到严重损害的人

undermine *v.* damage or weaken (sb. or sth.), esp. gradually or insidiously 暗中破坏,逐渐削弱

chastise *v.* rebuke or reprimand severely 厉声训斥,严厉谴责

play-by-play *n.* （Amer.）a detailed running commentary on a sporting contest 实况解说

rundown *n.* an analysis or summary of sth. by a knowledgeable person 分析,总结,概要,梗概

erratic *a.* not even or regular in pattern or movement; unpredictable 不稳定的,捉摸不定的, 无规律的

pitcher *n.* the player who delivers the ball to the batter 投手

high-five *v.* 举手击掌（两人以手合掌高举头顶以表示得意祝贺或问候的手势）

study *n.* （a study in）a thing or person that is an embodiment or good example of sth. 化身, 榜样,模范

base hit （棒球）安全打

rattle *v.* cause (sb.) to feel nervous, worried, or irritated （非正式）使窘迫不安,使惊慌失 措,烦扰;使恼火,激怒

enroll *v.* register (someone) as a member or student 登记,注册,使入伍（或入会,入学等）

bowling *n.* 保龄球运动

scenario *n.* a setting, in particular for a work of art or literature（艺术或文学作品中的）场景

fictionalize *v.* 把（历史事件等）编成小说,使小说化

stem from 来自,起源于,由……造成

live out 度过（某一段时间）,过（某种生活）

aspiring *a.* 有志气的,有抱负的

relegate *v.* consign or dismiss to an inferior rank or position 把……降级,把……置于次要地位

best *n.* the highest standard or level that sb. or sth. can reach 最高标准,最高水平,最佳状

态,最佳局面

interplay *n.* the way in which two or more things have an effect on each other 相互影响,相互作用

socialize *v.* mix socially with others 交往,交际

superb *a.* excellent 卓越的,杰出的,极好的

adulthood *n.* 成人期

unfailingly *ad.* 无穷尽地,经久不衰地

motivation *n.* the general desire or willingness of sb. to do sth. 积极性,干劲

arena *n.* a level area surrounded by seating, in which sports, entertainments, and other public events are held 场地

entrust *v.* assign the responsibility for doing sth. to (sb.) 委托给,托付给

incredible *a.* difficult to believe; extraordinary 难以置信的,非凡的

awesome *a.* inspiring great admiration or fear 令人敬畏的

thrill *n.* an experience that produces a sudden feeling of excitement and pleasure 引起兴奋 (或激动)的经历

Comprehension of the Text

1. Why does the basketball coach pull the "bleacher dad" aside and stop him?

   _____.

2. Why does the baseball coach hold different attitudes towards his son and the other players?

   _____.

3. What is the track girl's reaction to her parents' efforts in making her a star?

   _____.

4. According to the author, what do kids need?

   _____.

5. What lesson do you think the article will bring for parents?

   _____.

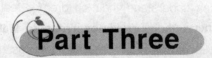

Part Three

Reading Comprehension (Skimming and Scanning)

Directions: *In this part, you will have 15 minutes to go over the passage quickly and answer the questions. For questions 1~7, mark Y (for YES) if the statement agrees with the information given in the passage; N (for NO) if the statement contradicts the information given in the passage; NG (for NOT GIVEN) if the information is not given in the passage. For questions 8~10, complete the sentences with the information given in the passage.*

Parenting and Children's Development

As people know, the family is a place in which children learn to interpret reality. In the families, parents serve as significant interpreters for children of information about the world and children's abilities. They are children's first teachers. Parents want their children to grow into socially mature individuals, and they may feel frustrated in trying to discover the best way to accomplish this development.

Parenting styles are broad patterns of child bringing up practices, values and behaviors. According to Diana Baumrind, four types of parenting styles are indulgent (more responsive than demanding), authoritarian (highly demanding and directive but not responsive), authoritative (both demanding and responsive), and neglectful (low in responsiveness and demandingness).

Children from authoritarian family are often aggressive, fearful, and anxious; they often have weak communication skills. Children associated with authoritative parenting, are happy, cheerful, self-controlled and can cope with stress. Children from indulgent family are aggressive, spoiled, and noncompliant; they have difficulties in peer relations. Children associated with neglectful parenting are lack of self-control, social incompetence and delinquency.

Children's emotions are often affected by parenting. Parents are kids' first important teachers. According to John Gottman, "Parents are kids' emotion coaches, and they teach their kids strategies to deal with life's ups and downs. Even more than IQ, emotional awareness and ability to handle feelings will determine one's success and happiness in all walks of life, including family relationships". So it's very important to use good parenting at home. Authoritative parenting is the best parenting style, because it is good for children's emotion development, and because authoritative parents acknowledge their children's feelings and accept them unconditionally, they can set acceptable standards, and they help to promote children's independence.

Authoritative parents can understand their children's feelings and teach them how to regulate them. They often help them to find appropriate ways to solve problems. John Gottmand said, "They don't ignore or deny their kids' feelings. Nor do they ignore or laugh at their children for emotional expression." They have knowledge of their children's feelings. Authoritative parents have a strong awareness of their own emotions and those of their loved one. John Gottman believes, "They can see value in their children's negative emotions; they have more patience when their children are angry, sad, or fearful."

Authoritative parents are concerned about their kids. They seem to be willing to spend time with a crying or impatient child, listening to their worries, empathizing with them, letting them vent their anger, or just cry it out. They are responsible parents.

Authoritative parents also expect maturity, promote independence and appropriate behavior of children. They teach children to calm down and focus attention. When they calm down, they can concentrate in finding ways to solve the problems. Psychologists say people are very easy to lose control when they get mad, so it is very easy to do wrong things. For example, my son is ten years old. He is very easy to get mad or excited. When he gets mad, I don't blame him. I know I have to calm down so that I can teach him to do so. I always tell him slowly and tenderly: "Can you tell me what's going on? Maybe I can help you. Don't worry. Mum is here with you. Let me help you to find a good way." Sometimes I teach him to do some exercise to relax. I teach him to do deep breathing when he is mad. After deep and slow inhalation and breathing for five to six times, he feels peaceful and relaxed. It really works. Learning to calm down and focus attention becomes increasingly important as the children mature. Learning to be calm also helps the child to concentrate in learning situations and to focus on the achievement of specific tasks. And, as a child grows, it's extremely helpful for learning how to share toys. This skill can make a big difference in a child's ability to enter new playgroups, make new friends, and handle rejection when peers turn away.

Although some people think authoritarian parenting is associated with school success, children from this kind of family are often aggressive, fearful, and anxious and have weak communication skills, because parents have too many restrictive, punitive disciplines for their children to follow. They are also rejecting children. My parents used authoritarian parenting in my family. There are three children in my family. My mother used the same style to us all. I don't think it is the best for parents or caretakers to use the same style, because different families have different children, even in the same family, children are different from each other. It's better for them to use eclectic parenting style. We didn't like authoritarian parenting, because we had not any opportunity to tell our feelings or argue. What we could do is "shut up" and "follow my words". According to John Gottman, "Family life is our first school for emotional learning". It's true. All of us have developed into different emotional persons. Both of my brothers are over forty now. They are really aggressive. They have problems in communication skills and fail to take activity. They also still use the same parenting to educate their children now. Especially my second elder brother, his family has lots of problems just because of his temper. He often yells to his children and fights with his wife. I am shy, fearful and have weak communication skills, too. I am afraid to express my opinion in public. Though, we are adults.

Now, we are all lacking of confidence. We are still under the shadow of this kind of parenting and have influence on our kids. According to Gottman, families with authoritarian parents "seem unable to function well either because they cannot set guidelines, or because they do not seek interests that involve places and persons outside the family". This makes it more difficult for children to develop self-knowledge and distinguish their own career goals from their parents' goals.

Good parenting can help parents to make good emotional kids and have a happy family. The authoritative style balances clear, high expectations with emotional support and recognition of children's autonomy. Children associated with this kind of family are happy, cheerful, self-controlled and can cope with stress. They have fewer behavior problems, and are better able

to bounce back from miserable experiences. Children can do better in terms of academic achievement, health, and peer relationships. Gottman believes "the children who learn to acknowledge and master their emotions are more self-confident as well as physically healthier. They also do better in school and are more likely to grow into emotionally healthy adults".

1. Parents act as important instructors for children of messages about the surroundings and their competence.
2. Children of parents who are neither responsive nor demanding are often aggressive, fearful, and anxious, and they often have weak communication skills.
3. Some expert suggests, "Parents are kids' emotion instructors, and they offer their kids strategies to handle life's ups and downs".
4. Parents who are high in responsiveness and demandingness always brush aside their kids' feelings and ignore or laugh at their children for emotional expression.
5. Psychologists say when people are in a state of crazy, they are most likely to lose control, which will surely result in subsequent troubles like doing wrong things.
6. Learning to be calm helps the child to devote the whole of himself to learning situations and to centering on the accomplishments of specific tasks.
7. One of our most important responsibilities as parents is to listen to our children, hearing not only their words, but also the feelings behind their words.
8. Parenting styles are broad patterns of child bringing up _____.
9. Authoritative parents also expect mature, promote independence and _____.
10. The authoritative style balances clear, high expectations with emotional support and recognition of _____.

Part Four

> **Directions:** *There is a passage in this section. This passage is followed by some questions. For each of them there are four choices marked A), B), C) and D). You should decide on the best choice.*

Bringing up Children

In bringing up children, every parent watches eagerly the child's acquisition (学会) of each new skill — the first spoken words, the first independent steps, or the beginning of reading and writing. It is often tempting to hurry the child beyond his natural learning rate, but this can set up dangerous feelings of failure and states of worry in the child. This might happen at any stage. A baby might be forced to use a toilet too early, a young child might be encouraged to learn to read before he knows the meaning of the words he reads. On the other hand, though, if a child is left alone too much, or without any learning opportunities, he loses his natural enthusiasm for life and his desire to find out new things for himself.

　　Patents vary greatly in their degree of strictness towards their children. Some may be especially strict in money matters. Others are severe over times of coming home at night or punctuality for meals. In general, the controls imposed represent the needs of the parents and the values of the community as much as the child's own happiness.

　　As regards the development of moral standards in the growing child, consistency is very important in parental teaching. To forbid a thing one day and excuse it the next is no foundation for *morality*（道德）. Also, parents should realize that "example is better than precept". If they are not sincere and do not practise what they *preach*（说教）, their children may grow confused, and emotionally insecure when they grow old enough to think for themselves, and realize they have been to some extent fooled.

　　A sudden awareness of a marked difference between their parents' principles and their morals can be a dangerous disappointment.

1. Eagerly watching the child's acquisition of new skills _____.

　　A. should be avoided

　　B. is universal among parents

　　C. sets up dangerous states of worry in the child

　　D. will make him lose interest in learning new things

2. In the process of children's learning new skills, parents _____.

　　A. should encourage them to read before they know the meaning of the words they read

　　B. should not expect too much of them

　　C. should achieve a balance between pushing them too hard and leaving them on their own

　　D. should create as many learning opportunities as possible

3. The second paragraph mainly tells us that _____.

　　A. parents should be strict with their children

　　B. parental controls reflect only the needs of the parents and the values of the community

　　C. parental restrictions vary, and are not always enforced for the benefit of the children alone

　　D. parents vary in their strictness towards their children according to the situation

4. The word "precept" (Line 3, Para. 3) probably means "_____".

　　A. idea　　　　　B. punishment　　　C. behavior　　　　D. instruction

5. In moral matters, parents should _____.

　　A. observe the rules themselves

　　B. be aware of the marked difference between adults and children

　　C. forbid things which have no foundation in morality

　　D. consistently ensure the security of their children

Part Five

Children's Day

Children's Day is celebrated in many parts of the world. It is a day to highlight the dignity of children and their need for love, care, and respect, and instill in the children a sense of independence and national pride. It is also a day to honor adults that have contributed to improving the lives of children.

In August 1925, some 54 representatives from different countries gathered together in Geneva, Switzerland to convene the first "World Conference for the Wellbeing of Children", during which the "Geneva Declaration Protecting Children" was passed. The proclamation made a strong appeal for the spiritual needs of children, relief for children in poverty, prevention of child labor, reassessing the way that children are educated and other issues related to the welfare of children around the world.

After the conference, various governments around the world designated a day, different in each country, as Children's Day, to encourage and bring joy to children as well as to draw the attention of society to children's issues.

Universal Children's Day is on November 20. First proclaimed by the UN General Assembly in 1954, it was established to encourage all countries to institute a day, firstly to promote mutual exchange and understanding among children and secondly to initiate action to benefit and promote the welfare of the world's children.

Many countries like China chose to celebrate the International Children's Day on June 1, which has been established in November 1949 at the International Democratic Women's League Council held in Moscow. The Day, which is also called the First of June, is explained as "an international memorial day that exists upon the purpose of securing lives and rights of children and encouraging their happiness and health".

However, Women's/Children's Day (formerly Children's Day) is celebrated in Taiwan, China on April 4. This day marks the restoration of Taiwan to Chinese rule in 1945 after half a century of Japanese occupation.

May 5 is Children's Day in Japan. It became a national holiday in 1948, but it has been a day of celebration in Japan since ancient times. It was traditionally a festival for boys. Girls have their own festival, held on March 3.

In India, the birthday of Jawaharlal Nehru is celebrated as Children's Day every year, on

November 14.

April 23 is the "National Sovereignty and Children's Day" in Turkey. It was Mustafa Kemal Aataturk, the Father of the Republic of Turkey who loved children so much, that started the Day, the same date when the Republic of Turkey was founded. On the Day, certain children are selected to take over the places of the government and even a lucky kid is the president of Turkey for a whole day!

Humor Prepared for You

Get a Job

One day shortly after I had come home from college, my father was outside doing yard work. He found a baby bird under a tree and assumed it had fallen from its nest. Wanting to return the tiny creature to its home, my dad went to get a ladder. When he got back, he found another baby bird on the ground.

Suddenly he heard a loud chirping from above. Looking up, my father saw the mother bird giving a third baby the boot from its nest. With that, Dad walked into our house, took one look at me watching television and barked, "Get a job!"

The Russian Baby

Morris and Becky were delighted when finally their long wait to adopt an infant came to an end. The adoption center called and told them they had a wonderful Russian baby boy, and the couple took him without hesitation.

On the way home from the adoption center, they stopped by the local college so they each could enroll in night courses. After they filled out the form, the registration clerk inquired, "Whatever make you study Russian?" The couple said proudly, "We just adopted a Russian baby and in a year or so he'll start to talk. We just want to be able to understand him without any interpreter."

Famous Sayings

A mother is not a person to lean on but a person to make leaning unnecessary.

—*D. C, Fisher, American female novelist*

母亲不是赖以依靠的人，而是使依靠成为不必要的人。—— 美国女小说家 菲希尔 D. C.

Happy are the families where the government of parents is the reign of affection, and obedience of the children the submission to love.　　—*Francis Bacon, British philosopher*

幸福的家庭中，父母靠慈爱当家，孩子也是出于对父母的爱而顺从大人。

——英国哲学家　弗朗西斯·培根

Unit Six

Stereotype

Despite the crucial role of physical appearance in forming first impressions, little research has examined the accuracy of personality impressions based on appearance alone. According to one study, personality is manifested through both static and expressive channels of appearance, and observers use this information to form accurate judgments for a variety of traits.

In this unit, you'll read:

- Prejudice Against the Obese and Some of Its Situational Sources
- Name Discrimination! How It Affects Job and Career Choices, Life Status, Overall Success
- Beauty Contestant Fights for Right of Self-Improvement
- Moral Decline
- Sayings about Proper Names and Nicknames

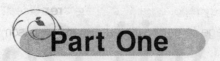

Part One

Pre-reading Questions
1. Could you explain the meaning of the word "stereotype"?
2. Have you experienced being discriminated just because of poor appearance?
3. How do the negative names influence job opportunities?

Prejudice Against the Obese and Some of Its Situational Sources

1   There can be little question that the growing number of overweight and obese Americans confront serious discrimination and prejudice. Situationist Contributors, Adam Benfrorado, Jon Hanson, and David Yosifon summarized the extent of the problem as follows:

2   For obese Americans, constant **stigmatization** and frequent discrimination are found in all aspects of daily life, including education, employment, health care, and interpersonal relationships... Parents provide significantly less **monetary** support for their overweight children than for their thin children in pursuing advanced education and that 28% of teachers involved in the study said that becoming obese was one of the worst things that could happen to a person. Unsurprisingly, fewer fat students end up going to college.

3   One scholar reviewed twenty-nine studies about the experiences of the obese in the workplace, and he found discrimination in nearly every aspect of the employment relationship, from hiring to wages to benefits. In fact, weight appears to elicit more **pervasive** discrimination than other appearance-related factors like gender, age, or race... Isolating weight and sex, one group of researchers found that the weight of an applicant explained 34.6% of hiring, whereas sex explained only 10.4%. In another set of experiments that studied how decisions about employee discharge were colored by social **stigmas**, participants demonstrated stronger negative feelings toward overweight employees than they did toward **ex-mental** patients or **ex-felons**.

4   The wage **differential** is equally startling, although the effect is far stronger in women. **Morbidly** obese white women have wages 24.1% lower than their standard weight counterparts, and moderately obese woman earn 5.9% less.

5   Much of the discrimination occurs in areas less noticeable than hiring or wages. In one study of people who were at least 50% above their ideal weight, more than a quarter reported that

they had been denied benefits like health insurance **on account of** their weight. Moreover, 24% of nurses in another study reported that they are "**repulsed**" by obese patients, so even when obese individuals manage to get health care there is reason to believe that it may not be the best.

6   Those situationist scholars argued that "the added discrimination reserved for the overweight and obese reflects our sense that those problems, more than the others, reflect personal choices" (that is, disposition, instead of situation):

7   When we look at the obese we see only their fat. We miss their intelligence, their kindness, and their strength, just as we miss the broader situational influences that led them to be overweight. We see a disposition that **reassuringly** explains their most salient feature — fat people are weak... Overweight people are frequently stereotyped as being socially **handicapped** and emotionally **impaired**, and as having negative personality traits. After all, who else would choose to look like that?

8   Such negative **stereotypes** attach early on. By nursery school, children show a preference for drawings of children in wheelchairs and with facial **disfigurements** to those of obese children; by the time they enter elementary school, they have already begun to construct causal concepts. In one study, children who were asked to describe a **silhouette** of an obese child used words like "dirty," "lazy," "ugly," "stupid," and "sloppy." According to another study, the quality of life for obese children is approximately the same as that of children undergoing chemotherapy for cancer... One researcher explained: "Obesity is an extremely socially stigmatized disease, and unlike some conditions, it's not something a child can hide." Evidence abounds that obese people are not wanted. Sixteen percent of adult Americans would abort a baby if they knew it would be untreatably obese, whereas 17% would abort if they were certain the child would be mentally retarded. In a 1988 study, students reported that they would rather marry someone who was an embezzler, a drug addict, a shoplifter, or a blind person than someone who was obese.

9   It seems strange that there could be so much discrimination against the overweight in a country with so many fat people. The explanation may be that the overweight, just like everyone else, have been convinced of the desirability of the waif body and the righteousness of the dispositionist message. They made a bad choice — or many bad choices — and now fairness demands that they pay the consequences. They look in the mirror and say, "Yes, it's true, I am disgusting;" "I brought all this discrimination on myself;" and "I have a decision to make, just like Dr. Phil says." This self-assessment shares much with the reflections of Milgram's subjects who left feeling that their own evil ways, and not the situation, were solely to blame for their behavior.

📖 Words and Expressions

stigmatize *v.* to accuse or condemn 使受耻辱；指责；污辱
monetary *a.* of or relating to money or currency 金融的；财政的

pervasive *a.* spreading throughout 无处不在的；遍布的

stigma *n.* a distinguishing mark of social disgrace 耻辱的标记，瑕疵

ex-mental patient 康复的精神病人

ex-felon *n.* 出狱的重罪犯

differential *a.* the difference between rates of pay for different types of labour 差异；工资级差

morbidly *ad.* in a morbid manner 病态地

on account of 由于

repulse *v.* to reject with coldness or discourtesy? 拒绝

reassuring *a.* restoring confidence and relieving anxiety 安慰的，鼓励的

handicap *v.* injure permanently 使(某人)行动和生活不正常

impair *v.* to reduce or weaken in strength, quality, etc. 损害，削弱

disfigurement *n.* the act of damaging the appearance or surface of sth. 毁容，缺陷，畸形

silhouette *n.* the outline of a solid figure (人的)体形

Background Information

Stereotype 刻板印象：A stereotype is a commonly held public belief about specific social groups, or types of individuals. The concepts of "stereotype" and "prejudice" are often confused with many other different meanings. Stereotypes are standardized and simplified conceptions of groups, based on some prior assumptions. To learn more about the stereotype, visit *http://en.wikipedia.org/wiki/Stereotype.*

Learn about Words

Often you can tell the meaning of a word from its context — the words around it. Please find the word in the paragraph that means：

1. unfair treatment of a person, racial group, minority, etc.; action based on prejudice (1)
2. excessively fat or fleshy (1)
3. place or set apart (3)
4. dismissal or release from an office, job, institution, etc. (3)
5. to give rise to; evoke (3)
6. causing surprise or fear (4)
7. a person that has the same position as sb. else in a different place or situation (4)
8. to refuse (oneself) things desired (5)
9. the natural qualities of a person's character (6)
10. to end a pregnancy early in order to prevent a baby from developing and being born alive (8)

Part Two

Reading Skill — Scanning

Scanning is a technique you often use when looking up a word in the telephone book or dictionary. You search for key words or ideas. In most cases, you know what you're looking for, so you're concentrating on finding a particular answer. Scanning involves moving your eyes quickly down the page seeking specific words and phrases. Scanning is also used when you first find a resource to determine whether it will answer your questions. Once you've scanned the document, you might go back and skim it.

When scanning, look for the author's use of organizers such as numbers, letters, steps, or the words, first, second, or next. Look for words that are bold faced, italics, or in a different font size, style, or color. Sometimes the author will put key ideas in the margin.

Reading off a computer screen has become a growing concern. Research shows that people have more difficulty reading off a computer screen than off paper. Although they can read and comprehend at the same rate as paper, skimming on the computer is much slower than on paper.

🔍 Skill-Specific Training

Move your eyes as quickly as possible down the page until you find the first impression of the following names on people.

John: _____.

Victoria: _____.

Tina: _____.

Dennis: _____.

Candy: _____.

Name Discrimination! How It Affects Job and Career Choices, Life Status, Overall Success

Silicon Valley Blogger

You may think this is far out, but bear with me a moment. Take a look at this table. It shows how you can be stereotyped according to your name.

What's In A Name?

Positive Names

People Thought They Were...	Female	Male
Intelligent	Abigail, Eleanor, Lisa, Meredith and Rebecca	Clifford, David, Edward, John, Samuel, Ned and Tim
Leaders	Ruth	Alexander, Dwight and Lance
Hardworking	Ada, Ingrid, Marie and Margaret	Jake, Manuel, Ron and Todd
Entrepreneurial and Professional	Lorraine and Sylvia	Gregory and Ted
Talented	Tina	Neil
Wealthy	Audrey, Paige and Victoria	Lucius, Edmond and Claude
Blue-Collar	Roxy	Arnie
Refined	Indira, Calista and Grace	Nigel, Alistair, Vaughn
Ambitious	Leigh	Cedric
Organized	Julianne	
Outgoing	Bernadette, Christy, Elaine, Gwen, Joy, Kathy, Kim, Patricia, Nancy and Wendy	Allen, Cole, Danny, Ed, Gary, Jim, Russ and Rob
Accountants (Nerdy)	Minerva and Ingrid	Myron and Reynold
Teachers	Trudy	Thomas
Wealthy Lawyers		Drew

Negative Names

People Thought They Were...	Name
Deceitful	Oswald
Awkward	Angus
Show-off	Don
Bratty	Dennis
A **Jerk**	Ace
Stubborn	Rolf
Two-faced	Vera
Bossy	Joyce and Myrna
Opinionated	Rhea and Maud
Old and Overweight	Dolores
Dumb	Candy, Kiki and Vanna

Source：*CareerBuilder.com and Behind The Name*

But what has this got to do with personal finance? Well actually, a lot. Stereotyping has its financial **ramifications** which have been recognized through several studies.

We live in a fairly prejudiced world. But "name discrimination" **takes the cake**. Maybe my diversified work place and my exposure to one of the most liberal work environments in the world (here in San Francisco, CA) has somehow **conned** me into thinking that things were cool at the office. Not to mention that all the companies I've worked for have solid **stances** on equal opportunity.

So I found it almost ridiculous that something that seemed so **arbitrarily** personal could stand in the way of your financial success and status. Apparently there are studies that prove that your NAME, of all things, can make a difference to your social and financial standing.

Well here are some specifics that prove that your name can **wreck** your chances of getting ahead, particularly if you have an *African-American sounding name*.

How A Name Affects Employment and Job Opportunities

A National Bureau of Economic Research Paper shows that job applicants with white names had a 50% chance of getting a callback over those who had African-American names. That is, traditional white sounding names only had to send 10 resumes to get one callback, while those that didn't had to send out 15 resumes per callback. One of their unsettling findings is that maybe it's employer bias in play, or the perception that race is tied to productivity.

Other facts from the study:

- Only resumes were reviewed; face to face meetings never took place.
- A white name's callbacks yielded the equivalent of eight additional years of experience.
- Residential address also mattered to some degree, with more callbacks received for resumes tied to wealthier, more educated or more-white zip codes.
- Names made a bigger impact on results than addresses did.
- Results were the same across occupation and industry categories covered in the experiment.
- For companies with the "equal opportunity" byline, results didn't seem to make a difference!
- Only when a name didn't provide a clue to race, were other elements of the resume considered.
- More education and more skills displayed on a resume with an ethnic sounding name didn't make a difference to the outcome.
- Names that indicated gender also had an effect on results.
- Names that worked in the experiment: Neil, Brett, Greg, Emily, Anne and Jill.
- Names that didn't work in the experiment: Tamika, Ebony, Aisha, Rasheed, Kareem and Tyrone.

Could initial quick screening of resumes by headhunters cause this discriminatory effect?

Imagine going through a huge pile of resumes which you need to whittle down to a manageable size. Without realizing it, an HR representative may be unwittingly applying their immediate impressions on the pile of paper before them. What else can they go on anyway?

How A Name Affects Housing Opportunities

Beyond snagging jobs, it turns out that name discrimination is also alive and well in the rental circuit. Another study by the Journal of Applied Social Psychology revealed these facts:

From 1,100 e-mail inquiries to Los Angeles-area landlords asking about vacant apartments advertised online, the traditional white sounding name **elicited** 89% of positive replies. A foreign sounding name brought in 66% of replies while the African-American name took in 56%. A landlord's positive reply consisted of a follow up appointment to show off the property for lease or an indication that the place was available.

How A Name Affects Career Choices

Yet another study has struck fear in the hearts of would-be parents. It turns out that kids with gender specific names become discouraged from certain educational interests thus affecting their long term course of study. What this means is that if you are named a girly sounding name, you end up avoiding math and the sciences. Sounds weird but true!

Girls who are given very feminine names, such as Anna, Emma or Elizabeth, are less likely to study math or physics after the age of 16, a remarkable study has found. The effect is so strong that parents can set twin daughters off on completely different career paths simply by calling them Isabella and Alex, names at either end of the spectrum. A study of 1,000 pairs of sisters in the US found that Alex was twice as likely as her twin to take math or science at a higher level.

Why would this happen? The explanation given is that like it or not, people have expectations of others based on their name. These expectations affect one's self-image and cause typecasting. I guess a feminine person is not supposed to be studying math or physics.

This typecasting also works with ugly sounding names or those names identified with lower class or status. Those with lower class names (spelled in an unusual way or with punctuations) would average 3 to 5 percent lower than others with conventional names. Again, this was caused by imposed expectations. From the study, it was scary to hear that teachers who first saw a class **roster** admitted that they couldn't help but form impressions of the children because of their names, before they all met.

Comprehension of the Text

1. What name is suitable for your boy if you expect him to be a teacher?

   _____

2. What is the reason that people with African-American names have less chance of getting a callback in job hunting?

   _____

3. Which has more influence on employment, sounding name or the wealthier residential address?

   _____.

4. In Los Angeles, will the landlords prefer renting their house to the person with traditional white sounding name or the foreign sounding name?

   _____

5. Between the twin Isabella and Alex, who is likely to be a scientist?

   _____

Words and Expressions

refined *a.* (of a person) polite, well educated and able to judge the quality of things 举止优雅的

bratty *a.* (an ill-mannered child) impolite 讨厌的，不服从的

jerk *n.* a dull stupid fatuous person 蠢人；傻瓜；笨蛋

stubborn *a.* refusing to comply, agree, or give in 顽固的；固执的

bossy *a.* always telling people what to do 好发号施令的，专横的

dumb *a.* slow to understand 愚蠢的

ramification *n.* (usu. pl.) one of the large number of complicated and unexpected results that follow an action or a decision (众多复杂而又难以预料的)结果，后果

take the cake 得奖，成为最佳者〈讽〉坏到极点

con *v.* to trick sb. 欺骗

stance *n.* a rationalized mental attitude 看法，立场，观点

arbitrarily *ad.* in a random manner 武断地；肆意地

wreck *v.* smash or break forcefully 毁坏；毁灭

elicit *v.* (written) to get information or a reaction from sb. 引出，探出

roster *n.* a list or register, esp. one showing the order of people enrolled for duty 名册

Part Three

> **Reading Comprehension (Skimming and Scanning)**
> **Directions:** *In this part, you will have 15 minutes to go over the passage quickly and answer the questions. For questions 1~7, mark Y (for YES) or N (for NO). For question 8~10, complete the sentences with the information given in the passage.*

Beauty Contestant Fights for Right of Self-improvement

In the struggle for individual rights in China, a young woman named Yang Yuan is creating a new category of entitlement that falls somewhere down the list from freedom of speech and voting. She is fighting for her right to enter a beauty contest after having had plastic surgery.

"Is it not good to make society full of beautiful people?" she asked wistfully in her small apartment.

Ms. Yang's plight, not likely to inspire outrage among international human rights advocates, has titillated the Chinese media as she has become the latest in a growing parade of young women (and at least one man) who have become instant celebrities after undergoing extensive cosmetic surgery.

These so-called artificial beauties, rather than provoking public alarm or debate, seem to be regarded as worthy product upgrades. Plastic surgery clinics are popping up around the country. Even some of the poorest young women from the countryside are willing to spend months of earnings for a procedure that gives their eyes a more rounded, Western look.

Beauty pageants, once banned as bourgeois "spiritual pollution," are now held across the country, among them the Miss World pageant. Shopping malls now hold underwear fashion shows. And the cosmetics giant L'Oréal saw sales in China jump by 70 percent last year.

Hung Huang, chief executive of a media group that publishes Chinese lifestyle magazines, said Chinese women had always emphasized appearance and beauty. She said the loosening of social controls, along with rising incomes, had unleashed pent-up demand and fueled a consumer boom. One government estimate calculated the beauty industry in China at $24 billion.

There does not seem to be much hesitation on the part of women to have cosmetic surgery, despite real risks. Government statistics reveal that more than 200,000 malpractice (玩忽职守) lawsuits have been filed during the past decade over botched operations, many of them conducted by surgeons with little oversight or training. In March, the state media reported that new government regulations were under review.

For many women, the decision to have cosmetic surgery is less about vanity than practicality, rooted in the belief that a more attractive appearance will help them find a better job or spouse in a more competitive society.

Ms. Yang, who is 19, was tall and striking before her surgery, and had started a modeling career after graduating from high school. But she was not satisfied with her face and said makeup artists had suggested plastic surgery. She also had entered a handful of beauty contests without success.

"I wanted to be equal to other beautiful women," Ms. Yang said. "That's why I had plastic surgery."

"Everybody wants natural beauty, but nobody is perfect," Ms. Hao wrote in a diary entry carried by the Chinese press. "Everybody has flaws, but now we can have shortcuts to beauty."

In February, Ms. Yang underwent a four-hour surgery in Beijing for her eyes, nose, mouth and chin. She timed the surgery so that she would be able to recuperate before the opening round of the Miss Intercontinental Beijing contest in May. It worked: she advanced from the opening round to become one of 30 finalists. But she was later disqualified after contest organizers learned about her surgery.

Ms. Yang was distraught. Her plastic surgery clinic had used her face in advertisements, and she made no attempt to conceal it. "I was speechless and really disappointed," she said. "I did the plastic surgery because of the pageant, and I was disqualified because of it."

She took her case to the news media and soon the Chinese press was carrying images of a tear rolling down her surgically improved face. Contest organizers made an overture to accept her back into the contest, but she said she felt insulted by how they had handled it. She has since filed a lawsuit on the grounds that her reputation was damaged and that her rights were violated because the contest rules made no mention of prohibiting plastic surgery.

In her apartment, she grimly envisioned a world where "artificial beauties" faced discrimination. "I just want to first get back my rights," Ms. Yang said. "I hope that in the future there will be a niche in society for me."

Not to worry: an entrepreneur has announced a new beauty contest scheduled for August. Only artificial beauties will be allowed to enter.

1. Whether Yang Yuan has the right to enter a beauty contest has not been dealt with often before.

2. Ms. Yang's struggle for individual rights have attracted so much attention domestically.

3. Beauty shows are always popular across the country.

4. Many women don't have hesitation to do the plastic surgery because it involves no risk with the advance of modern technology.

5. Many women do the cosmetic surgery mostly because of the feeling of excessive pride.

6. Although Ms. Yang succeeded to be one of 30 finalists, she was prohibited to go further in the contest after organizers learned about her surgery.

7. Ms. Yang felt being insulted although the contest organizers accepted her back.

8. After knowing her plastic surgery clinic had used her face in _____, Ms. Yang made no attempt to conceal it.

9. Ms. Yang filed a _____ against the organizers, claiming that her reputation was damaged and her rights were violated.

10. Ms. Yang hopes that in the future there will be a _____ in society for her.

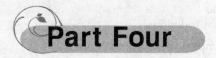

Part Four

Directions: *There is a passage in this section. This passage is followed by some questions. For each of them there are four choices marked A), B), C) and D). You should decide on the best choice.*

Moral Decline

The decline in moral standards — which has long concerned social analysts — has at last captured the attention of average Americans. And Jean Bethke Elshtain, for one, is glad.

The fact the ordinary citizens are now starting to think seriously about the nation's moral climate, says this *ethics*（伦理学）professor at the University of Chicago, is reason to hope that new ideas will come forward to improve it.

But the challenge is not to be underestimated. Materialism and individualism in American society are the biggest obstacles. "The thought that 'I'm in it for me' has become deeply rooted in the national consciousness," Ms. Elshtain says.

Some of this can be attributed to the disintegration of traditional communities, in which neighbors looked out for one another, she says. With today's greater mobility and with so many couples working, those bonds have been weakened, replaced by a greater emphasis on self.

In a 1996 poll of Americans, loss of morality topped the list of the biggest problems facing the U. S. and Elshtain says the public is correct to sense that: Data show that Americans are struggling with problems unheard of in the 1950s, such as classroom violence and a high rate of births to unmarried mothers.

The desire for a higher moral standard is not a *lament*（挽歌）for some nonexistent "golden age," Elshtain says, nor is it a *wishful*（一厢情愿的）longing for a time that denied opportunities to women and minorities. Most people, in fact, favor the lessening of prejudice.

Moral decline will not be reversed until people find ways to counter the materialism in society, she says. "Slowly, you recognize that the things that matter are those that can't be bought."

1. Professor Elshtain is pleased to see that Americans _____.
   A. have adapted to a new set of moral standards
   B. are longing for the return of the good old days
   C. have realized the importance of material things
   D. are awakening to the lowering of their moral standards

2. The moral decline of American society is caused mainly by _____.
   A. its growing wealth
   B. the self-centeredness of individuals
   C. underestimating the impact of social changes
   D. the prejudice against women and minorities

3. Which of the following characterizes the traditional communities?
   A. Great mobility.   B. Concern for one's neighbors.
   C. Emphasis on individual effort.   D. Ever-weakening social bonds.

4. In the 1950s, classroom violence _____.

A. was something unheard of   B. was by no means a rare occurrence

C. attracted a lot of public attention   D. began to appear in analysts' data

5. According to Elshtain, the current moral decline may be reversed _____.

A. if people can return to the "golden age"

B. when women and men enjoy equal rights

C. when people rid themselves of prejudice

D. if less emphasis is laid on material things

Part Five

Reading for Pleasure

Sayings about Proper Names and Nicknames

曾经有一位中国人在一家豪华餐厅宴请一位美国人，这位美国人指着桌上的大转盘惊叫道："Wow! Look at the Chinese lazy Susan! She carries so many delicious dishes!"。这里老外用了 lazy Susan 来指代桌上的大转盘，那么为什么要把转盘称为"lazy Susan"呢？

这其中有来历。据说以前在美国有一个名叫 Susan 的女老板，她开了一家名叫 Susan Restaurant 的餐馆。餐馆的女服务员觉得为顾客一个个上菜夹菜很麻烦，而顾客自己取菜也不方便，于是就想到了一个主意。她做了一个可以旋转的圆盘放在桌子中间，让顾客自己取食。后来，这种手动旋转圆盘被称为 lazy Susan。在英语中"餐桌转盘"还有另一种说法即 dumbwaiter，千万不要按照字面意思翻译为"哑巴服务员"。

其实在英语中，含有人名的成语很多，但大多与人无多大关系，翻译时则不能想当然地按照字面意思翻译。

1. Jack of all trades (and master of none) 万金油，杂而不精的人

直译为"杰克什么都会"，但实际形容什么也不通的人。Jack 有勤杂工，伙计的意思。

2. dear John letter 绝交信

据说是约翰的情人写给约翰的信。美国曾经有过一首十分流行的歌曲，写的是一个女子既不忍心又不得不与男友分手的痛苦心情，其中开头的每一句都是 dear John。也有人认为其出处来自这里。

3. Columbus discovered America 陈年旧事，老生常谈

哥伦布于 15 世纪发现新大陆已经是人尽皆知的事，不再是什么新闻了。

4. a Judas kiss 奸诈，口蜜腹剑

犹大以吻耶稣为暗号，向坏人暗示此人是耶稣，从而出卖了耶稣。所以此语形容奸诈，口蜜腹剑。

5. Joe Miller 老掉牙的笑话

Joe Miller 于 1793 年出版了一本笑话集,这样的笑话还不老掉牙吗?

6. John Hancock 亲笔签名

源自美国政治家 John Hancock。他在《独立宣言》上的签名潇洒有力,引人注目。"Put your John Hancock here. "指"在此签上你的大名。"

7. David and Jonathan 生死与共的朋友,莫逆之交

据《圣经》记载,古以色列国王,耶稣的祖先 David,为建立统一的以色列王国,与 Jonathan 建立了深厚的友谊。

8. Jack shall have Jill. 有情人终成眷属。

9. Tom, Dick and Harry 张三,李四和王五,普通人

10. as old as Adam 非常古老

《圣经》记载,Adam 是上帝创造的第一个人。"和亚当一样老"自然是"非常古老"了。

11. rob Peter to pay Paul 拆东墙补西墙

12. John Bull 约翰牛

英国或英国人的绰号,表现典型的英国(人)的形象或特征,如顽强刚毅,固执冷峻,气势汹汹,精力旺盛。它会让人联想到头戴高礼帽,身穿夹克衫,足蹬长筒靴的矮胖英国绅士的形象。这个绰号为英国人自己所取,源自英国作家 John 的讽刺作品 *The History of John Bull*《约翰牛的生平》。

13. Uncle Sam 山姆大叔

这是美国的绰号。漫画里的美国常常以一个大叔式的人物出现,身材瘦长,身着红蓝白燕尾服和条纹裤,头戴花旗高帽,下巴长着山羊胡子。据说美国独立战争期间,纽约州有个老头叫 Sam Wilson,他开了一家肉制品厂,专门为美军供货。由于他爱国、热情、忠厚,大家都叫他 Uncle Sam,他自己也很喜欢这种叫法。政府每次收到他的货在验收合格后总习惯打上 US 的字样,恰好与 the United States 的缩写相符。后来人们就把 Uncle Sam 作为美国的绰号。

14. Aunt Sally 众矢之的,受人攻击、嘲讽的对象

在英国集贸市场上曾有一种叫 Aunt Sally 的木偶,鼻子歪斜,嘴里常常叼着烟斗,游客们朝烟斗投东西以打掉烟斗中奖。

15. Aunt Tom/Jane 专门讨好白人的黑人妇女

16. dumb Dora 傻姑娘,痴情女

17. Queen Anne is dead. 老生常谈

安妮女王已经死了,这是人人都知道的事情。

Humor Prepared for You

When I was six months pregnant with my third child, my three-year-old daughter came into the room when I was just getting ready to get into the shower. She said, "Mummy, you are getting fat!"

I replied, "Yes, honey, remember Mummy has a baby growing in her tummy(肚子)."

"I know," she replied. "But what's growing in your bum(屁股)?"

Famous Sayings

It is only shallow people who do not judge by appearances.

—*Oscar Wilde*

只有肤浅的人才不会以貌取人。

——奥斯卡·王尔德

What's in a name? That which we call a rose by any other name would smell as sweet.

—*William Shakespeare*

名称有什么关系呢？玫瑰不叫玫瑰，依然芳香如故。

——威廉·莎士比亚

Unit Seven

Work Smart, Not Hard

Most people work because it's unavoidable. They need to make enough money for necessities: food, rent, clothing, transportation, tuition, and so on. They spend about one-third of their lives at work, but they hate it. They complain and count the minutes until quitting time each day. By contrast, there are some people who actually enjoy work. They spend many extra hours on the job each week and often take work home with them. These workaholics are as addicted to their jobs as other people are to drugs or alcohol. Workaholism can be a serious problem. The lives of workaholics are usually stressful, and this tension and worry can cause health problems such as heart attacks or stomach ulcers. In addition, typical workaholics don't pay much attention to their families. They spend little time with their children, and their marriages may end in divorce. People should learn to coordinate life and work.

In this unit, you will read:
- Mayhew
- U.S. Workers Feel Burn of Long Hours, Less Leisure
- Six Secrets of High-Energy People
- Stress
- Are You a Workaholic

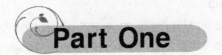

Part One

Pre-reading Questions
1. What's your ideal job in the future?
2. What jobs can you do after graduating from college?
3. Will you sacrifice your dream so as to keep a steady job?

Mayhew

William S. Maugham

1 The lives of most men are determined by their environment. They accept their circumstances amid which fate has thrown them not only with resignation but even with good will. They are like **streetcars** running contentedly on their **rails** and they despise the **sprightly flivver** that dashes in and out of the traffic and speeds so **jauntily** across the open country. I respect them; they are good citizens, good husbands, and good fathers, and of course somebody has to pay the taxes; but I do not find them exciting. I am fascinated by the men, few enough in all conscience, who take life in their own hands and seem to mould it to their own liking. It may be that we have no such thing as free will, but at all events we have the illusions of it. At a cross-road it does seem to us that we might go either to the right or to the left and, the choice once made, it is difficult to see that the whole course of the world's history obliged us to take the turning we did.

2 I never met a more interesting man than Mayhew. He was a lawyer in Detroit. He was an able and a successful one. By the time he was thirty-five he had a large and a lucrative practice, he had **amassed** a competence, and he stood on the threshold of a distinguished career. He had an acute brain, an attractive personality, and uprightness. There was no reason why he should not become, financially or politically, a power in the land. One evening he was sitting in his club with a group of friends and they were perhaps a little worse (or even better) for liquor. One of them had recently come from Italy and he told them of a house he had seen at Capri, a house on the hill, overlooking the Bay of Naples, with a large and shady garden. He described to them the beauty of the most beautiful island in the Mediterranean.

'It sounds fine,' said Mayhew. 'Is that house for sale?'

'Everything is for sale in Italy.'

'Let's send'em a cable and make an offer for it.'

'What in heaven's name would you do with a house in Capri?'

'Live in it,' said Mayhew.

3   He sent for a cable form, wrote it out, and **dispatched** it. In a few hours the reply came back. The offer was accepted.

4   Mayhew was no hypocrite and he made no secret of the fact that he would never have done so wild a thing if he had been sober, but when he was he did not regret it. He was neither an impulsive nor an emotional man, but a very honest and sincere one. He would never have continued from **bravado** in a course that he had come to the conclusion was unwise. He made up his mind to do exactly as he had said. He did not care for wealth and he had enough money on which to live in Italy. He thought he could do more with life than merely spend it on correcting the trivial quarrels of unimportant people back home in Detroit. He had no definite plan. He only wanted to get away from a life that had given him all it had to offer. I suppose his friends thought him crazy; some must have done all they could to **dissuade** him. He arranged his affairs, packed up his furniture, and started.

5   Capri is a **gaunt** rock of **austere** outline, bathed in a deep blue sea; but its vineyards, green and smiling, give it a soft and easy grace. It is friendly, remote, and **debonair**. I find it strange that Mayhew should have settled on this lovely island, for I never knew a man more insensible to beauty. I do not know what he sought there: happiness, freedom, or merely leisure; I know what he found. In this place which appeals so **extravagantly** to the senses he lived a life entirely of the spirit. For the island is rich with historic associations and over it **broods** always the enigmatic memory of Tiberius the Emperor. From his windows which overlooked the Bay of Naples, with the noble shape of Vesuvius changing color with the changing light, Mayhew saw a hundred places that recalled the Romans and the Greeks. The past began to haunt him. All that he saw for the first time (for he had never been abroad before,) excited his fancy; and in his soul stirred the creative imagination. He was a man of energy. Presently he made up his mind to write a history. For some time he looked about for a subject, and at last decided on a second century of the Roman Empire. It was little known and it seemed to him to offer problems analogous with those of our own day.

6   He began to collect books and soon he had an immense library. His legal training had taught him to read quickly, He settled down to work. At first he had been accustomed to foregather in the evening with the painters, writers, and suchlike who met in the little tavern near the Piazza, but presently he withdrew himself, for his absorption in his studies became more pressing. He had been accustomed to bathe in the bland sea and to take long walks among the pleasant vineyards, but little by little, **grudging** the time, he ceased to do so. He worked harder than he had ever worked in Detroit. He would start at noon and work all through the night till the whistle of the steamer that goes every morning from Capri to Naples told him that it was five o'clock and time to go to bed. His subject opened out before him, vaster and more significant, and he imagined a work that would put him forever beside the great historians of the past. As the years went by he was to be found seldom in the ways of men. He could be tempted to come out of his house only by a game of chess or the chance of an argument. He loved to set his brain against another's. He was widely read now, not only in history, but in philosophy and science;

and he was a skilful controversialist, quick, logical, and **incisive**. But he had good-humor and kindliness. Though he took a very human pleasure in victory, he did not **exult** in it to your mortification.

7   When first he came to the island he was a big, brawny fellow, with thick black hair and a black beard, of a powerful physique; but gradually his skin became pale and **waxy**; he grew thin and frail. It was an odd contradiction in the most logical of men that, though a convinced and **impetuous** materialist, he despised the body; he looked upon it as a **vile** instrument which he could force to do the spirit's bidding. Neither illness nor lassitude prevented him from going on with his work. For fourteen years he **toiled unremittingly**. He made thousands and thousands of notes. He sorted and classified them. He sat down to write. He died.

8   The body that he, the materialist, had treated so **contumeliously** took its revenge on him.

9   That vast accumulation of knowledge is lost for ever. Vain was that ambition, surely not an **ignoble** one, to set his name beside those of Gibbon and Mommsen. His memory is treasured in the hearts of a few friends, fewer alas! As the years pass on, and to the world he is unknown in death as he was in life.

10   And yet to me his life was a success. The pattern is good and complete. He did what he wanted, and he died when his goal was in sight and never knew the bitterness of an end achieved.

🔊 Words and Phrases

streetcar *n.* (N. Amer.)a tram (北美)有轨电车

rail *n.* a steel bar or continuous line of bars laid on the ground as one of a pair forming a railway track 铁轨,钢轨;轨道,铁路

sprightly *a.* (esp. of an old person) lively; full of energy (尤指老人)精力充沛的;充满活力的

flivver *n.* (N. Amer. informal, dated)a cheap car or aircraft, esp. one in bad condition (北美,非正式,旧)(尤指破旧的)廉价小汽车,廉价飞机

jaunty *a.* having or expressing a lively, cheerful, and self-confident manner 轻松活泼的;无忧无虑的;喜洋洋的

amass *v.* gather together or accumulate (a large amount or number of valuable material or things) over a period of time 积聚,积累

dispatch *v.* send off to a destination or for a purpose 派遣;发送

bravado *n.* a bold manner or a show of boldness intended to impress or intimidate 虚张声势,装作气势汹汹的样子

dissuade *v.* persuade (someone) not to take a particular course of action 劝阻

gaunt *a.* (of a building or place) grim or desolate in appearance (建筑物或地方)阴森的,荒凉的

austere *a.* having an extremely plain and simple style or appearance; unadorned 朴素的;无装饰的

debonair *a.* (of a man) confident, stylish, and charming（男子）温文尔雅的

extravagantly *a.* lacking restraint in spending money or using resources 奢侈的，挥霍的，铺张的

brood *v.* [no obj.]think deeply about sth. that makes one unhappy 沉思，念念不忘（尤指不愉快的事）

grudge *v.* be resentfully unwilling to give, grant, or allow (sth.)（因不满而）不愿意给（或允许）

incisive *a.* accurate and sharply focused（叙述）尖锐的，精准的

exult *v.* show or feel elation or jubilation, esp. as the result of a success（尤指因成功而）狂喜；欢欣鼓舞

waxy *a.* resembling wax in consistency or appearance 蜡质的；似蜡的

impetuous *a.* acting or done quickly and without thought or care 冲动的，鲁莽的，性急的，急躁的

vile *a.* (archaic)of little worth or value(古)不足道的，无价值的

toil *v.* work extremely hard or incessantly 苦干，辛勤劳动

unremitting *a.* never relaxing or slackening; incessant 不间断的；不松懈的

contumelious *a.* (archaic)(of behaviour) scornful and insulting; insolent（古）（行为）轻蔑的；侮辱性的；傲慢无礼的；侮慢的

ignoble *a.* not honourable in character or purpose 卑鄙的，可耻的

Background Information

William Somerset Maugham 毛姆（ January 1874 ～ December 1965） was an English playwright, novelist and short story writer. He was among the most popular writers of his era, and reputedly, the highest paid author during the 1930s.

Capri (Italian pronunciation：['kapri], pronounced /kə'pri:/ in English)卡鲁里 is an Italian island in the Tyrrhenian Sea off the Sorrentine Peninsula, on the south side of the Gulf of Naples, in the Campania region of southern Italy. It has been a resort since the time of the Roman Republic.

Learn about Words

Often you can tell the meaning of a word or phrase from its context — the words around it. Please choose the choice with the same meaning to the word used in the article.

1. feel contempt or a deep repugnance for（1）
2. an inner feeling or voice viewed as acting as a guide to the rightness or wrongness of one's behaviour（1）
3. producing a great deal of profit（2）

4. a person who pretends to be what he is not (4)

5. of little value or importance (4)

6. difficult to interpret or understand; mysterious (5)

7. comparable in certain respects, typically in a way which makes clearer the nature of the things compared (5)

8. a feeling of loss of prestige or self-respect; humiliation (6)

9. weak and delicate (7)

10. a state of physical or mental weariness; lack of energy (7)

Part Two

> **Reading Skill — Skimming**
>
> Skimming is to read quickly to identify the main idea of a passage.
>
> Skimming is used when you want to see if an article may be of your interest or to get the general idea of a passage.
>
> How to skim?
> - Read only selected sentences.
> - Read the first and last paragraphs of a text.
> - Read the first and last sentences of a paragraph.
> - Use textual clues such as:
>   - ☆ italicized or underlined words
>   - ☆ headlines or subtitles
>   - ☆ spacing and paragraphing

Skill-Specific Training

Before you read Part Two closely, skim the text to find the answers to the following questions in three minutes.

1. What is the passage mainly about?

2. Did U. S. workers put in more hours on work than major European workers in 2002?

3. What's the reason for U. S. productivity surpassing Europe and Japan for the first time since World War II?

4. Which day is Take Back Your Time Day?

5. How can employees solve the problem of overworking?

U. S. Workers Feel Burn of Long Hours, Less Leisure

Stephanie Armour

A **backlash** is building against America's work **epidemic**.

More employees are resisting companies' demands for longer hours on the job, the 24/7 pace of business that means operations never cease, and the surrender of leisure time to work because of new technology such as cell phones and e-mail.

"People are putting in 40 and 50 hours a week, and there's not enough time for anything," says Gretchen Burger, in Seattle, an organizer with Take Back Your Time, a grass-roots movement aimed at focusing attention on the issue of overwork. "There is an alternative."

Some workers, unwilling to clock extra hours without extra pay, are suing their companies over **alleged** overtime violations. In **fiscal** 2003, the Labor Department collected $212 million in back wages, which include overtime violations. That's a 21% increase over the record-setting amount collected in 2002.

Some economists also believe that many productivity gains of the 1990s can be attributed to longer work hours rather than the efficiency of new technology.

For the first time, industries that have been notorious for their taxing schedules are **scaling back**. New guidelines now limit the number of hours that medical residents can work. And starting Jan. 4, federal regulations will require many truck drivers to set aside more time for breaks.

Some **beleaguered** workers are also taking action, changing to less-demanding occupations or leaving corporations to start their own businesses, where they can feel more in control of their work lives. Others are scaling back to spend more time with families.

Working to the max

U. S. workers put in an average of 1,815 hours in 2002. In major European economies, hours worked ranged from about 1,300 to 1,800, according to the International Labor Organization (ILO). Hours were about the same in the USA as in Japan.

Combined weekly work hours for dual-earning couples with children rose 10 hours per week, from 81 hours in 1977 to 91 hours in 2002, according to a new study by the New York-based Families and Work Institute.

Employees feel the strain. Mounting research shows there's a tangible downside to overwork, from mental-health problems to physical **ailments** and job injuries caused by fatigue and stress. It's also a bottom-line issue: A study by the Economic Policy Institute found that **mandatory** overtime costs industry as much as $300 billion a year in stress- and fatigue-related problems.

Cody Mooneyhan, 31, can relate. He works as much as 14 hours a day, getting up at 4:30 a. m. and arriving home at 9:30 p. m. to work two jobs: senior writer for Vanguard Communications and assistant at the *American Journal of Pathology*. His wife, Renée, 31, works several nights a week as a social worker. His employers don't require long hours, but Mooneyhan feels he must work two jobs to support his three children: Sarah, 1, Zoe, 3, and Zack, 7.

He says he works to maintain a middle-class lifestyle, not to have luxuries. He lives in a three-bedroom town house, has a 7-year-old computer and owns a Toyota Tercel and a minivan.

Says Mooneyhan, of Germantown, Md.: "Being tired makes everything that much more stressful, but it's like having a baby. You get used to it. It's kind of sad. The kids sometimes ask, 'What's the deal with Dad? Does he still live here?' I've thought, 'This is going to kill me.'"

Output gains due to longer hours

Some doubt the effort to curb hours will cause the USA to adopt the more leisurely approach of Europe, where women in Sweden get 96 weeks of maternity leave and workers in France enjoy about five weeks of vacation a year.

"Good luck," says Stephen Roach, chief economist for Morgan Stanley in New York. He believes much of the accelerated productivity in the USA since the mid-1990s is due to longer work hours.

An ILO report in September found that U.S. productivity grew in 2002, surpassing Europe and Japan in annual output per worker for the first substantial period since World War II. The report found that the difference was due to the longer hours worked by Americans.

But much of that growth isn't picked up in government data measuring work hours, Roach says.

"This is work that happens outside the workplace," he says. "People work in planes, cars and at home."

Government data on hours worked don't capture time put in off the job, such as during weekends, or after-hours work that many salaried employees do on laptops, cell phones and e-mail. They also don't capture the overall rise in hours put in by families.

Even vacations are going by the wayside: Employees are handing companies more than $21 billion in unused vacation days each year, according to a study by Expedia.com.

Some efforts to curtail hours

A backlash to the overwork trend is building in Philadelphia, Boston, Seattle and other cities where dozens of events were held in the fall to mark the first Take Back Your Time Day. Organizers of the grass-roots movement want to establish the Oct. 24 event as an annual affair to draw attention to the issue of overwork. Several **jurisdictions,** including Seattle, officially proclaimed Oct. 24 as Take Back Your Time Day.

Efforts to ease the leisure-time shortage are also catching the attention of politicians. The U.S. Senate this year passed a resolution **designating** October as National Work and Family Month — a move that organizers of the Take Back Your Time movement say has put the work and home conflict onto the national stage.

Some companies are responding by allowing workers to customize schedules. Jennifer Maler, 29, is a tax compliance specialist at Ernst & Young. Working full time, she wanted more time for other passions, such as modeling and dancing. "I love what I do, but I felt like I was living at the office," Maler says.

So she asked — and got permission — to adopt a flexible work schedule. In 1999, she took a pay cut and began working a 30-hour week spread over three days.

"It's the best thing I ever did," says Maler, who works in New York. "It's given me the ability to stay with my career, and it's made me a more complete person."

Although the growing push to reclaim time sounds appealing to some employees, others say long hours and after-hour work have become so **ingrained** that change might be hard.

As chairman and CEO of HealthExpo, which organizes health fairs around the USA, Cynthia Ekberg Tsai, 47, of New York, often arrives at work before her team. After working through lunch, she may leave at 8 p.m. for dinner and return to the office until 1 a.m.

"I do not go to lunch, because it gives me the chance to keep on working. Do I have the sense that people are working harder? Yes," says Ekberg Tsai. "Most people overcommit. We haven't learned the magical word of 'no.'"

Comprehension of the Text

1. What actions do some tired workers take to avoid over-committing?

   _____.

2. Why does Cody Mooneyhan keep two jobs?

   _____.

3. What's Stephen Roach's opinion on the accelerated productivity in the USA?

   _____.

4. According to organizers of the Take Back Your Time movement, what put the work and home conflict onto the national stage?

   _____.

5. What's Jennifer Maler's opinion on taking a flexible work schedule?

   _____.

🐭 Words and Expressions

backlash *n.* a strong and adverse reaction by a large number of people, esp. to a social or political development(尤指人们对社会或政治运动的)强烈反对

epidemic *n.* a disease occurring in such a way that it is very common for a time 流行病

allege *v.* claim or assert that someone has done something illegal or wrong, typically without proof that this is the case(尤指无证据地)声称,断言(某人做非法事情或坏事)

fiscal *a.* of or relating to government revenue, esp. taxes 财政(尤指税收)的

scale back 按比例缩减,相应缩减

beleaguer *v.* lay siege to 包围,围困,围攻

ailment *n.* an illness, typically a minor one 微恙,小疾(尤指小病)

mandatory *a.* required by law or rules;compulsory 法律(或规则)规定的;强制的,必须遵守的

jurisdiction *n.* the official power to make legal decisions and judgments 司法权,裁判权

designate *v.* officially assign a specified status or ascribe a specified name or quality to 正式把……定为(或命名为);任命……为

ingrained *a.* (of a habit, belief, or attitude) firmly fixed or established; difficult to change (习惯,信仰,态度)根深蒂固的

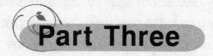

Part Three

> **Reading Comprehension**(Skimming and Scanning)
>
> **Directions**:*In this part*, *you will have* 15 *minutes to go over the passage quickly and answer the questions*. *For questions* 1~7, *mark Y* (*for YES*) *or N* (*for NO*). *For question* 8~10, *complete the sentences with the information given in the passage*.

Six Secrets of High-Energy People

There's an energy crisis in America, and it has nothing to do with fossil fuels. Millions of us get up each morning already weary over the day holds. "I just can't get started," people say. But it's not physical energy that most of us lack. Sure, we could all use extra sleep and a better diet. But in truth, people are healthier today than at any time in history. I can almost guarantee that if you long for more energy, the problem is not with your body.

What you're seeking is not physical energy. It's emotional energy. Yet, sad to say, life sometimes seems designed to exhaust our supply. We work too hard. We have family obligations. We encounter emergencies and personal crises. No wonder so many of us suffer from emotional fatigue, a kind of utter exhaustion of the spirit.

And yet we all know people who are filled with joy, despite the unpleasant circumstances of their lives. Even as a child, I observed people who were poor, or disabled, or ill, but who nonetheless faced life with optimism and vigor. Consider Laura Hillenbrand, who despite an extremely weak body, wrote the best-seller Seabiscuit. Hillenbrand barely had enough physical energy to drag herself out of bed to write. But she was fueled by having a story she wanted to share. It was emotional energy that helped her succeed.

Unlike physical energy, which is finite and diminishes with age, emotional energy is unlimited and has nothing to do with genes or upbringing. So how do you get it? You can't simply tell yourself to be positive. You must take action. Here are six practical strategies that work.

1. Do something new.

Very little that's new occurs in our lives. The impact of this sameness on our emotional energy is gradual, but huge: It's like a tire with a slow leak. You don't notice it at first, but eventually you'll get a flat. It's up to you to plug the leak — even though there are always a dozen reasons to stay stuck in your dull routines of life. That's where Maura, 36, a waitress, found herself a year ago.

Fortunately, Maura had a lifeline — a group of women friends who meet regularly to discuss their lives. Their lively discussions spurred Maura to make small but nevertheless life altering changes. She joined a gym in the next town. She changed her look with a short haircut and new black T-shirts. Eventually, Maura gathered the courage to quit her job and start her own business.

Here's a challenge: If it's something you wouldn't ordinarily do, do it. Try a dish you've never eaten. Listen to music you'd ordinarily tune out. You'll discover these small things add to your emotional energy.

2. Reclaim life's meaning.

So many of my patients tell me that their lives used to have meaning, but that somewhere along the line things went stale.

The first step in solving this meaning shortage is to figure out what you really care about, and then do something about it. A case in point is Ivy, 57, a pioneer in investment banking. "I mistakenly believed that all the money I made would mean something," she says. "But I feel lost, like a 22-year-old wondering what to do with her life." Ivy's solution? She started a program that shows Wall Streeters how to donate time and money to poor children. In the process, Ivy filled her life with meaning.

3. Put yourself in the fun zone.

Most of us grown-ups are seriously fun-deprived. High-energy people have the same day-to-day work as the rest of us, but they manage to find something enjoyable in every situation. A real estate broker I know keeps herself amused on the job by mentally redecorating the houses she shows to clients. "I love imagining what even the most run-down house could look like with a little tender loving care," she says. "It's a challenge — and the least desirable properties are usually the most fun."

We all define fun differently, of course, but I can guarantee this: If you put just a bit of it into your day, you energy will increase quickly.

4. Bid farewell to guilt and regret.

Everyone's past is filled with regrets that still cause pain. But from an emotional energy point of view, they are dead weights that keep us from moving forward. While they can't merely be willed away, I do recommend you remind yourself that whatever happened is in the past, and nothing can change that. Holding on to the memory only allows the damage to continue into the present.

5. Make up your mind.

Say you've been thinking about cutting your hair short. Will it look stylish—or too extreme? You endlessly think it over. Having the decision hanging over your head is a huge energy drain.

Every time you can't decide, you burden yourself with alternatives. Quit thinking that you have to make the right decision; instead, make a choice and don't look back.

6. Give to get.

Emotional energy has a kind of magical quality; the more you give, the more you get back. This is the difference between emotional and physical energy. With the latter, you have to get it to be able to give it. With the former, however, you get it by giving it.

Start by asking everyone you meet, "How are you?" as if you really want to know, then listen to the reply. Be the one who hears. Most of us also need to smile more often. If you don't smile at the person you love first thing in the morning, you're sucking energy out of your relationship. Finally, help another person — and make the help real, concrete. Give a massage (按摩) to someone you love, or cook her dinner. Then, expand the circle to work. Try asking yourself what you'd do if your goal were to be helpful rather than efficient.

After all, if it's true that what goes around comes around, why not make sure that what's circulating around you is the good stuff?

1. The energy crisis in America discussed here mainly refers to a shortage of fossil fuels.
2. People these days tend to lack physical energy.
3. Laura Hillenbrand is an example cited to show how emotional energy can contribute to one's success in life.
4. The author believes emotional energy is inherited and genetically determined.
5. Even small changes people make in their lives can help increase their emotional energy.
6. Ivy filled her life with meaning by launching a program to help poor children.
7. The real-estate broker the author knows is talented in home redecoration.
8. People holding on to sad memories of the past will find it difficult to _____.

9. When it comes to decision-making, one should make a quick choice without _____.

10. Emotional energy is in a way different from physical energy in that the more you give, _____.

Part Four

Directions: *There is a passage in this section. This passage is followed by some questions. For each of them there are four choices marked A), B), C) and D). You should decide on the best choice.*

Stress

"Humans should not try to avoid stress any more than they would shun food, love or exercise." Said Dr. Hans Selye, the first physician to document the effects of stress on the body. While here's on question that continuous stress is harmful, several studies suggest that challenging situations in which you're able to rise to the occasion can be good for you.

In a 2001 study of 158 hospital nurses, those who faced considerable work demands but coped with the challenge were more likely to say they were in good health than those who felt they couldn't get the job done. Stress that you can manage also boost *immune*（免疫的）function. In a study at the Academic Center for Dentistry in Amsterdam, researchers put volunteers through two stressful experiences. In the first, a timed task that required memorizing a list followed by a short test, subjects through a *gory*（血淋淋的）video on surgical procedures. Those who did well on the memory test had an increase in levels of immunoglobulin A, an antibody that's the body's first line of defense against germs. The video-watchers experienced a downturn in the antibody.

Stress prompts the body to produce certain stress hormones. In short bursts these hormones have a positive effect, including improved memory function. "They can help nerve cells handle information and put it into storage," says Dr. Bruce McEwen of Rockefeller University in New York. But in the long run these hormones can have a harmful effect on the body and brain.

"Sustained stress is not good for you," says Richard Morimoto, a researcher at Northwestern University in Illinois studying the effects of stress on longevity, "It's the occasional burst of stress or brief exposure to stress that could be protective."

1. The passage is mainly about _____.
   A. the benefits of manageable stress　　　B. how to cope with stress effectively

    C. how to avoid stressful situations   D. the effect of stress on memory

2. The word "shun" (Line 1, Para. 1) most probably means _____.

    A. cut down on   B. stay away from

    C. run out of   D. put up with

3. We can conclude from the study of the 158 nurses in 2001 that _____.

    A. people under stress tend to have a poor memory

    B. people who can't get their job done experience more stress

    C. doing challenging work may be good for one's health

    D. stress will weaken the body's defense against germs

4. In the experiment described in Para. 2, the video-watchers experienced a downturn in the antibody because _____.

    A. the video was not enjoyable at all

    B. the outcome was beyond their control

    C. they knew little about surgical procedures

    D. they felt no pressure while watching the video

5. Dr. Bruce McEwen of Rockefeller University believes that _____.

    A. a person's memory is determined by the level of hormones in his body

    B. stress hormones have lasting positive effects on the brain

    C. short bursts of stress hormones enhance memory function

    D. a person's memory improves with continued experience of stress

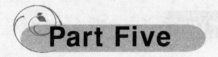

Part Five

Reading for Pleasure

Are You a Workaholic

    People who are addicted to work are similar to one another in some ways. Here is a list of ten characteristics of workaholics. Which ones apply to you? Check your answers with YES / NO.

  1. Do you get up early even if you go to bed late?

  2. Do you read or work while you eat?

  3. Do you make lists of things to do?

  4. Do you find it unpleasant to "do nothing"?

  5. Do you usually have a lot of energy?

6. Do you work on weekends and on holidays?

7. Can you work anytime and anywhere?

8. Do you prefer not to take vacations?

9. Do you think you probably won't want to retire?

10. Do you really enjoy your work?

If you answered "yes" to eight or more questions, you might be a workaholic.

How to Work Smart, Not Hard

- Assess everything that needs to be done.
- Make an outline.
- Consider your materials.
- Follow your plan and don't deviate from it - unless you must.
- Delegate to the right people at the right times.
- Work parallel.
- Control clients by communicating properly.
- Never willingly trap yourself into accepting a bad job.
- Know when it's time for a re-bid.
- Work as hard and as efficiently as possible, and finish each job as quickly as you can.
- Recognize the point of 'diminishing returns'.
- Finish strong.

Humor Prepared for You

I'm That Man's Tailor

A man went to see his doctor one day because he was suffering from pains in his stomach. After the doctor had examined him carefully, he said to him, "Well, there's nothing really wrong with you, I'm glad to say. Your only trouble is that you worry too much. Do you know, I had a man with the same trouble as you in here a few weeks ago, and I gave him the same advice as I'm going to give you. He was worried because he couldn't pay his tailor's bills. I told him not to worry his head about the bill any more. He followed my advice, and when he came to see me again two days ago, he told me that he now felt quite all right again."

"Yes, I know all about that," answered the patient sadly. "You see, I'm that man's tailor."

Famous Sayings

Happy is the man who is living by his hobby.

—*George Bernard Shaw*

醉心于某种癖好的人是幸福的。

——乔治·萧伯纳

Work while you work; play while you play; this is the way to be cheerful and gay.

—*A. D. Stoddart*

工作时工作，玩乐时玩乐，依此方法做，轻松又快乐。

——A. D. 斯道达特

You cannot burn the candle at both ends.

蜡烛不能两头都烧。／你不能一工作起来就废寝忘食。

Unit Eight

More to Life than Work

Today, many young people constantly focus on material possessions to win the "most important" part of life which is to enjoy life as much as possible. It's easy to buy into this philosophy that "life is too short not to live a little", but once one has forgotten what really matters, he is actually losing the track of what is life meant to be.

In this unit, you will read:

- What Do Young Jobseekers Want?
- How to Become a World Citizen, before Going to College
- Writing High Impact Resumes
- What Youngsters Expect in Life
- Life Description of a Chinese College Student

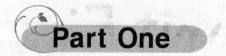

Part One

Pre-reading Questions

1. Have you ever made any career plans for yourself?
2. What kind of cities would you like to live in after graduation?
3. Which do you attach more importance to, a good job or a meaningful life?

What Do Young Jobseekers Want?
(Something Other Than the Job)

Lisa Belkin

1   Early this summer, Joshua J. Pelton decided that he was meant to live in Orlando, Fla. So he quit his sales job in Detroit, packed his car with all the **belongings** that fit, put the rest in storage, and drove southeast daydreaming about **sundrenched** winters and packed nightclubs.

2   "I didn't have much of a plan, but I knew I wanted to be here," said Mr. Pelton, 24, who, in his emphasis on where he lives rather than what he does there, is typical of his generation.

3   Time was when applying for a first job meant papering the country with resumes and **migrating** wherever the best offer might lead. But this latest generation of graduates has already shown itself to be a **peripatetic** bunch — traveling more widely and moving farther from home for college.

4   Add to that the emphasis that **Gen Y** puts on quality of life — perhaps more than any group that has come before — and it would follow that Gen Y looks for work differently, too.

5   "To our generation, it doesn't make sense to have a great job in a **crummy** city," said Mark Van Dyke, 25, describing his decision to move three years ago from the suburbs of Chicago to Bellingham, Wash., where he worked low-paying retail jobs before finding one in marketing, at Logos Bible Software. It was all worth it, he said, because his new hometown is "on the Pacific Ocean but driving distance from **snowboarding** on Mount Baker."

6   Sixty-five percent of 1,000 respondents aged 24 to 35 who were asked by the Segmentation Company, a division of the marketing **consultant** Yankelovich, said they preferred to "look for a job in the place that I would like to live," rather than "look for the best job I can find, the place where it is located is **secondary**."

7   They also told researchers that places must be safe, clean and green. The most-cited quality was tidiness and attractiveness (78 percent) followed by "will allow me to lead the life I want to lead" (77 percent).

8   Urban leaders are increasingly courting young workers, because as **baby boomers** retire,

Gen Y will have to fill the gap. Across the country, cities are **scrambling** to become the place that recent **grads** want to be.

9   In the last decade only 14 urban areas nationwide saw more of these workers move in than move out: Las Vegas; Austin, Tex.; Phoenix; Atlanta; Raleigh-Durham, N.C.; Charlotte, N. C.; Salt Lake City; Portland, Ore.; Denver; Orlando; Nashville; Dallas-Fort Worth; Miami-Fort Lauderdale; and Greensboro-Winston Salem, N.C.

How to join that list? "That's the question all our members are asking," said Carol Coletta, the president and chief **executive** of CEOs for Cities, a Chicago-based association of urban leaders.

10   Her group financed the Yankelovich study, titled "Attracting College-Educated Young Adults to Cities." Its advice? Spread the word that you are, in the words of the report, "clean, safe and green." Those qualities won't seal the deal, but without them, this age group won't even look.

11   This philosophy is leading cities to market themselves aggressively to young workers. Orlando, for instance, paid for its own investigation to find out what they want. The results convinced the city council to authorize $1.1 billion in July to build an arts center, an event center and to upgrade a sports arena.

12   Boston's mayor set up a task force to **poll** young adults about their needs, and intends to have their answers inform his development plan.

13   Memphis and Philadelphia, in turn, have created programs (called Mpact in Memphis and Innovation Philadelphia) that woo college students and young professionals, in the hope that they will feel socially welcome and politically connected, and stay.

14   Those who set their sights on a particular city, however, are not always looking for something that can be built or marketed. Many choose on a **gut** feeling.

15   Joy Portella had a "life **epiphany**" about two years ago, at 33, and decided to leave Manhattan, even though it is the center of her profession: international development. If she were deciding on just a "career move," she said, she would have stayed in New York or moved to Washington, D.C. Instead she chose a **counterintuitive** path and headed for Seattle.

16   Her move was "liberating," she said. "Before, all my moves had been initiated by things I had to do — jobs or academic programs." She **decamped** to Seattle out of desire alone, and now has a job she loves as the director of communications for Mercy Corps.

17   Ms. Portella knew little of Seattle when she decided to make her move. But she did have a job offer, having spent a year searching from 3,000 miles away.

18   That is not true of everyone. Mr. Pelton arrived in Orlando with no job prospects. He had sent out resumes while still in Detroit, but received no response. "I found that it's much easier to find a job when you are in that city," he said. He now works in group sales for the Walt Disney World **Resort**, and said the city fulfilled his hope that he could **reinvent** himself there.

19   "I can do my regular job, then I can go be a pirate at Magic Kingdom, or watch fireworks every night of the week if I want," he said. "Growing up in Michigan and staying there, I had an

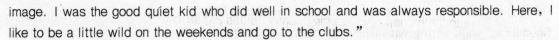

image. I was the good quiet kid who did well in school and was always responsible. Here, I like to be a little wild on the weekends and go to the clubs."

20   Casey Blalock, 24, is about to take the same leap any day now, moving from San Francisco to Seattle without a net. "I'm not looking to reinvent myself or find the meaning to life by moving," she wrote in an e-mail message. "But I do think I'll get to know myself better. I plan on finding a new job, volunteering, cooking, reading, hiking and enjoying a **crumpet** down at Pike Place Fish Market."

21   If it doesn't work out, she knows she can always set her sights elsewhere. Because an age group mobile enough to pick up and move once is just as likely to do so again.

22   Alan Caudill, now 31, moved from Pittsburgh to San Francisco five years ago, when the Internet start-up that employed him was **floundering** and he and his wife of two months realized they had never loved Pittsburgh.

23   "San Francisco culture was more us," he said. "I haven't been to an Applebee's, eaten fast food or drunk a Coors Light since we moved here (and I'm finally able to get a real burrito)."

24   While Mr. Caudill has found a job he enjoys, in software management at another start-up, he has also found that he enjoys the adventure of starting **anew**.

25   "We're thinking of doing it again," he said. "In the next few years we're debating moving either elsewhere in the country — we love D. C. , and Manhattan, and have family in Cleveland — or Europe or Latin America."

🔖 Words and Expressions

belongings *n.* something owned 动产；财物

sundrenched *a.* 阳光普照的

migrate *v.* move from one country or region to another 迁移；移往

peripatetic *a.* traveling esp. on foot 徒步游历的，漫游的

crummy *a.* of very bad quality 劣质的；低劣的；糟糕的

snowboarding *n.* the sport of moving over snow on a snowboard 滑雪板运动

consultant *n.* an expert who gives advice 顾问

secondary *a.* of second rank or importance or value 次要的，次等的

scramble *v.* to move hurriedly 快速爬行

grad *n.* a grad is a graduate 毕业生

executive *n.* a person responsible for the administration of a business 主管

poll *v.* get the opinions (of people) by asking specific questions 对……进行调查

gut *n.* prompted by (or as if by) instinct 本能的，直觉的

epiphany *n.* a moment of sudden insight or understanding 顿悟

counterintuitive *a.* contrary to what common sense would suggest 违反直觉的

decamp *v.* leave a camp; leave 离营；离开

resort *n.* a frequently visited place 度假胜地

reinvent *v.* create anew and make over 彻底改造，重新使用

crumpet *n.* raised muffin cooked on a griddle 一种松脆的圆饼

flounder *v.* walk with great difficulty（常指在水中）挣扎

anew *adv.* again but in a new or different way 再，重新

Background Information

1. Gen Y: The term Generation Y first appeared in an August 1993 Ad Age editorial to describe teenagers of the day, which they defined as separate aged 13～19（born 1974～1980）, as well as the teenagers of the upcoming ten years.

2. baby boomer: A person born during a baby boom, esp. one born in the U. S. between 1946 and 1965.

Learn about Words

Often you can tell the meaning of a word from its context — the words around it. Please find the word in the paragraph that means:

1. absent-minded; dreaming while awake (1)
2. a summary of your academic and work history (3)
3. the selling of goods to consumers; usu. in small quantities (5)
4. the trait of being neat and orderly (7)
5. obtain or provide money for (10)
6. the work of inquiring into sth. thoroughly (11)
7. to improve, especially sth. that was old or outdated (11)
8. bring into being; participate in the development of (16)
9. the possibility of future success (18)
10. someone who robs at sea (19)

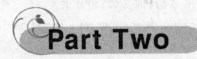

Part Two

Reading Skill — Scanning

Scanning is a technique you often use to search for key words or ideas. In most cases, you know what you're looking for, so you're concentrating on finding a particular answer. Scanning involves moving your eyes quickly down the page seeking specific words and phrases. When scanning, look for the author's use of organizers such as numbers, letters, steps, or the words, first, second, or next. Look for words that are bold faced, italics, or in a different font size, style, or color. Sometimes the author will put key ideas in the margin.

Skill-Specific Training

Directions: *Underline the years, numbers, persons, countries, regions and other information in the following questions first, and then scan the following passage for answers to those questions.*

1. Why did Ms. Sullivan defer her admission to American University?

   _____

2. What is the percentage of the college students who graduate in 4 years according to US National Center for Education Statistics?

   _____

3. What would clinics in Costa Rica offer more for students who are interested in medicine according to Ms. Bull?

   _____

4. How did Casey J. Krieger view her one semester experience in India?

   _____

5. How long did Sam Coggeshall stay in New Zealand?

   _____

6. What does the book "*The Gap-Year Advantage*" describe?

   _____

7. Who is Global Learning Across Borders trying to help with an after-school program?

   _____

8. How would overseas travels help young Americans according to Mr. Eastman?

   _____

How to Become a World Citizen, before Going to College

Tanya Mohn

Four jobs. Seventy hours a week. All summer. That has been Erin Sullivan's schedule since graduating from high school. (Dinner was often in her car, driving from **life-guarding** to baby-sitting.)

But it has been worth it, said Ms. Sullivan, 18, of Lawrenceville, N. J., who was to leave this weekend for Latin America on a mostly self-financed "gap year" of volunteering, home stays and Spanish lessons before attending college in fall 2007. "I want a better idea what I'm going for before I go," said Ms. Sullivan, who is **deferring** admission to American University.

In the United States, as most of high school graduates are now settling into college dorms, recently an increasing number of middle-class students, like Ms. Sullivan, are opting to take a gap year before or during college, and many students of various financial backgrounds now pay all or part of the cost. And as college costs soar, more families see the moves as good investments, because their children often return more focused.

As it is, many freshmen don't stay in college for long. "About 30 percent of freshmen don't see sophomore year. It's like World War I **trench warfare**," said Brian R. Hopewell, a college consultant on Cape Cod. "That's the dirty little secret many don't take into account."

Data from the US National Center for Education Statistics indicates that only 35 percent of students graduate in four years. Many take as long as five or six.

"Parents are thinking twice before writing **hefty** tuition checks," said Holly Bull, president of the Center for **Interim** Programs, in Princeton, N. J., which helps students plan gap years. Despite increased pressure to have their children attend good colleges, many boomer-generation parents seem more open to gap-year options than their **predecessors** were.

It makes economic sense for students to explore their interests before college, **advocates** of gap years say; freshmen who do so are less likely to party too much, fail courses or change majors repeatedly — all of which can result in more time needed to graduate, and more expense.

And gap years can help build resumes: students who are interested in medicine have more contact with patients volunteering in clinics in Costa Rica, for example, than they can in the United States, Ms. Bull said. And, on various foreign trips, they can **attain** a level of fluency in a new language.

Many students learn valuable life skills by earning and handling money during gap years, said Gail Reardon, founding director of Taking Off, a Boston consulting firm that also helps students plan gap years.

"One mother said 'I don't know what you did to her, but before she wouldn't use an A. T. M. Now she'll go anywhere, often taking the cheapest way to get place to place,' " Ms. Reardon said. "We **spoon-feed** our kids and they don't develop any sense that they can do things. And once they do it, it changes everything."

Many families do not view a gap year as an **extravagance**.

"It was the best investment we could have made in her life," said Dale B. Krieger, a financial adviser, who estimated the cost for his daughter's year at $30,000 for a semester in India, a month in Italy and a semester in New York, taking art classes and serving as an **intern** at a museum.

"That's definitely well put," said his daughter, Casey J. Krieger, 19. "The experience was definitely an eye-opener, and fascinating. And it really changed my life." She is now a freshman at the School of the Museum of Fine Arts in Boston.

Average costs for a gap year run about $10,000 to $12,000, which includes any **consultants'** fees you might pay.

Foreign trips, of course, can mean expenses beyond air fare, program fees and spending money. Among the possible extras are health and medical insurance, and expenses for documents like passports and visas.

Students often combine a costly overseas group program in the fall with a cheaper one in the spring. Among the least expensive are service programs or internships.

But some programs are free, except for travel expenses. A recent internship at a school for the deaf in Vermont offered room and board in exchange for work and the chance to learn American Sign Language.

Some students may initially have unrealistic expectations.

"Some guy told me a year in a tent in the **wilderness** would cost $1,000" in New Zealand, said Sam Coggeshall, 20, of Princeton, about a New Zealander he had met. His parents knew better. "He thought he'd get to the airport and ask somebody for a job or find work online," said Susan Henoch, his mother. "I don't think so." They hired a consultant.

After graduating from high school in 2004, her son headed to New Zealand, where he spent the year **tending** sheep, working in conservation (as part of a program called Willing Workers on Organic Farms — going from farm to farm to work for room and board). The year cost roughly $7,000, including air fare. But one year wasn't enough, said Mr. Coggeshall, who went back to New Zealand and spent his second year volunteering at an elementary school in Wellington and living in a rented apartment. The cost was about $5,000, including air fare.

Both years, he bought an international student identity card through STA Travel, which offers discounted air fares and flexible return policies. This month, he begins his freshman year at the University of Oregon in Eugene.

"If you do your research, there are a wide variety of financial opportunities," said Rae Nelson, who with her husband, Karl Haigler, wrote "The Gap-Year Advantage" (St. Martin's Griffin, 2005). The book describes resources for low-cost programs, student discounts and other money-saving tips.

"Financial obstacles remain the No. 1 barrier of at least 50 percent of students who apply," said John Eastman, executive director of Global Learning Across Borders, a nonprofit group based in New York that focuses on international programs.

The group recently started a **pilot** after-school program to reach out to low-income students, who have historically been **underrepresented** in study-abroad programs.

"It can't be viewed as a luxury," Mr. Eastman said, adding that overseas travel was important for helping young Americans become "culturally competent and globally aware." Mr. Krieger became chairman of this organization after his daughter's positive overseas experience.

Caitlin Thurrell, 18, of Meredith, N. H., received a scholarship for half the $8,950 program fee for a semester in India, offered by Global Learning Across Borders, by agreeing to be a student ambassador when she returns, visiting schools to talk about her experiences. She also sought backing from local organizations, like the Rotary Club and the town newspaper, offering to serve as a foreign **correspondent**.

🔊 Words and Expressions

life-guard *n.* a person employed to rescue people in danger in the water 救生员

defer *v.* to delay or cause to be delayed 推迟，延期

trench *n.* a deep ditch or furrow 战壕

warfare *n.* the act, process, or an instance of waging war 战争状态；作战

hefty *a.* big and strong 重的；异常大的

interim *a.* temporary 暂时；临时

predecessor *n.* a person who precedes another, as in an office 前任，前辈

advocate *v.* to support or recommend publicly 提倡；主张

attain *v.* to achieve or accomplish 获得；完成

spoon-feed *a.* to feed with a spoon 用匙喂的；娇养的

extravagance *n.* wasteful spending 奢侈；挥霍

intern *n.* internship; getting practical experience in a job 实习

consultant *n.* an expert who gives advice 顾问

wilderness *n.* a wild, uninhabited region 荒地，荒野

tend *v.* to care for somebody or something 照料，看护

pilot *a.* done on a small scale to see if successful 试验性的；引导的

underrepresented *a.* inadequately represented 代表名额不足的

correspondent *n.* a journalist employed to provide news stories 通讯员，记者

Comprehension of the Text

1. Why do some parents support to pay for a gap year for their children?
   _____.

2. Why do gap years make economic sense for students according to the article?
   _____.

3. What extra fees could foreign trips cause?
   _____.

4. What did Sam Coggeshall do in New Zealander?
   _____.

5. What obstacles remain to be the top barriers for half of the students who apply?
   _____.

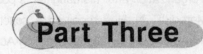

Part Three

Reading Comprehension (Skimming and Scanning)

Directions：*In this part, you will have 15 minutes to go over the passage quickly and answer the questions on Answer Sheet 1. For questions 1~7, choose the best answer from the four choices marked A), B), C) and D). For questions 8~10, complete the sentences with the information given in the passage.*

Writing High Impact Resumes

Surranna Sandy

In today's job market, the resume — a document that provides an overview of your experience, education and skill set — is the number one request of potential employers.

Research has shown that job seekers without a top-quality resume face long and difficult job searches, while those with polished, professionally written resumes multiply their chances of obtaining their desired positions. In the highly competitive job market, human resources managers and recruiting professionals are inundated with hundreds of resumes for a single position. Resume Solutions research has determined that on average, an employer spends 10-30 seconds reviewing a resume before determining whether it warrants further consideration. In such a competitive landscape it is critical that job seekers make a good first impression as a viable candidate by submitting a high impact resume that cuts through the noise and shows your value to each employer.

As a job seeker, your resume and cover letter must convince a recruiter that you are the perfect candidate for the vacancy without overloading the document with irrelevant data. In order to attract attention in the job marketplace and distinguish yourself from the competition, your resume needs to creatively highlight your work history, achievements, education and capabilities. Many new job applicants capture their career history in the Curriculum Vitae (CV) format. Unfortunately, the CV is only accepted for academic or research related positions and is too cumbersome for private sector jobs. Further, various components of the CV such as marital status, a photograph and other personal data is not relevant in the labour market and in fact may eliminate you as a potential candidate.

Your resume should answer the following questions: What expertise do you offer a potential employer? What added value you brought to your prior employers through measurable achievements? What education qualifications and certifications do you bring?

How do you write a high impact resume?

A resume that generates results should be relevant to an employer's needs, and emphasize the qualifications that are job, field or industry specific. To illustrate, if you are seeking a role as an Accountant but also possess experience in sales, it is advisable to focus primarily on your accounting knowledge rather than highlighting your sales talents. Another important consideration is to conduct comprehensive industry research prior to applying to jobs so that you are aware of the key job-specific requirements that employers are seeking.

To be effective, a resume should be concise and to the point. It is critical that you do not prepare a resume that consists of a laundry list of responsibilities for each job you have ever held or one which includes company jargon. In a document that is no longer than three pages (two is preferable), you need to convey to a prospective employer the contributions you made in each of your past roles. Do not use long-winded sentences or dated terminology. An example of what not to do: "Dear sirs, with your permission, herein is included my resume and cover letter, in accordance with your request for someone of my esteemed talents which are in line with your organization's long-term goals." Employers do not want to read long, cumbersome or jargon-laden sentences. Be specific and to the point.

To generate interest from a potential employer, you need demonstrate strategically your defining career moments and business and leadership successes, while outlining measurable results. Depending on your previous positions, this can be shown through examples of ways in which you have reduced costs, improved efficiency, solved problems or any other illustrations of how the organization benefited from your past performance. It is recommended that you include goals you overachieved such as delivering a project ahead of schedule and below budget, improving your staff performance or helping to retain key client accounts.

A high impact, effective resume will:
- Demonstrate how you will meet an employer's needs
- Convey the qualifications and abilities you offer for the job you want
- Show results and your qualifications in action
- Identify your career path
- Be attractive to the reader through a professional format
- Be concise and easy to read
- Let the reader see your skills, knowledge and abilities
- Be grammatically correct and spelling error free

As a certified professional resume writer working with clients from diverse backgrounds and ability levels, my primary objective is to increase my client's marketability by presenting their unique core competencies, personal talents, strengths and accomplishments in a way that engages the reader and compels them to invite my clients for an interview. However, it is critical that we are honest in the way we present our clients' skills and as such, we never exaggerate their capabilities and successes. You should ensure you do the same when writing your new resume. At all times be honest and relevant with no exaggerations of any details. This may include job titles, education levels, accomplishments and abilities.

What's included in a professional resume?

To be effective, it is critical that your resume effectively links your qualifications to a specific job target. It should outline your career progression, education & training, technical and personal skills, languages spoken, professional affiliations, awards & recognition, and any community involvement.

A basic resume layout should open with a profile or qualification summary to summarize who you are and what you have to offer to a potential employer. It should be tailored to the specific industry and job category you are seeking. Many large and medium-size companies employ technology to gather, store and filter resumes, using keyword searches to identify qualified applicants. You can include industry keywords within the text of the summary, as a stand-alone section, or incorporated throughout your resume.

Typically, your next section should list your employment history in reverse chronological order — listing the most recent job first, followed by second most recent and so on. For each job, you should summarize your varying responsibilities and provide details on measurable results.

Your education follows the details of your employment history. When listing your education, ensure that the institution is clearly stated, the degree qualification is detailed and the year of graduation is included. Only degrees and diplomas from accredited institutes should be included. Your education section can also include any additional courses, certificates and professional development you have obtained.

Additional sections for your resume could include technical skills, affiliations and other job relevant data. Please note, you should not include religious or political affiliations and personal details such as date of birth, marital status, SIN numbers or a personal photograph.

Your success in securing high quality interviews and job offers is critically dependent on your effectiveness in conveying your qualifications and core expertise to potential employers. Before you begin to craft your resume, I suggest that you take the time to develop an in-depth inventory of your hard and soft skills. Many job seekers find this process challenging, and for those of you having difficulty communicating your skills on paper, turning to a professional resume writer may be the answer. Companies such as Resume Solutions, whose Certified Professional Resume Writers are members of Professional Association of Resume Writers and Career Coaches and the Career Management Alliance, are pledged to uphold the highest standards of professionalism, writing quality and ethical behavior when providing guidance to job seekers. As such, they can be an important partner in your job search strategy.

1. What is the number one request of potential employers according to the article?
   A. Resume   B. Experience   C. Education   D. Skill
2. Which of the following statements is NOT true about top-quality resumes?
   A. Top-quality resumes would multiply job seekers' chances.
   B. Top-quality resumes would attract employers' attention.
   C. Top-quality resumes help make a good impression.
   D. Top-quality resumes guarantee the job seekers good opportunities.
3. If you are seeking a role as an Accountant but also possess experience in sales, you should focus on _____.
   A. both accounting knowledge and sales talents
   B. either accounting knowledge or sales talents
   C. accounting knowledge

D. sales talents

4. In order to make a resume effective, job seekers are advised to _____.

A. list the responsibilities for each past job

B. use more than three pages

C. list contributions they made in past jobs

D. use long-winded sentences

5. How to demonstrate your business successes in the past in a resume?

A. To outline detailed successful results.

B. To show how organization benefited from your past performance.

C. To include the goals you wanted to achieve.

D. To show you finished a project on schedule.

6. What is the author's primary objective as a professional resume writer?

A. To help his clients present their unique core competencies.

B. To compel the reader to invite his clients for an interview.

C. To help his clients exaggerate some of their capabilities.

D. To ensure his clients to provide honest and relevant information.

7. Which of the following statements is NOT true about a profile summary?

A. It should be put at the opening part of a resume.

B. It should summarize what you have to offer to a potential employer.

C. It should cover more job categories you are seeking.

D. It should include industry keywords within the text.

8. When listing your education, you should only include your degrees and diplomas from _____.

9. In your resume, you should not list the information that is related to _____.

10. Before you begin to design your resume, the author suggests that you take the time to make a list of your _____ skills.

Part Four

> **Directions**: *There is a passage in this section. This passage is followed by some questions. For each of them there are four choices marked A), B), C) and D). You should decide on the best choice.*

What Youngsters Expect in Life

According to a survey, which was based on the responses of over 188,000 students, today's traditional-age college freshmen are "more materialistic and less *altruistic* (利他主义的)" than at any time in the 17 years of the poll.

Not surprising in these hard times, the student's major objective "is to be financially well off. Less important than ever is developing a meaningful philosophy of life." It follows then that today the most popular course is not literature or history but accounting.

Interest in teaching, social service and the "altruistic" fields is at a low. On the other hand, enrollment in business programs, engineering and computer science is way up.

That's no surprise either. A friend of mine (a sales representative for a chemical company) was making twice the salary of her college instructors her first year on the job — even before she completed her two-year associate degree.

While it's true that we all need a career, it is equally true that our civilization has accumulated an incredible amount of knowledge in fields far removed from our own and that we are better for our understanding of these other contributions — be they scientific or artistic. It is equally true that, in studying the diverse wisdom of others, we learn how to think. More important, perhaps, education teaches us to see the connections between things, as well as to see beyond our immediate needs.

Weekly we read of unions who went on strike for higher wages, only to drive their employer out of business. No company; no job. How shortsighted in the long run!

But the most important argument for a broad education is that in studying the accumulated wisdom of the ages, we improve our moral sense. I saw a cartoon recently which shows a group of businessmen looking puzzled as they sit around a conference table; one of them is talking on the *intercom* (对讲机): "Miss Baxter," he says, "could you please send in someone who can distinguish right from wrong?"

From the long-term point of view, that's what education really ought to be about.

1. According to the author's observation, college students _____.
   A. have never been so materialistic as today
   B. have never been so interested in the arts
   C. have never been so financially well off as today
   D. have never attached so much importance to moral sense
2. The students' criteria for selecting majors today have much to do with _____.
   A. the influences of their instructors
   B. the financial goals they seek in life
   C. their own interpretations of the courses
   D. their understanding of the contributions of others
3. By saying "While it's true that... be they scientific or artistic" (Lines 1~3, Para. 5), the author means that _____.
   A. business management should be included in educational programs
   B. human wisdom has accumulated at an extraordinarily high speed

C. human intellectual development has reached new heights

D. the importance of a broad education should not be overlooked

4. Studying the diverse wisdom of others can _____.

A. create varying artistic interests

B. help people see things in their right perspective

C. help improve connections among people

D. regulate the behavior of modern people

5. Which of the following statements is true according to the passage?

A. Businessmen absorbed in their career are narrow-minded.

B. Managers often find it hard to tell right from wrong.

C. People engaged in technical jobs lead a more rewarding life.

D. Career seekers should not focus on immediate interests only.

Part Five

Reading for Pleasure

Life Description of a Chinese College Student

1. Differences between high school and college life

The main difference is the incredible increase in free time. In high school，every day was a constant *grind*（教师严令学生用功；灌输）and I never had any free time. In college I have a *surplus*（过剩）. Instead of classes six hours a day，they take up a mere three hours. I'm no longer forced to sit in the same building all day. This newfound time provides many luxuries that can easily be abused. I can be productive or *goof of*（不认真工作）.

2. Most difficult part of college life

Time management! There were many times this semester when I had to write a paper and heard my friends were going to a party. That always happened on days that I'd had time to get work done but had wasted it instead. Then I couldn't go out.

3. Biggest fear

My biggest fear was how to adjust to this new freedom. I knew living on my own meant my parents were not going to be breathing down my neck to do my work. They were not going to have me home at a certain hour. I was in complete control. These two aspects of being on my

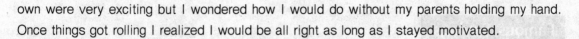

own were very exciting but I wondered how I would do without my parents holding my hand. Once things got rolling I realized I would be all right as long as I stayed motivated.

4. Advice for freshman

Stay on top of things; don't get so caught up in the social atmosphere of college that you get behind in your studies — remember what you're there for. There is nothing worse than approaching the end of a semester and realizing you have *procrastinated*（耽搁）so much you have an impossible mountain of work. No one needs that added stress.

Humor Prepared for You

Job Interviews

Reaching the end of a job interview, the human resources person asked the hot-shot young engineer, fresh out of MIT, "And what starting salary were you looking for?"

: The engineer coolly said, "In the neighborhood of $125,000 a year, depending on the benefits package."

The interviewer said, "Well, what would you say to a package of 5 weeks vacation, 14 paid holidays, full medical and dental, company matching retirement fund to 50% of salary, and a company car leased every 2 years — for starters, say, a red Corvette?"

The engineer tried to control his excitement, but sat straight up and said, "Wow! Are you kidding?"

"Yeah," the interviewer shrugged, "But you started it."

Overworked

But... I'm tired because I'm overworked.

The population of this country is 18 million. 8 million are retired. That leaves 10 million to do the work. There are 6 million in school, which leaves 4 million to do the work. Of this there are 1.5 million unemployed, leaving 2.5 million to do the work. Take from that 1,180,000 people who work for government departments and that leaves 1,320,000 people to do the work. 480,000 are in the armed forces, which leaves 840,000 to do the work. At any time, there are 179,000 people in hospitals, leaving 661,000 people to do the work. At the moment, there are 660,998 people in prisons.

That leaves just two people to do the work.

You and me.

And you're sitting at your computer reading jokes!

Famous Sayings

Genius is one percent inspiration, ninety-nine percent perspiration.

—*Thomas Edison*

天才是百分之一的灵感，百分之九十九的汗水。

——托马斯·爱迪生

Being busy does not always mean real work. The object of all work is production or accomplishment and to either of these ends there must be forethought, system, planning, intelligence, and honest purpose, as well as perspiration. Seeming to do is not doing.

—*Thomas Edison*

忙并不总是意味着你在好好工作。所有工作的目的是生产或者说完成目标。达到他们中的任何一个都必须预先计划，系统规划，需要智慧、纯粹的目的和汗水。看起来在做并不有效。

——托马斯·爱迪生

Let us realize that the privilege to work is a gift, that power to work is a blessing, that love of work is success.

—*David O. McKay*

让我们认清有权工作是一项恩赐，有能力工作是一项祝福，喜爱工作就是成功。

——大为奥·麦基

Unit Nine

Success Doesn't Come Easy

You hear and read all of the success stories. People typically talk about how they went after what they wanted, their personal goals and their dreams and they made it happen. One thing that they ignored in talking about is the hardships that they had to endure. If you want success, you would need patience, persistence, an open mind, a will to learn and it would help if you can accept help.

In this unit, you will read:

- The Secret of My Success
- Be Strong: How to Deal with Pain and Hardships in Your Life
- Bosses Say 'Yes' to Home Work
- The Bussiness of America Is Bussiness
- Two Chinese Idioms

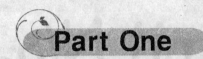

Part One

The Secret of My Success

Harley Hahn

1 People often ask me for advice on how to be successful. 'Is there a secret?' they say.

2 As we all know, real success comes slowly and is due to a number of different factors all coming together over a period of years. Being successful takes intelligence, natural talent, knowledge, skill, hard work, smart choices, **persistence** and luck.

3 Although there is no real shortcut, there is a secret: a secret so powerful that you can use it to open doors that might otherwise be closed, and to influence people to help you time and again. In fact, I would go **as far as** to say that this is the secret that has a lot to do with my success.

4 The secret is simple: Write thank-you notes.

Making a Friend at IBM

5 Years ago, when I was just starting as a professional writer, I also worked as a computer consultant. One day, I happened to read in a computer magazine that IBM was having a big conference for consultants a few hours from where I lived. I decided it would be a good idea to attend the conference, so I drove there to see if I could get in.

6 Once I arrived, my request to attend the conference led me to Bill, the IBM person who was organizing the conference. Bill was a nice enough fellow, but he didn't want to let me in. He said the conference was only for professional consultants and was by invitation only.

7 Well, I can be persistent when I need to, and finally Bill agreed to let me attend some of the conference sessions. "You can go to the afternoon workshops," he said **grudgingly**, "but you can't go to the dinner or to anything else." However, I wasn't going to complain. I did **show up**, uninvited, to an invitation — only conference for important consultants, and I felt lucky that anyone would even talk to me.

8 During the conference, I found out Bill's mailing address at IBM, and the minute I got home

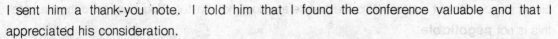

I sent him a thank-you note. I told him that I found the conference valuable and that I appreciated his consideration.

9   Over the years, I got to know Bill a lot better, and I found out he was a wonderful, thoughtful man. However, at the time, I didn't know him at all. All I knew was that he responded to my note by allowing me to <u>register</u> with the IBM Consultant Relations department as an officially recognized consultant.

10   During the next few years, I was not only invited to IBM's conferences, I was able to spend time with Bill and the various people he worked with. He had a lot of experience, and I spent many hours listening to his stories and learning from him. Bill **went out of his way** to **set up** meetings for me with important IBM <u>executives</u> and to introduce me to influential consultants. He helped me in so many important ways, I can't even begin to list them all. And when the time came that the IBM Consultant Relations department needed to build their own computer network, they hired me as a consultant to come to their headquarters and do the work for them.

Why Thank-You Notes Are So Effective

11   I would like to believe that I was **hot stuff**. After all, it's pleasant to think that Bill was able to talk to me for only a few moments and see what a truly valuable human being I was. The <u>plain</u> truth, however, was that the consultant's conference was filled with people who were more knowledgeable, more experienced, better known and far more important than me. But I had one advantage.

12   Out of several hundred guests, I was one of the few who bothered to take the time to thank IBM for having me. IBM (and Bill) went to a lot of trouble and spent a lot of money for these people, and I was the only one who took a few minutes to send a thank-you note.

13   Why are such notes so effective? Although it is easy to sit down and write a short note, hardly anyone does, and the moment you do, you **set** yourself **apart** from the crowd. Moreover, people like Bill work hard. How do you think they feel when someone takes the time to thank them for a job well done, or for spending a little extra time doing something special for someone?

14   How would you feel? You would feel great, and you would never forget the person who took the trouble to write the note that made you feel so good.

When Should You Write a Thank-You Note

15   Good manners require you to write a thank-you note whenever someone:
- Sends you a gift
- Entertains you at their home
- Does you a kindness
- Offers you an important opportunity

16   The first two situations are straightforward. Whenever you receive a gift and whenever you have been entertained at someone's home, you must write a thank-you note. The

circumstances do not matter. Who the people are does not matter. You must send them a note: this is not **negotiable**.

17   If you do not feel like it ("I didn't want to go in the first place, and the food was terrible, and my hostess didn't even seem to notice when her baby **threw up** all over my new blouse"), **console** yourself with the thought that you are being polite. Writing thank-you notes is what well-mannered people do, and it is good manners that separate us from the rest of the animal kingdom.

18   When someone does you a kindness, you may or may not be obliged to send him a thank-you note. In general, you do not have to write a note to thank someone for doing his job properly. For example, say you are looking for a book at the library, and the librarian is polite and efficient. She is merely doing her job, and you do not need to send her a note (although you should be gracious and thank her at the time).

19   Suppose, however, you have a special request, one that requires the librarian to put in an unusual amount of effort helping you. Once you receive that help, it would be the mark of a real gentleman or lady to send a written thank-you note. When you do, I guarantee that (1) your note will make the librarian very happy, and (2) you will **stand out** because very few people bother to write such notes.

20   So, when someone helps you, how do you know when you should write a thank-you note? The answer is simple.

The Best Reason to Write Thank-you Notes

21   So far I have given you several good reasons to write thank-you notes. First, you will be showing gratitude to people who deserve your thanks. Second, people will respond to your good manners. Through the years, this will result in many new opportunities, which will help you become successful.

22   In addition, when someone sends you a gift, writing a thank-you note tells the person that you received the gift. If you have ever sent something that was never acknowledged, you will know how important it is for someone to know that his or her gift arrived safely.

23   These are all good reasons to write thank-you notes, but there is one more that is even more important.

24   Imagine that you have to choose a person with whom you are going to spend a lot of time. You have **narrowed the choices down** to two people who, superficially, seem the same. But then you find out that one person always writes thank-you notes, and the other person doesn't.

25   If you are like me, you would choose the thank-you note person. After all, doesn't it seem likely that such a person would be more gracious, friendly, and better-mannered, and isn't that just the type of person we all like to be around?

26   When you get in the habit of thanking people for their gifts and for their help, you yourself become a gracious, friendly, well-mannered person. Yes, it does take time to write thank-you notes, and it is not always convenient. But over the years, putting in that effort that will change

you for the better — and you do spend a lot of time with yourself.

27　Perhaps, then, that is the real secret of success.

📖 Words and Expressions

persistence *n.* the fact of continuing to try to do sth. in spite of difficulties or opposition, in a way that can seem unreasonable 坚持；执着；执意

as far as used when you are asking or talking about the degree to which sth. is true or possible（问到或谈及程度时说）有多大，直（至）

grudgingly *ad.* unwillingly, reluctantly 不情愿的，勉强的

show up（informal）to arrive where you have arranged to meet sb or do sth. 如约赶到；出现，露面

go out of one's way（**to do sth.**）to make a special effort to do sth 特地；格外努力

set up to arrange for sth to happen 安排；策划

hot stuff（informal, especially Br E）a person who is very skilful at sth 技艺很高的人；高手

set...apart to make sb/sth different from or better than others 使与众不同；使突出；使优于……

negotiable *a.* that you can discuss or change before you make an agreement or a decision 可协商的；可讨论的

throw up to vomit 呕吐

console *v.* to give comfort or sympathy to sb who is unhappy or disappointed 抚慰，慰藉

stand out to be very easy to see or notice by looking or sounding different from other things or people 引人关注，与众不同

narrow（**sth.**）**down**（**to sth.**）*v.* to reduce the number of possibilities or choices 把（可能性或范围）缩小到；缩小范围

📖 Background Information

1. IBM（国际商业机器公司）IBM is short for International Business Machines Corporation, the leading American computer manufacturer, with a major share of the market both in the United States and abroad. Its headquarters are in Armonk, N. Y.

　　It was incorporated in 1911 as the Computing-Tabulating-Recording Company in a consolidation of three smaller companies that made punch-card tabulators and other office products. In 1933 IBM purchased *Electromatic* Typewriters, Inc. , and thereby entered the field of electric typewriters, in which it eventually became an industry leader.

　　IBM's specialty was mainframe computers—i. e. , expensive medium- to large-scale computers that could process numerical data at great speeds. Since 2000, IBM has placed one of its supercomputers consistently at or near the top of the industry's list of most powerful machines as measured by standardized computation tests. In addition to producing supercomputers for governments and large corporations, IBM's supercomputer division, in cooperation with the Toshiba Corporation and the Sony Corporation of Japan, designed the Cell Broadband Engine. Developed over a four-year period beginning in 2001, this advanced computer chip has multiple applications, from supercomputers to Toshiba high-definition televisions to the Sony Playstation 3 electronic game system. IBM also designed the computer chips for the Microsoft Corporation Xbox 360 and the Nintendo Company Wii game systems. IBM became the first company to generate more than 3,000 patents in one year (2001) and, later, more than 4,000 patents in one year (2008). The company now holds more than 40,000 active patents, which generate considerable income from royalties.

2. Harley Hahn — As a writer, philosopher, humorist and computer expert, Harley has written 30 books that have sold more than 2 million copies. He has also written numerous articles, essays and stories on a wide variety of topics, including romance, philosophy, economics, culture, medicine and money. Much of his writing is available on his Web site, the book — *Harley Hahn's Internet Yellow Pages* — was the first Internet book in history to sell more than 1 million copies. Two of his other books *Harley Hahn's Internet Insecurity* and *Harley Hahn's Internet* Advisor have been nominated for a Pulitzer Prize. These books, along with others, have made him the best-selling Internet author of all time.

His work and my papers — including a complete set of all my books — is archived by the Special Collections Department of the library at the University of California at Santa Barbara.

Harley has a degree in Mathematics and Computer Science from the University of Waterloo, in Canada, and a graduate degree in Computer Science from the University of California at San Diego. He also studied medicine at the University of Toronto Medical School. He has been the recipient of a number of honors and awards, including a prestigious National Research Council (Canada) post-graduate scholarship.

📖 Learn about Words

A. *Often you can tell the meaning of a word from its context — the words around it. Find the word in the paragraph that means.*

1. someone who has a lot of experience and whose job is to give advice and training in a particular area (5)

2. continuing to do sth., although it is difficult (7)

3. simple and easy to understand (16)

4. an offer, price, contract that and can be discussed and changed before being agreed on (16)

5. to make someone feel better when they are feeling bad or disappointed (17)

B. *A word may have more than one meaning depending on the way it is used. Decide which meaning fits the word as it is used in the paragraph. Write the letter of the meaning you choose.*

6. register (9)

   A. to record a name or details about sb. or sth. in an official list

   B. to show or express a feeling

   C. to officially state your opinion about sth. so that everyone knows what you think or feel

7. executive (10)

A. someone who has an important job as a manager in a company or business

B. the part of a government that is responsible for making sure that new laws and other decisions are done in a way they have been planned

C. the group of people in a political organization, society etc that makes the rules and makes sure that they work in the way they were planned

8. plain (11)

A. without anything added or without decoration; simple

B. showing clearly and honestly what you think about sth., without trying to hide anything

C. very clear, and easy to understand or recognize; obvious

9. gracious (18)

A. having the kind of expensive style, comfort and beauty that only rich people can afford

B. behaving in a polite, kind and generous way, esp. to people of lower class

C. a word meaning kind and forgiving, used to describe God

10. bother (19)

A. to make someone feel slightly worried or upset

B. to upset or frighten someone by repeatedly trying to hurt them, touch them sexually

C. to make the effort to do sth.

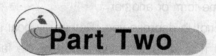

Part Two

> **Reading Skill — Predicting the Writer's Ideas**
>
> Predicting is using the text to guess what will happen next. Then readers confirm or reject their prediction as they read. Predicting is a reading strategy used before and during reading.

Skill-Specific Training

As you read the passage, try to predict the general direction of the writer's thinking. There are a few questions inserted in the passage to guide you. Be sure to answer them before you go on to the next section of the passage.

Be Strong: How to Deal with Pain and Hardships in Your Life

Prediction 1

When looking at the title of the passage and the picture, you will probably find that the text is about:

A. *a story about one's life experiences*

B. *advices on how to deal with pain and hardships*

C. *stories of great people*

Every now and then life throws us in the deep end and tells us to swim. We find ourselves in **overwhelming** situations that we don't know how to deal with. It might be the death of a loved one, a personal illness or a case of serious **depression**. In this post I want to give you a few ways to deal with the pain and hardships that you will **encounter** in your life. I hope it will inspire you just a little bit.

THE INEVITABILITY OF HARDSHIP

Prediction 2

When you read this subtitle of the passage, probably you will be prepared to read:

A. *a justification of the inevitable hardships everyone will encounter in their lives*

B. *a list of frequent things that bring trouble to people*

C. *the writer's hardships in life*

The first thing I want to talk about is the fact that pain and hardships are inevitable. No one can escape them. Every single one of us, at some point in our life, will experience pain, suffering and hardships of some form or another.

My goal in saying this is not to depress you. Rather my goal is to inspire you. How is this inspiring you might ask? Well it is simple. Being aware of the fact that you will experience, suffering is a cause for hope because, unlike many other people, you now have a chance to prepare for it. And people who prepare are never as badly affected as those who don't.

Suffering, pain and hardships are inevitable. Make sure your preparation for them is also just as inevitable. This is the most important step.

HOW TO DEAL WITH PAIN AND HARSHIPS IN YOUR LIFE

Prediction 3

What follows the subtitle in the following is probably:

A. *specific advices based on your current background*

B. *advices of common sense*

C. *advices gained from the writer's own experience*

The tips that I am about to give you come from two places, my own personal experience and the experiences of history's greatest **meditation** masters. Sometimes it is better to hear some **pithy** and real tips as opposed to some dry and theoretical ones. I will try, therefore, to keep these as practical as possible.

REALIZE THAT IT IS YOUR HARDSHIPS THAT MAKE YOU BETTER

Prediction 4

From the above paragraphs and the subtitle, we may expect the main part of the passage, which will be :

A. your hardships to be experienced in the future

B. a justification of the subtitle by the writer's story (stories)

C. hardships encountered by most people

Picture this. You are in the center of the Indian desert. You are just out of high school; young, naive and **egotistical**. You are on a bit of a spiritual journey but at the same time looking for adventure. And then after just arriving in a place miles from anywhere you wake up in the middle of the night **vomiting, convulsing** and shaking. You are days from a hospital and you are really sick. Things start to look **bleak**.

That is the situation I found myself in on my first trip to India. I had eaten some poisonous food and for the next three days I lay in bed sick as a dog. It didn't matter what I did, nothing seemed to help. I started to get quite frightened as I knew I was too sick to travel and there were no doctors around. But then something amazing happened, I was paid a visit by a very high Tibetan Lama. **Turned out** he was on a teaching tour in the area and my friend had told him that I was sick. He came into my room and said one thing and one thing only. I have never ever forgotten it as it had such a profound impact on my life. He said:

"I am not interested in how much money you have or what family you belong to. I am interested in how you deal with hardships. That is the only thing that matters. That **defines** your future. "

It is the truest thing anyone has ever said to me about suffering and hardships. It is the hardships that define your character. Everyone is charming and lovely when the birds are **chirping** and the flowers are **blooming** but hardly anyone is **compassionate**, patient and loving when they are sick, ill or under pressure. How you deal with hardships determines your character.

If you want to learn to deal with pain and hardship you need to realize that you have an amazing opportunity to grow as a person. You can prove to yourself that you are strong. You can show yourself that you have strength of character and will-power. The amazing thing about hardships and pain is that they present you with a rare opportunity to grow into a strong and decent human being.

REALIZE THAT PAIN AND HARSHIPS WON'T LAST

There is a great truth in this universe that **applies to** everything. There is no corner of the world that it does not touch, no depth of the ocean that it does not find, no planet in space that it cannot reach. That truth applies to everyone and everything. That truth is impermanence.

Nothing lasts.

We have heard it all before. What goes up must come down. What comes together must eventually part. What is composite will soon break. What is **accumulated** will one day be **dispersed**. Everything in our universe is impermanent. Nothing can escape it.

As depressing as this sounds it also has an upside. The next time you are going through some pain or hardships you can remind yourself that it won't last. You can look at everything in history and feel secure in knowing that, no matter how bad things seem now, the problems won't last forever. What a wonderful thing! Like all things, suffering is also impermanent.

REALIZE THAT YOU ARE NOT ALONE

Prediction 5

What follows this section will probably be:
A. *some people are physically together with you*
B. *your family are always together with you*
C. *a section which concludes the passage by a justification that your hardships are and will be encountered by other people, rather than yourself.*

There is something very powerful about knowing that other people are going through what you are going through. Realizing that you are not alone is an extremely good way to deal with pain and hardships.

Let's take the example of someone with severe depression. Depression can make you feel pretty alone. In fact, 90% of the time depression makes you feel so isolated and **self-orientated** that you don't have a thought about other people for long stretches of time. I was a bit like this in my teen years.

But when you open up to the fact that you are not alone you get a **boost** of some really powerful strength, You get a sense of **community**, of friendship, of companionship — even if you haven't met anyone else with the condition. Just knowing that there are other people out there like you can really make you feel good.

The next step in this idea is to realize that thousands of other people have gone through what you are going through and come out the other end. They have made it through and won. They haven't died, lost hope or given up. They have faced the very same thing as you (whatever it is) and they have come out the other end. Never forget this.

Words and Expressions

overwhelming *a.* so powerful that you can not resist it or decide how to react 无法抗拒的

depression *n.* the state of feeling very sad and without hope 抑郁；沮丧；消沉

encounter *v.* to experience sth., esp. sth. unpleasant or difficult, while you are trying to do sth. else 遭遇,遇到(尤指令人不快或困难的事)

meditation *n.* the practice of thinking deeply in silence, esp. for religious reasons or in order to make your mind calm 冥想;沉思

pithy *a.* (of a comment, piece of writing, etc.) short but expressed well and full of meaning 言简意赅的;精炼的

picture *v.* to image sb./sth.; to create an image of sb./sth. in your mind 想象;设想;回忆

egotistical *a.* the practice of talking and thinking about oneself excessively because of an undue sense of self-importance 念念不忘自我,言必称"我";自负;自大

vomit *v.* to bring food from the stomach back out through the mouth 呕吐

convulse *v.* to cause a sudden shaking movement in sb.'s body 使痉挛(或抽筋)

bleak *a.* not hopeful or encouraging 无望的;令人沮丧的

turn out to be discovered to be; to prove to be 原来是;证明是;结果是

define *v.* to describe or show sth. accurately 阐明;明确;界定

chirp *v.* (of small birds and some insects) to make short high sounds 叽叽喳喳叫

bloom *v.* to produce flowers 开花

compassionate *a.* feeling or showing sympathy for people who are suffering 有同情心的

apply to (sth.) to use sth. or make sth. work in a particular situation 应用;使用

accumulate *v.* to gradually get more and more of sth. over a period of time 积累;积聚

disperse *v.* to move apart and go away in different directions 分散;疏散;驱散

orientate *v.* to direct sb./sth. towards sth.; to make or adapt sb./sth. for a particular purpose 面对;使适应

boost *v.* something that helps or encourages sb./sth. 帮助;激励

community *n.* the feeling of sharing things and belonging to a group in the place where you live 共享;共有

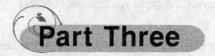

Part Three

> **Reading Comprehension** (Skimming and Scanning)
> **Directions:** *In this part, you will have 15 minutes to go over the passage quickly and answer the questions on Answer Sheet 1. For questions 1~7, choose the best answer from the four choices marked A), B), C) and D). For questions 8~10, complete the sentences with the information given in the passage.*

Bosses Say 'Yes' to Home Work

Rising costs of office space, time lost to stressful commuting, and a slow recognition that workers have lives beyond the office-all are strong arguments for letting staff work from home.

For the small business, there are additional benefits too — staff are more productive, and happier, enabling firms to keep their headcounts（员工数） and their recruitment costs to a minimum. It can also provide a competitive advantage, especially when small businesses want to attract new staff but don't have the budget to offer huge salaries.

While company managers have known about the benefits for a long time, many have done little about it, skeptical of whether they could trust their employees to work to full capacity without supervision, or concerned about the additional expenses teleworking policies might incur as staff start charging their home phone bills to the business.

Yet this is now changing. When communications provider Inter-Tel researched the use of remote working solutions among small and medium-sized UK businesses in April this year, it found that 28% more companies claimed to have introduced flexible working practices than a year ago.

The UK network of Business Links confirms that it too has seen a growing interest in remote working solutions from small businesses seeking its advice, and claims that as many as 60～70% of the businesses that come through its doors now offer some form of remote working support to their workforces.

Technology advances, including the widespread availability of broadband, are making the introduction of remote working a piece of cake.

"If systems are set up properly, staff can have access to all the resources they have in the office wherever they have an internet connection," says Andy Poulton, a business advisor at Business Link for Berkshire and Wiltshire. "There are some very exciting developments which have enabled this."

One is the availability of broadband everywhere, which now covers almost all of the country (BT claims that, by July, 99.8% of its exchanges will be broadband enabled, with alternative plans in place for even the most remote exchanges). "This is the enabler," Poulton says.

Yet while broadband has come down in price too, those service providers targeting the business market warn against consumer services masquerading（伪装） as business friendly broadband.

"Broadband is available for as little as ￡15 a month, but many businesses fail to appreciate the hidden costs of such a service," says Neil Stephenson, sales and marketing director at Onyx Internet, an internet service provider based in the north-east of England. "Providers offering broadband for rock bottom prices are notorious for poor service, with regular breakdowns and heavily congested（拥堵的） networks. It is always advisable for businesses to look beyond the price tag and look for a business — only provider that can offer more reliability, with good support." Such services don't cost too much — quality services can be found for upwards of ￡30 a month.

The benefits of broadband to the occasional home worker are that they can access email in real time, and take full advantage of services such as internet-based backup or even internet-based phone services.

Internet-based telecoms, or VoIP (Voice over IP) to give it its technical title, is an interesting tool to any business supporting remote working, not necessarily because of the promise of free or reduced price phone calls (which experts point out is misleading for the average business), but because of the sophisticated voice services that can be exploited by the remote worker — facilities such as voicemail and call forwarding, which provide a continuity of the company image for customers and business partners.

By law, companies must "consider seriously" requests to work flexibly made by a parent with a child under the age of six, or a disabled child under 18. It was the need to accommodate employees with young children that motivated accountancy firm Wright Vigar to begin promoting teleworking recently. The company, which needed to upgrade its IT infrastructure(基础设施) to provide connectivity with a new, second office, decided to introduce support for remote working at the same time.

Marketing director Jack O'Hern explains that the company has a relatively young workforce, many of whom are parents: "One of the triggers was when one of our tax managers returned from maternity leave. She was intending to work part time, but could only manage one day a week in the office due to childcare. By offering her the ability to work from home, we have doubled her capacity — now she works a day a week from home and a day in the office. This is great for her, and for us as we retain someone highly qualified."

For Wright Vigar, which has now equipped all of its fee-earners to be able to work at maximum productivity when away from the offices (whether that's from home, or while on the road), this strategy is not just about saving on commute time or cutting them loose from the office, but enabling them to work more flexible hours that fit around their home life.

O'Hern says: "Although most of our work is client-based and must fit around this, we can't see any reason why a parent can't be on hand to deal with something important at home, if they have the ability to complete a project late in the day."

Supporting this new way of working came with a price, though. Although the firm was updating its systems anyway, the company spent 10~15% more per user to equip them with a laptop rather than a PC, and about the same to upgrade to a server that would enable remote staff to connect to the company networks and access all their usual resources.

Although Wright Vigar hasn't yet quantified the business benefits, it claims that, in addition to being able to retain key staff with young families, it is able to save fee-earners a substantial amount of "dead" time in their working days.

That staff can do this without needing a fixed telephone line provides even more efficiency savings. "With Wi-Fi (fast, wireless internet connections) popping up all over the place, even on trains, our fee-earners can be productive as they travel, and between meetings, instead of having to kill time at the shops," he adds.

The company will also be able to avoid the expense of having to relocate staff to temporary offices for several weeks when it begins disruptive office renovations(翻新) soon.

Financial recruitment specialist Lynne Hargreaves knows exactly how much her firm has saved by adopting a teleworking strategy, which has involved handing her company's data management over to a remote hosting company, Datanet, so it can be accessible by all the company's consultants over broadband internet connections.

It has enabled the company to dispense with its business premises altogether, following the realization that it just didn't need them any more. "The main motivation behind adopting home working was to increase my own productivity, as a single mum to an 11-year-old," says Hargreaves. "But I soon realized that, as most of our business is done on the phone, email and at off-site meetings, we didn't need our offices at all. We're now saving £16,000 a year on rent, plus the cost of utilities, not to mention what would have been spent on commuting."

1. What is the main topic of this passage?
   A. How business managers view hi-tech.
   B. Benefits of the practice of teleworking.
   C. How to cut down the costs of small businesses.
   D. Relations between employers and employees.

2. From the research conducted by the communications provider Inter-Tel, we learn that _____.
   A. attitudes toward IT technology have changed.
   B. more employees work to full capacity at home
   C. more businesses have adopted remote working solutions
   D. employees show a growing interest in small businesses

3. What development has made flexible working practices possible according to Andy Poulton?
   A. Reduced cost of telecommunications.   B. Improved reliability of internet service.
   C. Access to broadband everywhere.   D. Availability of the VoIP service.

4. What is Neil Stephenson's advice to firms contracting internet services?
   A. They contract the cheapest provider.
   B. They look for reliable business-only providers.
   C. They contact providers located nearest to them.
   D. They carefully examine the contract.

5. Internet-based telecoms facilitates remote working by _____.
   A. offering sophisticated voice services
   B. providing calls completely free of charge
   C. helping clients discuss business at home
   D. giving access to emailing in real time

6. The accountancy firm Wright Vigar promoted teleworking initially in order to _____.
   A. attract young people with IT expertise to work for it
   B. present a positive image to prospective customers

C. reduce operational expenses of a second office

D. support its employees with children to take care of

7. According to marketing director Jack O'Hern, teleworking enabled the company to _____.

    A. minimise its office space   B. keep highly qualified staff

    C. enhance its market image   D. reduce recruitment costs

8. Wright Vigar's practice of allowing for more flexible working hours not only benefits the company but helps improve employees' _____.

9. With fast, wireless internet connections, employees can still be _____ while traveling.

10. Single mother Lynne Hargreaves decided to work at home mainly to _____.

Part Four

> **Directions:** *There is a passage in this section. This passage is followed by some questions. For each of them there are four choices marked A), B), C) and D). You should decide on the best choice.*

The Bussiness of America Is Bussiness

President Coolidge's statement, "The business of America is business," still points to an important truth today — that business institutions have more *prestige* (威望) in American society than any other kind of organization, including the government. Why do business institutions posses this great prestige?

One reason is that Americans view business as being more firmly based on the ideal of competition than other institutions in society. Since competition is seen as the major source of progress and prosperity by most Americans, competitive business institutions are respected. Competition is not only good in itself, it is the means by which other basic American values such as individual freedom, equality of opportunity, and hard work are protected.

Competition protects the freedom of the individual by ensuring that there is no *monopoly* (垄断) of power. In contrast to one, all-powerful government, many businesses compete against each other for profits. Theoretically, if one business tries to take unfair advantage of its customers, it will lose to competing business which treats its customers more fairly. Where many businesses compete for the customers' dollar, they cannot afford to treat them like inferiors or slaves.

A contrast is often made between business, which is competitive, and government, which is a monopoly. Because business is competitive, many Americans believe that it is more supportive of freedom than government, even though government leaders are elected by the people and business leaders are not. Many Americans believe, then, that competition is as important, or even more important, than democracy in preserving freedom.

Competition in business is also believed to strengthen the ideal of equality of opportunity. Competition is seen as an open and fair race where success goes to the swiftest person regardless of his or her social class background. Competitive success is commonly seen as the American alternative to social rank based on family background. Business is therefore viewed as an expression of the idea of equality of opportunity rather than the *aristocratic* (贵族的) idea of inherited privilege.

1. The statement "The business of America is business" probably means "_____".
   A. The business institutions in America are concerned with commerce
   B. Business problems are of great importance to the American government
   C. Business is of primary concern to Americans
   D. America is a great power in world business

2. Americans believe that they can realize their personal values only _____.
   A. when given equality of opportunity
   B. through doing business
   C. by protecting their individual freedom
   D. by way of competition

3. Who can benefit from business competition?
   A. Honest businessmen.
   B. Both businessmen and their customers.
   C. People with ideals of equality and freedom.
   D. Both business institutions and government.

4. Government is believed to differ strikingly from business in that government is characterized by _____.
   A. its absolute control of power
   B. its function in preserving personal freedom
   C. its role in protecting basic American values
   D. its democratic way of exercising leadership

5. It can be inferred from the passage that the author believes _____.
   A. Americans are more ambitious than people in other countries
   B. in many countries success often depends on one's social status
   C. American businesses are more democratic than those in other countries
   D. businesses in other countries are not as competitive as those in America

Reading for Pleasure

Two Chinese Idioms

Sleep on Brushwood and Taste Gall

During the Spring and Autumn period（770～476BC）, the State of Wu launched an attack against the State of Yue. The King of Wu was seriously wounded and soon died. His son Fu Chai became the new king. Fu was determined to get revenge. He drilled his army rigidly until it was a perfect fighting force. Three years later, he led his army against the State of Yue and caught its king Gou Jian. Fu took him to the State of Wu.

In order to avenge his father's death, Fu let him live in a shabby stone house by his father's tomb and ordered him to raise horses for him. Gou pretended to be loyal to Fu but he never forgot his humiliation. Many years later, he was set free. Gou secretly accumulated a military force after he went back to his own state. In order to make himself tougher he slept on firewood and ate a gall-bladder before having dinner and going to bed every night. At the same time he administered his state carefully, developing agriculture and educating the people. After a few years, his country became strong. Then Gou seized a favorable opportunity to wipe out the State of Wu.

Later, people use it to describe one who endures self-imposed hardships to strengthen one's resolve to realize one's ambition.

卧薪尝胆

春秋时期,吴国和越国之间进行了一场战争,吴王不幸受了重伤,不久就死了。他的儿子夫差作了吴国的新国王,他发誓要替父亲报仇。于是,他严格的操练他的士兵,把他们训练成了一支非常厉害的军队。三年以后,他对越国发动了战争,抓住了越王勾践,把他带回了吴国。

为了复仇,夫差让勾践住在他父亲墓旁的破石屋里天天看墓、喂马。勾践表面上服从,心里面却想着复仇。几年以后,勾践被放回越国。他立刻开始秘密聚集一支军队。为了提醒自己不要忘了报仇,他睡在柴上,还每天在吃饭睡觉前尝一尝苦胆。同时,他专心治理国家,大力发展农业,加强民众教育。几年后,越国又变得强大起来,然后,勾践抓住一个适当的机会消灭了吴国。

后来,人们用它来形容人刻苦自励以达到自己定下的目标。

If You Work at It Hard Enough, You Can Grind an Iron Rod into a Needle

This legend is about Li Bai, a great poet in the Tang Dynasty.

Li Bai was naughty and disliked study when he was a child. One day he saw an old woman grinding an iron rod on a big stone when he was playing by a river. Driven by curiosity, Li Bai came up and asked, "What are you doing, granny?"

"Grinding an iron rod," said the old woman without stopping grinding.

"Then what for?" he asked again.

"To make a sewing needle," was the answer.

"What?!" little Li Bai was puzzled, "you want to grind so big a rod into a needle?! It will take many years."

"This doesn't matter. As long as I persevere in doing so, there is nothing / cannot achieve in the world. Certainly I can make a needle from the rod."

Deeply moved by what the old woman said, Li Bai took effort to study since then and finally became one of the greatest poets in China.

You can also say: Constant dropping wears away a stone. Little strokes fell great oaks. Perseverance spells success.

只要功夫深,铁杵磨成针

宋·祝穆《方舆胜览·眉州·磨针溪》:世传李白读书象耳山中,学业未成,即弃去,"过是溪,逢老媪方磨铁杵,问之,曰:'欲作针。'太白感其意,还卒业"。

Humors Prepared for You

Secret of Your Success

"Sir, what is the secret of your success?" a reporter asked a bank president.

"Two words."

"And, sir, what are they?"

"Right decisions."

"And how do you make right decisions?"

"One word."

"And, sir, what is that?"

"Experience."

"And how do you get experience?"

"Two words."

"And, sir, what are they?"

"Wrong decisions."

Famous Sayings

It is not the strongest of the species that survives, nor the most intelligent, but rather the one most adaptable to change.

—*Charles Darwin*

在自然界中能幸存下来的，不是最强大的，也不是最聪明的，而是最能适应改变的。

——达尔文

Our greatest weakness lies in giving up. The most certain way to succeed is always to try just one more time.

—*Thomas Edison*

放弃是我们最大的弱点。成功的方法只不过是失败之后再尝试一次。

——爱迪生

Unit Ten

Peace, Not War

Modern man has brought this whole world to an awe-inspiring threshold of the future. He has reached new and astonishing peaks of scientific success. He has produced machines that think and instruments that peer into the unfathomable ranges of interstellar space. Yet, in spite of these spectacular strides in science and technology, and still unlimited ones to come, something basic is missing. There is a sort of poverty of the spirit which stands in glaring contrast to our scientific and technological abundance. The richer we have become materially, the poorer we have become morally and spiritually. We have learned to fly the air like birds and swim the sea like fish, but we have not learned the simple art of living together as brothers.

In this unit, you will read:

- Why Did President Truman Drop the Atomic Bomb?
- There Will Never Be a "Victor" in Iraqi War
- Beginning Anew
- A New Era Began at Alamogordo
- Meng Jiangnv Weep over the Great Wall

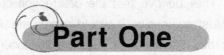

Part One

Pre-reading Questions

1. What do you think of the dropping of atomic bombs on Hiroshima and Nagasaki in World War II?
2. Is it the only way to end World War II by dropping the atomic bombs?
3. Could you point out the disastrous effects brought about by war?

Why Did President Truman Drop the Atomic Bomb?

Many think President Truman could have used some other means to compel Japanese surrender than atomic bombs. Is this the case?

1 At the end of World War II, few questioned Truman's decision to drop the atomic bombs on Hiroshima (广岛) and Nagasaki (长崎). Most Americans accepted the obvious reasoning: the atomic bombings brought the war to a more timely end. They did not have a problem with over one hundred thousand of the enemy being killed. After all, the Japanese attacked America, and not **the other way round**. In later years, however, many have begun to question the conventional wisdom of "Truman was saving lives," putting forth theories of their own. However, when one examines the issue with great attention to the results of the atomic bombings and compares these results with possible alternatives to using said bombs, the line between truth and fiction begins to clear. Truman's decision to use the atomic bomb on Japan was for the purpose of saving lives and ending the war quickly in order to prevent a disastrous land invasion.

2 The people who are now questioning Truman's motives are often known as **Revisionists**, because they attempt to **revise** common perceptions of history, proposing **alternate** theories and **motives**. As early as 1946 they begin to postulate new ideas, but their words only began to receive **credence** in the late 1960s and early 1970s. Revisionists **contend** that Truman either had **ulterior** motives in the dropping of the atomic bombs or that he used these bombs on Japan for an entirely different reason, one that had nothing to do with saving lives.

3 Most people who were alive at the time of the Hiroshima and Nagasaki bombings, especially veterans, **subscribe** to the "traditional" belief that Truman decided to drop the atomic bombs on Japan for solely military reasons. A timely end to the war would mean that no land invasion of Japan is necessary. Such an invasion would have been extraordinarily costly in terms of not only American lives, but also in terms of Japanese dead. Ending the war quickly would return soldiers to their homes and allow Americans to begin a life of **normality** again.

4   The Revisionists, however, believe that Truman had either **partially** or entirely different reasons for bombing Japan. They believe that the destruction of two Japanese cities would accomplish several things. Most obviously, it would punish the Japanese for the bombing of Pearl Harbor and the **atrocious** treatment of American prisoners of war. Also, an atomic bombing of Japan is also the only thing that would justify the expense of **the Manhattan Project**. If this expense was not justified, Truman would have faced a Congressional inquiry into the **misappropriation** of $2 billion. Not only did he want to avoid Congressional hearings, but he also wanted another term of office. His chances of reelection would have been **nil** if it were learned by the general public that he wasted money and American lives by **shelving** a weapon that could have ended the war more quickly. The final Revisionist claim is that Truman wanted to give the U. S. an edge in the coming Cold War by showing that he was not afraid to use these weapons of mass destruction.

5   They also say that Truman should have chosen one of the several available ways to compel a Japanese surrender without an atomic bombing of two cities. The most obvious alternative is an American invasion of Japan. **Olympic** was the code-name given to the planned American invasion of Kyushu (九州), one of the four Japanese home islands, if an atomic bomb were not available by late October. Two separate estimates exist to **rate** the number of American **casualties** that would result from such an invasion. A joint war plans committee comprised of the army and navy came to the conclusion that 46,000 Americans would die in an invasion of Kyushu and later Honshu (本州). The number of American wounded averaged three to one during the later years of the war, so according to this estimate, 175,000 American casualties were not **out of the question**. However, these figures were based on such **tentative** intelligence that George Marshall, the army's chief of staff, **bluntly** rejected them.

6   A second estimate proposed by **Admiral** Leahy was much higher. The invasion of Iwo Jima caused 6,200 American deaths, and the U. S. outnumbered the Japanese by four to one. Okinawa (冲绳) cost 13,000 U. S. servicemen, and they outnumbered the Japanese by two and one-half to one. These 13,000 men made up more than 35% of the U. S. landing force. Consequently, Admiral Leahy came to the conclusion that it was absurd to think that any less than 35% of the American force that invaded Japan would be killed. Based on the estimate of 560,000 Japanese soldiers on Kyushu as of early August, Leahy predicted that at very minimum over 250,000 American soldiers would lie dead as a result of an invasion of the Japanese islands.

7   It was later found that the troop strength on Kyushu was greatly under-estimated, and that by August 6 the Japanese had over 900,000 men stationed on Kyushu, nearly twice as many as thought. Leahy's estimates that the Americans would have a **preponderance**, when in fact the 767,000 American soldiers who would comprise the landing force were already greatly outnumbered three months before Operation Olympic was actually to begin. By November, Japanese troop strength could easily double or triple, making between 500,000 and 1,000,000 American deaths **conceivable**.

8　These numbers do not even begin to **account for** the Japanese dead. In Okinawa, twice as many Japanese were killed as Americans. It is therefore plausible that between 100,000 (according to the earliest estimate) and two million soldiers would die in an invasion. This number does not include Japanese civilians dead, which could conceivably have been even higher than the number of dead soldiers.

9　The Japanese army was already training its civilians to fight with sharpened bamboo poles. According to **samurai** tradition, there was no more honorable way to die than to do so for Japan and the emperor, and the civilians were quite prepared to take this philosophy to heart. Using sharpened **pikes** the Japanese could easily prevent a military government from being effective in those towns which the U. S. captured. Further, and even more brutal, was the training of young children to be "Sherman carpets." Japanese children were to be **strapped** with **TNT** and throw themselves under American tanks, thereby dying in the most honorable way possible—by killing the enemy. It can be assumed that at least as many civilians would have died as soldiers, bringing the totals somewhere around 200,000 to four million Japanese dead, along with the 50,000 to one million American dead, totaling 250,000 to five million total dead.

10　It was hoped that the Japanese military would **capitulate** once American forces occupied the Tokyo Plain, but it is possible that they would fight to the last man. On Saipan, nearly 900 Japanese killed themselves rather than be taken prisoner by Americans. Such was the Japanese philosophy to fight to the last man. If an entire nation was compelled to launch suicide attacks against the occupying army, it is conceivable that many, many millions of Japanese civilians would die.

11　In order to make an accurate comparison between the dropping of the atomic bombs and Operation Olympic, one must be adequately knowledgeable of the destruction that took place in the atomic bombings of Hiroshima and Nagasaki. The Hiroshima bombing killed about 66,000 people and devastated 4. 4 square miles, over two-thirds of the city. The Nagasaki bombing killed about 39,000 people, and destroyed half the city, bringing the total to 105,000 Japanese dead.

12　Of the Revisionist theories, the most common one is that Truman simply wanted to impress Stalin by dropping the atomic bomb. This is simply not the case. The most imperative thing on Truman's mind as he let the bombings go forward was that they would prevent a land invasion of Kyushu and the massive loss of life, both American and Japanese, which would accompany such an invasion. Ironically, atomic bombs were to be used to clear the beach heads for Operation Olympic, if an invasion would have been necessary. Scientists had assured Truman, erroneously, that sufficient radiation would have cleared from the beaches to allow American soldiers to land in safety. Even if Truman had chosen to invade instead of using the atomic bombs on Hiroshima and Nagasaki, they would still have been used, just in a different capacity. Furthermore, if Truman had wanted to impress Stalin, he would not have told Stalin that the United States had "produced a bomb of extraordinary power." Instead, he would have let the shock have its effect on both the Soviet Union and on Japan.

13   The only way anyone can judge Truman's motives in dropping the atomic bomb is by analyzing the result of his decision. No one can know, even by reading his personal diary, the exact reasons he had for using the bomb. It was likely a combination of many: punishment, justification of cost, saving lives, and ending the war as quickly as possible. However, it is evident that in the "grand scheme of things" the use of the atomic bomb saved lives. About 105,000 Japanese lost their lives in Hiroshima and Nagasaki. While this is a high number, the number who died in the American bombing **raids** on the six largest Japanese cities is far greater, about 250,000. Consequently, such a large number of deaths is by no means unprecedented. An invasion of Japan would possibly have cost between 250,000 and three million Japanese and American lives and ended the war four months later, at the very earliest. It may be concluded that no more people died in the atomic bombings than would have in an invasion of Kyushu, and that said bombings did have the effect of ending the war more quickly. Truman's motives, therefore, cannot be **called into question in light of** the results of his decision. At least in this case, the end justifies the means.

🔍 Words and Expressions

the other way round in the opposite position, direction or order; the opposite situation 颠倒过来;相反;反过来

revisionist *n.* a person who are different from, and want to change, the main ideas or practices of sth. 修正主义者

revise *v.* to change sth. in order to correct or improve it 修改,修订

alternate *a.* happening or following one after the other regularly 交替的,轮流的

motive *n.* a reason for doing sth. 动机

credence *n.* a quality that an idea or a story has that makes you believe it is true 可信性,真实性

contend *v.* to say that sth. is true, esp. in an argument 声称,主张,认为

ulterior *a.* existing beyond what is obvious or admitted; intentionally hidden 隐秘不明的;有意隐瞒的;别有用心的

subscribe *v.* to agree with or support an opinion, a theory, etc. 同意,赞同

normality *n.* a situation where everything is normal or as you would expect it to be 正常,正常状态

partial *a.* being or affecting only a part; not total 部分的,不完全的

atrocious *a.* horrifyingly wicked 凶恶的;残暴的

misappropriation *n.* money set aside (as by a legislature) for a specific purpose 据为己有,占有,挪用(指定用途的一笔拨款)

nil *n.* nothing 无,零

shelve *v.* hold back to a later time 将……搁在一边

rate *v.* to have or think that sb./sth. has a particular level of quality, value, or number etc. 评估;评价;计算

casualty *n.* a person killed or injured in a war or accident (战争或事故中的)伤亡者

out of the question impossible or not allowed and therefore not worth discussion 不可能;不允许;不值得讨论

tentative *a.* not definite or certain because you may want to change it later 试探性的；试验的；尝试性的

bluntly *ad.* in a very direct way, without trying to be polite or kind 直言地,单刀直入地

admiral *n.* the supreme commander of a fleet 海军将领，舰队司令

preponderance *n.* a superiority in numbers or amount 数量上的优势

conceivable *a.* that you can imagine or believe 可想到的，可相信的，可想象的

account for 说明(解释)……原因

samurai *n.* a Japanese warrior who was a member of the feudal military aristocracy（日本封建时代的)武士,武士阶级

pike *n.* a sharp point (as on the end of a spear)（昔日士兵用的）矛

strap *n.* a strip of leather or strip of similar material for binding things together or holding sth. in position 挎带，肩带；背带

capitulate *v.* surrender under agreed conditions 投降

raid *v.* a sudden short attack 突然袭击

call into question to doubt sth. or make others doubt sth. 怀疑;引起怀疑

in light of sth. [in the light of sth.（Brithish E)] after considering sth. 考虑到;鉴于

☞ Background Information

1. the Manhattan Project: "The Manhattan Project: Making the Atomic Bomb" is a short history of the origins and development of the American atomic bomb program during World War II. Beginning with the scientific developments of the pre-war years, the monograph details the role of United States government in conducting a secret, nationwide enterprise that took science from the laboratory and into combat with an entirely new type of weapon. The monograph concludes with a discussion of the immediate postwar period, the debate over the Atomic Energy Act of 1946, and the founding of the Atomic Energy Commission.

2. Olympic: the code-name(代号)given to the planned American invasion of Kyushu

3. TNT: (TriNitroToluene) explosive consisting of a yellow crystalline compound that is a flammable toxic derivative of toluene[化]三硝基甲苯,烈性炸药

☞ Learn about Words

Often you can tell the meaning of a word from its context — the words around it. Please find the word in the paragraph that means.

1. the ability to use one's experience and knowledge in order to make sensible decisions or judgments. (1)

2. sth. that you can choose to do or use instead of sth. else (1)

3. to suggest that sth. might have happened or to be true (2)

4. to give an acceptable explanation for sth. that other people think is unreasonable (4)

5. to force people to do sth. (5)

6. shared, owned by, or involving two or more people or groups (5)

7. to be more in number than another group (6)

8. able to be believed or imagined (7)

9. reasonable and seems likely to be true (8)

10. very important and needing immediate attention or action (12)

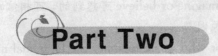

Part Two

> **Reading Skill — Denotation and Connotation**
>
> Denotation is the literal meaning of a word — what we find in a dictionary (本义). Connotation, on the other hand, is the implied meaning of a word — what a word suggests to us, or what it makes us feel or think (言外之意). In order to fully understand figurative language, or figures of speech, we need to be aware of the context in which the words appear.
>
> Generally speaking, the more we perceive the connotations of the words, the more we can understand how a writer wants us to feel or think.

Skill-Specific Training

Read the following sentences taken from the passage, paying close attention to the underlined words, each of which has a number of connotations. Give the denotation of the word and its connotation in the context.

1. The results of the poll, which reached its highest number since the conflict began in 2003, showed that the majority of its respondents wants a timetable for troop withdrawal, but inexplicably, that they're <u>split</u> on whether the U S will win the war or not.

   Denotation _____

   Connotation _____

2. Unfortunately, for the thousands of young, American military members who are dying on a daily basis — and their respective families — Bush refuses to <u>see</u> the conflict for what it is...

   Denotation _____

   Connotation _____

3. As a matter of fact, I am downright furious that Bush has been constantly <u>feeding</u> the public — and the parents of thousands of deceased American service members — a continuous pack of lies concerning the Middle East situation — while simultaneously

trying to justify his decision-making.

Denotation _____

Connotation _____

4. If Gorge Bush thinks that the United States will ever be <u>embraced</u> by Iraq, he is even
   more idiotic than I — or anyone else — ever imagined.

Denotation _____

Connotation _____

5. I also find Bush's notion of peace in the war <u>torn</u> country as, absolutely ludicrous.

Denotation _____

Connotation _____

There Will Never Be a "Victor" in Iraqi War

Eric Williams

I was **sitting around** the other day **contemplating** what my next non-sports column
would be about when I thought of the ongoing **atrocity** that has come to be known as "The Iraqi
War." Then, just as I began to **formulate** my thoughts on the subject, which I will share
shortly, I read an article about the results of the latest CNN **poll** on the war — which showed
that 60 percent of Americans now oppose the war — or should I say — invasion.

The results of the poll, which reached its highest number since the conflict began in 2003,
showed that the majority of its respondents wants a timetable for troop withdrawal, but
inexplicably, that they're **split** on whether the U. S. will win the war or not.

My problem with the war in general — and the immeasurable millions of Americans who are
both supporting the war — as well as **idiotic** president, George Bush — is that these people
genuinely believe that the U. S. will walk away from this "war" being **hailed** as either,
"victorious" or some kind of "heroes for humanity".

Well, I am **unequivocally** convinced that no member of the U. S. Armed forces will be
viewed as heroic outside of U. S. soil and am **vehemently** going on record to inform president
Bush and his supporters, that there will never be a " winner" in this tragic conflict of
philosophical- and religious-difference.

Unfortunately, for the thousands of young, American military members who are dying on a
daily basis — and their respective families — Bush refuses to see the conflict for what it is —
and unwanted **infringement** on the rights — and way of life — of an entire nation — and one
that was started on the basis of a lie (the search for weapons of mass destruction) although
that fact seems to have been forgotten by a multitude of Americans.

As a matter of fact, I am downright furious that Bush has been constantly **feeding** the
public — and the parents of thousands of deceased American service members — a continuous
pack of lies concerning the Middle East situation — while simultaneously trying to justify his
decision-making.

"I know that some of my decisions have led to terrible loss and one of those decisions has been taken lightly," Bush said in an interview. "I know that this war is controversial, yet being your president requires doing what I believe is right and accepting the consequences". Bush talks a good game, however, he is not the one who has to be informed that his son or daughter — or spouse, won't be coming home because they were killed in a senseless war that no one but Bush himself, wanted. It is estimated that, since the beginning of the invasion in 2003, approximately 30,000 Iraqi civilians and nearly 2,200 American service members, have died in the war, but Bush maintains that by remaining in the region to help the Iraqis form a democratic government, "means that America has an **ally** of growing strength in the fight against terror."

What a joke!

If Gorge Bush thinks that the United States will ever be **embraced** by Iraq, he is even more idiotic than I — or anyone else — ever imagined.

"We fully recognize that the Iraqis must step up and form a unity government so that those who went to the polls to vote, recognize that a government will be in place to respond to their needs. We also recognize that vacuums in the political process create opportunity for **malfeasance** and harm," the president said.

"I don't expect everybody to agree with my decision to go into Iraq, but I do want the people to understand... that failure in Iraq is not an option. Failure in Iraq would make the security situation for our country worse, and... success in Iraq will begin to lay the foundation of peace for generations to come."

I also find Bush's notion of peace in the war torn country as, absolutely **ludicrous**. Between the numerous factions like the Shiites (什叶派) and Sunnis (逊尼派), who, have their own internal issues, Iraq is closer to civil war than peace — and for Bush to even suggest otherwise — makes him out to be the bold-faced liar that he is.

I mean, it's one thing to truthfully go into a country and **overrun** it because of whatever political agenda happens to be **on the docket** at the time, but for the Bush administration to boldly lie its way into overtaking Iraq in a search for "weapons of mass destruction" (which, by the way, they have never found) is another thing altogether.

According to the results from the Opinion Research Corporation poll, conducted last week on behalf of CNN, 61 percent of the people polled said they believed at least some U. S. troops should be withdrawn from Iraq by the end of the year. Of those, 26 percent said they would favor the withdrawal of all troops, while 35 percent said not all troops should be withdrawn. Another 34 percent said they believed the current level of troops in Iraq should be maintained.

Although the Pentagon hopes to be able to reduce U. S. troop levels as Iraqi security forces become more capable of defending their own country, (which will never be a certainty) it is unclear when that point will be reached.

"It is also important for every American to understand the consequences of pulling out of Iraq before our work is done," Bush said. "We would abandon our Iraqi friends and signal to the world that America cannot be trusted. (I wonder why?) We would hand Iraq over to enemies who have **pledged** to attack us and the global terrorists' movement would be **emboldened** and more dangerous than ever before. To retreat before victory would be an act of **recklessness** and **dishonor** (and) I will not allow."

While Bush has now acknowledged setbacks and surprises in the war and has taken some responsibility for ordering the invasion on the basis of inaccurate intelligence, he has fully convinced himself — and millions of Americans in the process — that this war is still "winnable" and that there are only two options for the U.S. at this point — victory or defeat.

"Not only can we win the war in Iraq — we are winning the war in Iraq," Bush said. "The need for victory is larger than any president or political party because the security of our people is in the balance. I do not expect you to support everything I do but tonight I have a request: Do not give in to despair and do not give up on this fight for freedom."

Once again, if George Bush truly thinks that this is a "war" that can be "won," he is sadly mistaken. Thousands of Iraqi civilians are dead. Parents have lost children and children have lost their parents. Thousands of U.S. service members have died and their families have to cope with their losses. I won't even get into the untold number of soldiers who will return to the U.S. minus limbs or with psychological problems that will haunt them for the rest of their lives.

If George Bush thinks this is "winning" a war, I'd hate to see what he considers "losing."

One thing's for sure, "winning" has never felt this horrible.

Comprehension of the Text

1. What's the result of the latest CNN poll on the Iraqi War?

   _____.

2. According to the writer, who will be the "winner" in this war? And why?

   _____.

3. How many people have died in the war according to the passage?

   _____.

4. According to the latest CNN Poll, how many people are in favor of the withdrawal of all troops?

   _____.

5. Can you use your own words to describe George Bush's idea of the Iraqi War?

   _____.

🐾 **Words and Expressions**

sit around 闲坐

contemplate *v.* reflect deeply on a subject 沉思；默想；考虑

atrocity *n.* a terrible, cruel and violent act, esp. in war 邪恶，暴行

formulate *v.* to create or prepare sth. carefully, giving particular attention to details 构想出，规划

poll *n.* an inquiry into public opinion conducted by interviewing a random sample of people 民
意调查

split *a.* divided in opinions 分歧的，不统一的

idiotic *a.* very stupid 十分愚蠢的；白痴般的

hail *v.* praise vociferously 赞扬(为)······

unequivocal *a.* expressing your opinion or intention very clearly and firmly 表达明确的；毫不含糊的

vehement *a.* showing very strong feelings, esp. anger 强烈的，激烈的

infringement *n.* breaking a law or rule 侵权，侵害，违法行为

feed *v.* to give advice, information, etc. to sb. /sth. 提供(意见或信息等)；灌输

ally *n.* a friendly nation 盟军，同盟国

embrace *n.* the act of clasping another person in the arms (as in greeting or affection) 拥抱；拥护

malfeasance *n.* misconduct or wrongdoing, esp. by a public official 不正当，不法行为，渎职

ludicrous *a.* laughable or hilarious because of obvious absurdity or in congruity 荒唐[滑稽]可笑的

overrun *v.* to seize the positions of and defeat conclusively 占领，侵害，踩蹦

on the docket 在审理中

pledge *v.* promise solemnly and formally 保证；誓言

embolden *v.* to make sb. feel braver or more confident 使增加勇气；使更有胆量

recklessness *n.* actions of lack of care about danger and the possible results 无所顾忌；鲁莽

dishonor *n.* a loss of honour or respect because you have done sth. immoral or unacceptable 耻辱；丢脸

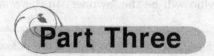

Part Three

> **Reading Comprehension (Skimming and Scanning)**
> **Directions:** *In this part, you will have 15 minute to go over the passage quickly and answer the questions. For questions 1～7, mark Y (for YES) if the statement agrees with the information given in the passage; N (for NO) if statement contradicts the information given in the passage; For question 8～10, complete the sentences with the information given in the passage.*

Beginning Anew

Thich Nhat Hanh

One moment can change a whole lifetime
One life can change eternity.

One stranger befriended,
One broken heart mended
One child loved, one captive set free.

Michael Stern, *in the song "One World"*

We may want to help those in need. We may want to love children who are hungry, disabled, or abused, to relieve them of their suffering. We carry that love in our heart and hope that someday we will be able to realize it. But when we actually contact these children, they may be difficult to love. They may be rude, they may lie, they may steal, and our love for them will fade. We had the idea that loving children who need our help would be wonderful, but when confronted with the reality, we cannot sustain our love. When we discover that the object of our love is not lovable, we feel deep disappointment, shame, and regret. We feel as though we have failed. If we cannot love a poor or disabled child, who can we love?

A number of Plum Village residents of Vietnamese origin want to go back to Vietnam to help the children and the adults there. The war created much division, hatred, and suspicion in the hearts of the people. These monks, nuns, and laypeople want to walk on their native land, embrace the people, and help relieve them of their suffering. But before they go back, they must prepare themselves. The people they want to help may not be easy to love. Real love must include those who are difficult, those who have been unkind. If they go back to Vietnam without first learning to love and understand deeply, when they find the people there being unpleasant, they will suffer and may even come to hate them.

You think you can change the world, but do not be too naive. Don't think that the moment you arrive in Vietnam, you will sit down with all the conflicting factions and establish communication immediately. You may be able to give beautiful talks about harmony, but if you are not prepared, you will not be able to put your words into practice. In Vietnam there are already people who can give very good Dharma talks, who can explain how to reconcile and live in harmony. But we should not only talk about it. If we do not practice what we preach, what can we offer anyone?

Eight years ago, I organized a retreat for American veterans of the Vietnam War. Many of the men and women at that retreat felt very guilty for what they had done and witnessed, and I knew I had to find a way of beginning anew that could help them transform. One veteran told me that when he was in Vietnam, he rescued a girl who had been wounded and was about to die. He pulled her into his helicopter, but he was not able to save her life. She died looking straight at him, and he has never forgotten her eyes. She had a hammock with her because, as a guerrilla, she slept in the forest at night. When she died, he kept the hammock and would not let it go. Sometimes, when we suffer, we have to cling to our suffering. The hammock symbolized all his suffering, all his shame.

During the retreat, the veterans sat in a circle and spoke about their suffering, some for the first time. In a retreat for veterans, a lot of love and support is needed. Some veterans would not do walking meditation because it reminded them too much of walking in the jungles of

Vietnam where they could step on a mine or walk into an ambush at any time. One man walked far behind the rest of us so that if anything happened, he would be able to get away quickly. Veterans live in that kind of psychological environment.

On the last day of the retreat, we held a ceremony for the deceased. Each veteran wrote the names of those whom he or she knew had died and placed the list on an altar we constructed. I took a willow leaf and used it to sprinkle water on the names and also on the veterans. Then we did walking meditation to the lake and held a ceremony for burning the suffering. That one veteran still did not want to give up his hammock, but finally he put it on the fire. As it burned, so did all the guilt and suffering he had held for so long in his heart.

Another veteran told us that almost everyone in his platoon had been killed by the guerrillas. Those who survived were so angry that they baked cookies with explosives in them and left them alongside the road. When some Vietnamese children saw them, they ate the cookies, and the explosives went off. They rolled around on the ground in pain. Their parents tried to save their lives, but there was nothing they could do. That image of the children rolling on the ground, dying because of the explosives in the cookies, was so deeply ingrained in this veteran's heart that now, twenty years later, he still could not sit in the same room with children. He was living in hell. After he had told this story, I gave him the practice of "Beginning Anew."

"Beginning Anew" is not easy. We have to transform our hearts and our minds in very practical ways. We may feel ashamed, but shame is not enough to change our hearts. I said to him, "You killed five or six children that day? Can you save the lives of five or six children today? Children everywhere in the world are dying because of war, malnutrition and disease. You keep thinking about the five or six children whom you killed in the past, but what about the children who are dying now? You still have your body; you still have your heart; you can do many things to help children who are dying in the present moment. Please give rise to your mind of love, and in the months and years that are left to you, do the work of helping children." He agreed to do it, and it has helped him transform his guilt.

"Beginning Anew" is not to ask for forgiveness. "Beginning Anew" is to change your mind and heart, to transform the ignorance that brought about wrong actions of body, speech and mind, and to help you cultivate your mind of love. Your shame and guilt will disappear, and you will begin to experience the joy of being alive. All wrongdoing arises in the mind. It is only through the mind that wrongdoing can disappear.

1. A number of Plum Village residents want to go back to Vietnam to help people there.
2. The minute people arrive in Vietnam, they will establish communication right away.
3. The Writer organized a retreat for American veterans of the Vietnam War several years ago.
4. One veteran kept a hammock of a Vietnamese guerrilla.
5. During the retreat, the veterans sat in rows and spoke about their suffering.
6. On the last day of the retreat, each veteran wrote the names of those whom he or she

knew had died on a piece of paper and set it on fire right away.

7. One veteran couldn't sit in the same room with children because he put poison in cookies for children during the war.

8. The writer stated that children everywhere are dying because of _____ and disease.

9. The writer persuaded the guilty veteran into giving rise to his mind of love, and do the work of _____.

10. "Beginning Anew" is to change people's _____, to transform the ignorance, and to help people cultivate mind of love.

Part Four

> **Directions**: *There is a passage in this section. This passage is followed by some questions. For each of them there are four choices marked A), B), C) and D). You should decide on the best choice.*

A New Era Began at Alamogordo

Before 1945, hardly anyone outside of New Mexico had ever heard of Alamogordo. In 1960 its population numbered 21,723. Ever since 1898, when the town had been built by the Southern Pacific Railroad, Alamogordo had been a lonely town. The land around it was largely desert, and largely empty.

Because it was isolated and because the weather was almost always clear and peaceful, a spot of desert near Alamogordo was chosen as the last site for the first atomic bomb ever exploded. The secret name of the test was Zeo.

At dawn on July 16, 1945, the atomic bomb was set off. Observers agreed that they had witnessed something unlike anything ever seen by men before, a huge, colorful fireball, more brilliant than the sun flashing as it rose for miles into the air. Never before had men released so much power at one time, nor had any nation ever possessed weapon as terrible and destructive as the atomic bomb.

For several weeks, the test was kept secret. When an atomic bomb was dropped from an American plane on Hiroshima, Japan, newspapers and radio stations all over America told of the test of the bomb in New Mexico. Almost everybody was amazed to learn where the bomb had been made and tested; the deserts of the Southwest had hidden the secret well.

When news of the atomic bomb and its destructiveness was announced, people all over the world wondered what other new weapons were being prepared in the New Mexico desert. Some people doubted that the secret of making atomic bombs could be kept from other countries. Some even doubted the wisdom of using so powerful a weapon. But no one doubted that a new kind of war — and a new kind of world — had begun at Alamogordo, one summer morning in 1945.

1. What is the main topic of this passage?

    A. The secret of Alamogordo.

    B. A new kind of war.

    C. The destructive force of the first atomic bomb.

    D. The selection of the test site for the first atomic bomb.

2. Which of the following is the main reason for choosing Alamogordo as the test site?

    A. It always had an enjoyable climate.

    B. It was connected to other cities by a railway.

    C. Its location would hide the secret well.

    D. It was situated in southwestern New Mexico.

3. When was the atomic bomb dropped on Hiroshima?

    A. As soon as the secret was revealed.　　B. At dawn on July 16, 1945.

    C. Immediately after the test.　　D. Several weeks after the test.

4. After the first atomic bomb explosion, everybody agreed that _____.

    A. it was wise to choose Alamogordo as the test site

    B. man had entered the age of nuclear warfare

    C. it was not wise to use such a powerful weapon

    D. it was not possible to keep the technology of making atomic bombs secret

5. The tone of this passage is one of _____.

    A. anxiety　　B. satisfaction

    C. encouragement　　D. fear

Part Five

Reading for Pleasure

Meng Jiangnv Weep over the Great Wall

This story happened during the Qin Dynasty (221BC～206BC). There was once an old man named Meng who lived in the southern part of the country with his wife. One spring, Meng sowed a seed of bottle gourd in his yard. The bottle gourd grew up bit by bit and its vines climbed over the wall and entered his neighbor Jiang's yard. Like Meng, Jiang had no children and so he became very fond of the plant. He watered and took care of the plant. With tender care of both men, the plant grew bigger and bigger and gave a beautiful bottle gourd in autumn. Jiang plucked it off the vine, and the two old men decided to cut the gourd and divide it by half. To their surprise when they cut the gourd a pretty and lovely girl was lying inside! They felt happy to have a child and both loved her very much, so they decided to bring the child up together. They named the girl Meng Jiangnv, which means Meng and Jiang's daughter.

As time went by, Meng Jiangnv grew up and became a beautiful young woman. She was very smart and industrious. She took care of old Meng and Jiang's families, washing the clothes and doing the housework. People knew that Meng Jiangnv was a good girl and liked her very much. One day while playing in the yard, Meng Jiangnv saw a young man hiding in the garden. She called out to her parents, and the young man came out.

At that time, Emperor Qin Shihuang (the first emperor of Qin) announced to build the Great Wall. So lots of men were caught by the federal officials. Fan Qiliang was an intellectual man and very afraid of being caught, so he went to Meng's house to hide from the officials. Meng and Jiang liked this good-looking, honest, and good-mannered young man. They decided to wed their daughter to him. Both Fan Qiliang and Meng Jiangnv accepted happily, and the couple was married several days later. However, three days after their marriage, officials suddenly broke in and took Fan Qiliang away to build the Great Wall in the north of China.

It was a hard time for Meng Jiangnv after her husband was taken away — she missed her husband and cried nearly every day. She sewed warm clothes for her husband and decided to set off to look for him. Saying farewell to her parents, she packed her luggage and started her long journey. She climbed over mountains and went through the rivers. She walked day and night, slipping and falling many times, but finally she reached the foot of the Great Wall at the present Shanhaiguan Pass.

Upon her arrival, she was eager to ask about her husband. Bad news came to her, however, that Fan Qiliang had already died of exhaustion and was buried into the Great Wall! Meng Jiangnv could not help crying. She sat on the ground and cried and cried. Suddenly with a tremendous noise, a 400 kilometer-long (248-mile-long) section of the Great Wall collapsed over her bitter wail. The workmen and supervisors were astonished. Emperor Qin Shihuang happened to be touring the wall at that exact time, and he was enraged and ready to punish the woman.

However, at the first sight of Meng Jiangnv Emperor Qin Shihuang was attracted by her beauty. Instead of killing her, the Emperor asked Meng Jiangnv to marry him. Suppressing her feeling of anger, Meng Jiangnv agreed on the basis of three terms. The first was to find the body of Fan Qiliang, the second was to hold a state funeral for him, and the last one was to have Emperor Qin Shihuang wear black mourning for Fan Qiliang and attend the funeral in person. Emperor Qin Shihuang thought for a while and reluctantly agreed. After all the terms were met, Emperor Qin Shihuang was ready to take her to his palace. When the guarders were not watching, she suddenly turned around and jumped into the nearby Bohai Sea.

This story tells of the hard work of Chinese commoners, as well as exposes the cruel system of hard labor during the reign of Emperor Qing Shihuang. The Ten-Thousand-Li Great Wall embodied the power and wisdom of the Chinese nation. In memory of Meng Jiangnv, later generations built a temple, called the Jiangnv Temple, at the foot of the Great Wall in which a statue of Meng Jiangnv is located. Meng Jiangnv's story has been passed down from generation to generation.

孟姜女哭长城

　　秦始皇统一中国后，征集了数十万民夫，于公元前 214 年将秦、燕、赵三国北边的城墙连通、修缮合一，这便是举世闻名的万里长城。孟姜女万里寻夫送寒衣，哭倒长城八百里的传说就发生在那个时候.

　　古时候，孟老汉和姜老汉互为邻居，仅一墙之隔。一年春天，孟老汉在自己院中种了一颗葫芦籽，经过浇水、施肥精心培育，葫芦秧长得肥壮、高大，从墙头爬过去，到姜老汉的院里结了个很大的葫芦，有几十斤重。等葫芦熟后，姜老汉拿刀把它切开，突然见里边躺着个又白又胖、非常可爱的女娃娃，姜老汉喜出望外，奔走相告，村里人听说后，纷纷前来观看这新鲜事，可是孟、姜两老汉却因此产生了矛盾，吵得不可开交。孟老汉非常坚定地说："这葫芦是我亲自种下的，胖女孩该归我。"姜老汉却固执地说："这葫芦结在我的院子里，这女娃该是我的。"吵了三天三夜，难解难分，毫无结果，后经村里人调解为：女娃娃属于两家共同的，轮流居住，共同扶养，并取了个"孟姜女"的名字。

　　光阴似箭，日月如梭，转眼间十多年过去了，孟、姜两家老人为现已长大成人的孟姜女选了个女婿叫范杞梁，选定良辰吉日，准备成亲。天有不测风云，成亲之日，新郎、新娘正要拜堂，突然从门外闯进几个衙役，一拥而上把新郎范杞梁当民夫抓走了。

　　原来，当时由于秦始皇在全国各地抽调大批民夫修筑长城，日日夜夜拼命干，民夫们被累死、饿死的不计其数，为了加快工程速度，他们又到处抓民夫补充，范杞梁也被发配去充当修长城的民夫了。

　　转眼一年过去了，范杞梁杳无音信，急得孟姜女饭吃不下，觉睡不着，不知如何是好，跟两家老人商量后，决定去找丈夫，发誓找不到丈夫绝不回家。她带上干粮和给丈夫特制的御寒衣服上路了。一路上，风吹雨淋、日晒霜打、饥寒交迫、步履艰难，经过千难万险的万里跋涉，终于找到了修长城的地方，一打听才知道，为修长城死了许多人，丈夫范杞梁早就累死了，并被埋在长城下，尸骨都找不到了。这一消息如同晴天霹雳，孟姜女顿时就伤心地恸哭起来，泪如泉，声如雷，哭得惊天动地，天昏地暗，眼看着长城一段段的倒塌，哭到哪里塌到哪里，足有八百里长。这下可急坏了工程总管，急忙去报告正来此巡查工程进展的秦始皇。秦始皇赶忙去见孟姜女寻问根由。一见之后，便被她的美貌迷住了，非要封她为"正宫娘娘"。孟姜女虽然怒火满腔，但还是压住心头仇恨，灵机一动，将计就计地非要秦始皇答应她三个条件，才能当"正宫娘娘"。一要找到丈夫范杞梁的尸体；二要为其丈夫举行国葬；三要秦始皇为范杞梁披麻戴孝、打幡送葬。秦始皇听罢孟姜女提的三个条件，思索片刻，为了得到美貌的孟姜女，便硬着头皮答应下来。孟姜女戴着孝拜了为筑城而死的范杞梁坟墓后，宿愿已偿，面对滚滚的渤海，纵身一跃，投海自尽了。

　　孟姜女哭长城的故事，很快就被人们所传颂，人们为纪念她，在山海关附近的一个山头上，给她修了坟、建了庙，取名为"姜女庙"。孟姜女万里寻夫送寒衣，哭倒长城八百里的故事家喻户晓，流传至今。

Humors Prepared for You

Then, the US president, George Bush gets a call from NASA: "Mr. President! The Russians have landed on the Moon!"

The next day NASA calls again: "Sir! The Russians are starting to paint the Moon red!"

Bush treats the issue with little interest, NASA, the US Air Force, the Navy, the Army, the Marines are all alarmed and push Bush to do something about it.

The third day, they assault him: "Mr. President, we have to do something, they already painted half of the Moon red!"

Bush doesn't give much attention to all the noise and fuss around him...

The fourth day, the US Congress starts a meeting on the subject, accusing Bush of ignorance: "They have painted the Moon red! It's as red as the communist flag, red red red!"

Bush: "O. K. guys, let's write Coca-Cola on it now!"

Famous Sayings

The worst sin towards our fellow creatures is not to hate them, but to be indifferent to them.

—George Bernard Shaw

我们对别人所犯的最大的罪过不是怨恨他们，而是对他们漠然处之。

——肖伯纳

You must be the change you want to see in the world.

—Mahatma Gandhi

想要世界有所改变，你就必须要以身作则

——甘地

If there is light in the soul, there will be beauty in the person.
If there is beauty in the person, there will be harmony in the house.
If there is harmony in the house, there will be order in the nation.
If there is order in the nation, there will be peace in the world.

修身，齐家，治国，平天下。

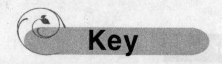

Key

Key to Unit One

Part One

1. permanent   2. profound   3. arduous   4. assimilation   5. mushroom
6. celebrity   7. plague   8. flock   9. ingrain   10. perpetuate

Part Two

Skill-Specific Training

Main idea of Para. 1: We will help you distinguish fantasy from fact about life in the United States.

Main idea of Para. 2: Life is not so leisurely in the United States.

Main idea of Para. 5: The rules of social behaviour in the United States are confusing.

Main idea of Para. 8: Racial and ethnic prejudice is a reality in the United States.

Main idea of Para. 10: There is de facto social stratification in America.

Main idea of Para. 15: Some American students are less prepared academically than others, but there are many academically prepared and highly competitive American students.

Comprehension of the Text

1. Because they will feel guilty about doing nothing or spending long periods of time relaxing or talking with friends.

2. Because there are many legal and bureaucratic restrictions and social rules governing their activities.

3. Although the majority of Americans can be considered to belong to the middle class, there is a small, wealthy upper class and a growing underclass.

4. That depends. They are generally not embarrassed or angered by being told they are wrong, as long as the criticism is stated in a friendly and respectful way.

5. No. Even "poor" American students own a lot of things, from cars and computers to stereo and skis. Material goods are easy to acquire in a consumer-orientated, credit-driven society, but they do not necessarily indicate great wealth.

Part Three

1. B   2. D   3. C   4. B   5. C
6. A   7. D
8. they felt it was not within their constitutional power
9. the virtue of the North against the evil slave owners of the South
10. The National Dry Retail Goods Association

Part Four

1. D   2. B   3. D   4. C   5. B

Key to Unit Two

Part One

1. litter   2. elevate   3. rigorous   4. boost

5. conscientious   6. inertia   7. scrutiny   8. condone

9. stout   10. elite

Part Two

Skill-Specific Training

1. C   2. A   3. B

Comprehension of the Text

1. Five.   2. Backstroke.   3. Bob Bowman

4. His victories came in the 200-meter freestyle, 200-meter backstroke and 100-meter butterfly.

5. His endurance.

Part Three

1. Y   2. Y   3. N   4. Y

5. Y   6. Y   7. N   8. swifter

9. doping   10. stamina

Part Four

1. B   2. C   3. A   4. C

5. B

Key to Unit Three

Part One

1. solitude   2. usher   3. inspire   4. indestructible

5. confide   6. animated   7. console   8. heir

9. fray   10. elude

Part Two

Skill-Specific Training

1. F   2. O   3. F   4. O

5. O

Comprehension of the Text

1. Oliver Barrett the Third, a father. Oliver Barrett the Fourth, a son, and also a law school student. Jennifer Cavilleri, an Italian Radcliffe student.

2. They always quarrel with each other, and they don't show respect for each other.

3. He thinks his son should first finish the law school and their love should be tested by time.

4. That's an irony, which means Oliver should have done better than that.

5. It means neither of them wants to start a conversation and they remain silent.

Part Three

1. Y	2. N	3. N	4. Y
5. Y	6. Y	7. N	8. gender stereotypes
9. black identity	10. multiracial intimacy		

Part Four

1. C	2. D	3. B	4. D
5. A			

Key to Unit Four

Part One

1. naked	2. legend	3. represent	4. liking
5. material	6. possession	7. schedule	8. soar
9. suicide	10. inevitable		

Part Two

Skill-Specific Training

1. unfathomable：impossible to be understood or measured 深奥的，难解的

2. inexpressible：too great to be expressed 难以形容的

3. reclaim：to claim back or to get sth. back 要求收回

4. distress：misery, suffering 苦恼；痛苦

5. berth：rest；tie up the boat 停靠；停泊

6. decline：refuse or turn down 拒绝

7. overflowing：having much or more than enough of sth. 溢出的；充满的

8. coerce：force；to cause to do through pressure 强制；迫使

Comprehension of the Text

1. Love is a gift.

2. They should accept the gift of love for what it was, and then move on.

3. You should feel honored that love came and called at your door, and gently decline t he gift you cannot return. Do not take advantage; do not cause pain

4. The author means that love can be made to grow only by giving it away and people should learn to be someone who generates love not someone who only seeks love.

5. There is nothing you can do and there is nothing you should do, because love has its time, its own season, and its own reason for coming and going.

Part Three

1. C	2. A	3. D	4. C
5. A	6. B	7. D	
8. hopes and aspirations	9. high-school essay	10. most honest emotions	

Part Four

1. B   2. C   3. C   4. B

5. D

Key to Unit Five

Part One

1. mischief   2. stimulate   3. potentiality   4. exhortation

5. antithesis   6. counseling   7. permissiveness   8. nurture

9. exceed   10. mediocre

Part Two

Skill-Specific Training

1. a nervous person   2. a detailed analysis   3. the next sports star

4. amateur sports-lovers who have never won before

5. showing themselves

6. the valuable opportunity of helping our children grow

Comprehension of the Text

1. Because the dad is damaging his son's nerves and undermining the coach's authority.

2. Because the coach has too high expectations to his son.

3. She throws up before every meet and secretly writes long poems about frustration, weakness and worthlessness.

4. Kids need to play and be praised for trying their best and for putting themselves "out there."

5. Parents should not place far too much emphasis on their children's athletic achievements.

Part Three

1. Y   2. N   3. Y   4. N

5. N   6. Y   7. NG

8. practices, values and behaviors   9. appropriate behavior of children

10. children's autonomy

Part Four

1. B   2. C   3. C   4. D

5. A

Key to Unit Six

Part One

1. discrimination   2. obese   3. isolate   4. discharge

5. elicit   6. startling 7. counterpart 8. deny

9. disposition   10. abort

Part Two

Skill-Specific Training

1. intelligent
2. wealthy
3. talented
4. bratty
5. dumb

Comprehension of the Text

1. Thomas.
2. It is employer bias in play or the perception that race is tied to productivity.
3. Sounding name.
4. The traditional white sounding name.
5. Alex.

Part Three

1. Y
2. Y
3. N
4. N
5. N
6. Y
7. Y
8. advertisements
9. lawsuit
10. niche

Part Four

1. D
2. B
3. B
4. A
5. D

Key to Unit Seven

Part One

1. despise
2. conscience
3. lucrative
4. hypocrite
5. trivial
6. enigmatic
7. analogous
8. mortification
9. frail
10. lassitude

Part Two

Skill-Specific Training

1. It tells that U. S. workers work hard and rest less.
2. Yes, they did.
3. Longer hours worked by Americans.
4. Oct. 24
5. Learn to say no.

Comprehension of the Text

1. Changing to less-demanding occupations, leaving corporations to start their own businesses, or scaling back to spend more time with families.
2. He must work two jobs to support his three children.
3. He believes much of the accelerated productivity is due to longer work hours.
4. The U. S. Senate passed a resolution designating October as National Work and Family Month.
5. She thought that's the best thing she ever did.

Part Three

1. N   2. N   3. Y   4. N
5. Y   6. Y   7. NG
8. move forward   9. looking back   10. the more you get back

Part Four

1. D   2. B   3. C   4. B
5. C

Key to Unit Eight

Part One

1. daydream   2. resume   3. retail   4. tidiness
5. finance   6. investigation   7. upgrate   8. initiate
9. prospect   10. pirate

Part Two

Skill-Specific Training

1. She wanted to get a better idea what she was going to university for before she went.

2. 35 percent

3. Clinics in Costa Rica would offer more contact with patients to students who are interested in medicine.

4. The experience was definitely an eye-opener, and fascinating for her and it really changed her life.

5. Two years.

6. The book describes resources for low-cost programs, student discounts and other money-saving tips

7. Low-income students

8. He said, overseas travel was important for American young people to become "culturally competent and globally aware."

Comprehension of the Text

1. And as college costs soar, more families see the moves as good investments, because their children often return more focused.

2. Gap years experience will cause freshmen to less likely party too much, fail courses or change majors repeatedly.

3. Among the possible extras are health and medical insurance, and expenses for documents like passports and visas.

4. He spent his first year tending sheep, working in conservation and his second year volunteering at an elementary school.

5. Financial ones.

Part Three

1. A 　　　　2. D 　　　　3. C 　　　　4. C

5. B 　　　　6. A 　　　　7. C

8. accredited institutes 　　　　9. religious or political affiliations

10. hard and soft

Part Four

1. A 　　　　2. B 　　　　3. D 　　　　4. B

5. D

Key to Unit Nine

Part One

1. consultant 　　2. persistent 　　3. straightforward 　　4. negotiable

5. console 　　　6. A 　　　　7. A 　　　　8. C

9. B 　　　　10. C

Part Two

1. B 　　　　2. A 　　　　3. B 　　　　4. B

5. C

Part Three

1. B 　　　　2. C 　　　　3. C 　　　　4. B

5. A 　　　　6. D 　　　　7. B 　　　　8. home life

9. productive 　　10. increase her own productivity

Part Four

1. C 　　　　2. D 　　　　3. B 　　　　4. A

5. B

Key to Unit Ten

Part One

1. wisdom 　　2. alternatives 　　3. postulate 　　4. justify

5. compel 　　6. joint 　　　7. outnumber 　　8. conceivable

9. plausible 　　10. imperative

Part Two

Skill-Specific Training

1. to be divided physically into parts or groups; to be divided in opinions

2. to be able to use your eyes to look at things and know what they are; to consider

3. to give food to a person or animal; to say or tell sth.

4. to hold your arms around someone and hold them in a friendly or loving way; to start to believe in a religion or political system

5. to damage sth. such as paper or cloth by pulling it too hard or letting it touch sth. sharp; to be very badly affected by sth.

Comprehension of the Text

1. 60 percent of Americans oppose the war.
2. There will never be a "winner" in this tragic conflict of philosophical — and religious — difference.
3. Approximately 30,000 Iraqi civilians and nearly 2,200 American service members.
4. 26 percent.
5. He thinks the war is winnable, and he thinks they are fighting for freedom.

Part Three

1. Y	2. N	3. Y	4. Y
5. N	6. N	7. N	8. war, malnutrition
9. helping children	10. mind and heart		

Part Four

1. A	2. C	3. D	4. B
5. B			

Comprehension of the Text

1. 60 percent of Americans oppose the war.

2. There will never be a "winner" in this tragic conflict of philosophical — and religious — difference.

3. Approximately 30,000 Iraqi civilians and nearly 2,300 American servicemembers.

4. 26 percent.

5. He thinks the war is winnable, and he thinks they are fighting for freedom.

Part Three

1. Y   2. N   3. Y

5. N   6. N   7. N   war, malnutrition

9 helping children   10. mind and heart

Part Four

1. A   2. C   3. D

5. H